A Rake's Flattery

."As for your looks, Miss Talcott, you don't do yourself justice. Do you know your eyes are huge and entrancing, capturing every tint of sea and sky? I find your freckles delightful, like flecks of cinnamon in cream. Your hair reminds me of a sunset over the Irish Sea; I would love to see it spilling around your shoulders. As for your figure . . ."

His gaze roved boldly over her, and she found her heart beating quickly. And not unpleasantly.

"That is quite enough," she said, mortified that the heat he conjured up in her must be shining clearly in her face. "You've only convinced me that you are an expert flatterer."

"I only spoke the truth," he said, eyes dark with amusement and something more disturbing.

Saving Lord Verwood

Elena Greene

A SIGNET BOOK

SIGNET
Published by New American Library, a division of
Penguin Group (USA) Inc., 375 Hudson Street,
New York, New York 10014, U.S.A.
Penguin Books Ltd, 80 Strand,
London WC2R 0RL, England
Penguin Books Australia Ltd, 250 Camberwell Road,
Camberwell, Victoria 3124, Australia
Penguin Books Canada Ltd, 10 Alcorn Avenue,
Toronto, Ontario, Canada M4V 3B2
Penguin Books (N.Z.) Ltd, Cnr Rosedale and Airborne Roads,
Albany, Auckland 1310, New Zealand

Penguin Books Ltd, Registered Offices:
80 Strand, London WC2R 0RL, England

First published by Signet, an imprint of New American Library,
a division of Penguin Group (USA) Inc.

First Printing, May 2004
10 9 8 7 6 5 4 3 2 1

Chapter One

*G*ulls shrieked, their voices fierce and mournful in the distance. Sheep bleated closer by. The morning mist curled around Penelope Talcott as she carefully picked her way along the rough, sloping lane that wound its way up the Downs from the sea. She pulled her cloak around her against the damp, then turned and looked back down the way she had come. Yesterday, this vantage point had afforded a fine view of Brighton, with its elegant terraces and the outlandish domes of the Royal Pavilion, all backed by a sea sparkling in the July sun. Today, the prospect was wreathed in an unseasonable fog.

Pen sighed. It seemed she had brought her sketchbook in vain. Moreover, coming here alone was likely to bring Aunt Mary's recriminations down on her head. But she could not have dragged her maid along with her, not when poor Susan was suffering from a cold, and to miss her morning walk was to miss the best part of the day. Well, if she couldn't draw, she could still relish the solitude, the sea breezes, the smell of the damp earth and the grass on the open, treeless hillside.

She walked on, then paused, feeling a sudden sense of foreboding. Above her, a large figure loomed in the mist, still at some distance. She could faintly hear the clomping of boots. Most likely it was some farm laborer or shepherd. So why did she feel ready to jump out of her skin, like a nervous hare?

On impulse, she turned and scrambled over the low stone

wall that separated the track from a broad sheep pasture, hoping she hadn't been seen. She crouched, setting the basket that held her blanket, sketchbook, and chalks down beside her. Now she could hear the man's footsteps more clearly. She kept very quiet, watching through a chink in the wall as the man's outline slowly became more distinct. A big man, dressed in a laborer's smock, a rough sack slung over his shoulder. His eyes, small and pale blue in a broad and weather-beaten face, framed with pale dirty hair. Just a farm laborer, she told herself. Yet her sense of dread increased as he approached. Her heart continued to hammer in her chest as he passed her hiding place and continued out of sight down the track, into the mist.

She stood and brushed grass off her dress with trembling fingers. Aunt Mary often chided her for her active imagination, but Pen could not rid herself of the feeling that the man presented some sort of threat. She took a deep breath, telling herself not to be such a nervous ninny. After she waited a few minutes, the sense of evil, if evil it was, decreased. Limbs still trembling slightly, she started to make her way down the hillside, avoiding sheep droppings and the occasional gorse bush as best she could, making for the gate at the bottom of the field. Best not to climb over the wall again and risk tearing her dress, even if it was her oldest and shabbiest. The breeze picked up as she walked, and the mists parted slightly.

Then she became aware of the sound of hoofbeats somewhere to her left. She turned her gaze in their direction to see a tall gentleman approaching, riding a dark horse. Was he the source of her unease? She didn't think so; in fact, something seemed familiar about the pair.

Could it be Lord Verwood? One of Aunt Mary's gossiping bosom bows had said he'd come to Brighton, and that he was currently paying court to a virtuous married lady. So like him to be meddling where he was not wanted! She hoped they would not meet again, for he never failed to disturb her tranquility.

Distracted, Pen allowed her foot to slip. She went down, tumbling a half-dozen yards and coming to a stop at the bottom of the pasture, a short distance from the gate. Right in the path of the horse and rider, approaching at a brisk canter. She lay stunned, unable to breathe, unable to will her limbs to move in the few precious seconds before she was trampled.

The horseman must have seen her in time, for he reined in his mount a few yards away. He glanced down at her with familiar, penetrating eyes of a brown so dark they were almost black, and her earlier suspicion was confirmed.

"My dear Miss Talcott!" exclaimed Lord Verwood, dismounting from the same beautiful bay she'd seen him ride before. "Have you injured yourself?"

He came forward, his horse's reins looped around one arm, and knelt down beside her. She sat up, trying to catch her breath, and shook her head.

"You know, you really must rid yourself of this distressing habit you have of tumbling down in front of me," he said, the amusement in his voice thinly veiled.

"I . . . could not . . . help it," she said between breaths. Heat flooded her face as she looked up into his. At least this time he did not look as angry as on that occasion in Hyde Park when she had first met him.

"Of course not," he replied in a soothing tone. "I am certain you could not help flinging yourself at my feet in Hyde Park, either. On that occasion, if I recall correctly, you were there to berate me for making off with your friend. I cannot imagine your purpose now."

"Had I known you would ride here this morning," she said, straightening her bonnet, "I should not have come this way."

"A pity," he said with a smile. "Perhaps you will tell me what you *are* doing here all by yourself?"

"I merely wished to go for a walk, and my maid is unwell," she said, accepting his arm as he helped her to her feet and trying to ignore the strength in his clasp. "Who are you to lecture me on propriety?"

"I am the last man in the world to lecture any female on propriety. I am merely curious."

She picked up her basket and turned to walk toward the gate. He chose to lead his horse beside her, making her uncomfortably conscious of his broad shoulders and muscular limbs, which a perfectly tailored blue coat and creaseless breeches did nothing to disguise.

"So tell me. Are you enjoying Brighton, Miss Talcott?"

"Not at all."

"I suppose, unlike your relations, you have no taste for expensive frivolity."

"I suppose *you* have come to Brighton for your health," she said, making no attempt to veil her sarcasm.

"Of course."

"Then you must take the waters of St. Anne's Well. According to Dr. Relhan, they are most beneficial to bodies 'laboring under the consequences of irregular living and illicit pleasures.' "

He laughed aloud. "Touché, Miss Talcott. You are no doubt correct, and I shall seek out St. Anne's Well instantly. I only trust the waters are not too vile for my palate."

She remained silent. A minute or two and they would reach the gate. She would be rid of him.

"How are your friends, Lady Catherine and Miss Hutton—er, Lady Amberley, I should say?"

A lump came to Pen's throat at the thought of Catherine, so happy with her Mr. Woodmere up in the Lakes, and Juliana, who had last written to her from Venice, where she and her new husband, the Earl of Amberley, were taking their honeymoon. They had become fast friends while at Miss Stratton's select school for young ladies, where they'd been dubbed the "Three Disgraces." Pen would never forget how Cat and Jule had defended her against the catty set on her arrival at the school, or the madcap escapades they'd drawn her into, like the time they had run away to a local fair disguised as boys.

"My friends are very well," she replied simply.

"I am glad to hear it."

There was an odd tone in Verwood's silky voice, sincere but also somehow regretful. Each time he had become involved in her friends' affairs, he'd claimed to have good intentions. Pen still did not know whether to believe him. Did he cherish a *tendre* for one of them? Or was it merely his pride that smarted after he'd twice been foiled in his mysterious schemes?

"I trust your nose has completely healed?" she asked, determined to keep the conversation to prosaic matters.

"Thank you, yes."

She glanced over and noted that his handsome profile showed no sign now of the punishment it had received a few months earlier at the hands of a rival for Juliana's favors. It was a mistake to look. Her eyes were irresistibly drawn to his high forehead, dramatically arched brows, his rather long nose and chin and wide sensual lips, features that all seemed too strong individually but made for a masculine, beautiful whole.

Drat! Now he was smiling at her wickedly, as if he found her attractive as well. Why did he make the effort? She was no acclaimed Beauty, like Catherine or Juliana, or the most recent object of his desires, Lady Everton. Small, redhaired, and freckled, Pen could have no power to attract such a connoisseur of the female sex, even if she wished to do so.

Verwood was dangerous; it was even said that he'd seduced and abandoned a young lady of quality. Pen was not the sort of fool who thought it romantic to reform a rake; she had set her heart on quite a different sort of man. Cyril Welling had all the qualities she desired in a husband; he was honest, trustworthy, and kind. What did it matter that Verwood was so darkly beautiful, his tall person so well-formed that she ached to sketch him, to capture every expression, the curve and shading of every muscle?

She increased her pace, desperately summoning up the image of Cyril to her mind in an effort to banish her consciousness of Lord Verwood. She did not go more than a few steps before tumbling face-first onto the muddy ground once more.

"What the devil—" Verwood cursed behind her. She rolled over, and saw him release his horse and come to her once more.

"Are you all right?" he asked, kneeling beside her.

She nodded, having had the wind knocked out of her again. He put one arm around her shoulder and helped her to sit up. She gasped, and inhaled the mingled scent of cloves, lavender, and horses.

"I cannot . . . imagine how I could have been so . . . clumsy . . . again," she said.

"Shh . . . do not move," he commanded softly. Obedient but puzzled, she watched as he sprang up and went toward the wall. Then she saw the strong, slender cord tangled around her ankle.

Tracing it with her eyes, she saw that it had been fastened between the stone wall and a gorse bush, at just the proper height to trip up an unwary walker. Or a horse.

Heart thudding again, she watched Verwood pace along the wall, peering over it. Then Verwood turned and strode to the gate, turning his head to gaze up and down the lane. He returned to her, his expression grim.

"This," she gestured toward the cord, "was not intended for me, was it?"

He shook his head, then knelt to remove the cord from her foot. A tingle rose from her ankle where his deft hands touched her stocking. She tried to ignore it, but her face warmed as he gently wiped the dirt from her cheek with his handkerchief, then helped her up once more.

Then an image assaulted her: Verwood and his horse lying broken and mangled on the cold ground, their grace and beauty destroyed forever. Her knees buckled, and Verwood held her close against him to keep her from falling. She took in a gulp of air, comforted by the feel of his warm, living, breathing body against hers. She stared up at him for a moment, then before she knew what was happening, he lowered his head and brushed her lips with his. For an instant new and potent sensations surged through her. Then Verwood lifted his head and smiled, looking odiously self-satisfied.

After a dazed moment she jerked out of his arms. "What do you take me for, some sort of—of trollop?" she demanded, voice shaking with embarrassment and fury. "Why did you do that?"

"The temptation was irresistible," he said, grinning. "You must forgive me. I shan't do it again—unless you desire it, of course."

"Certainly not," she said, shocked. "It is not the time for such nonsense. Have you forgotten that someone has just tried to do you a serious injury?"

"No. I must thank you," he said in a more sober tone. "Had I galloped into this, my horse and I would certainly have gone tail over top. You spared us a most embarrassing fall."

She glanced over at his horse, calmly cropping grass nearby.

"I am not an idiot, my lord. It could have been far worse than a mere fall. You could have broken your neck."

He said nothing, but the lines around his mouth tightened. Her mind raced. After her fall he had carefully surveyed their surroundings. Why?

"You do not think . . . that someone could have been waiting behind the wall, to—to?"

To finish off the job.

It was too lurid to say, so far from anything she had ever experienced. He continued to look grave and did not deny it, as she half-hoped. She lifted a hand to her mouth as a faint sense of nausea stole over her.

"Do not look so distressed. There is no one nearby. If anyone was here, he was frightened off by the presence of a witness."

"Who would wish to harm you?" she asked, her voice breaking. "Who would have known you would ride this way?"

He shrugged, from ignorance or a desire to keep his own counsel. Knowing his reputation, Pen felt certain he had his enemies. But what could he have done to merit an attempt on his life? How could he look so calm?

"Don't you even care that someone tried to hurt you?" she demanded.

"Does the thought fill you with dismay, Miss Talcott? I confess, I'm delighted." He even smiled.

"You are *mad.*"

"No, merely touched by your concern. I had no idea you had so much charity for me."

"I should be so concerned for any fellow being in danger."

"Of course." His smile froze. "But your concern is misplaced. I assure you, I can take care of myself."

"Even though it was my presence that saved you this time."

"I am not so easily disposed of."

Had there been previous attempts? "What will you do?"

"The less you know, the better. Your aunt will be looking for you. Is it not time you returned to town?"

It felt like a snub. She'd saved his life, he'd kissed her, and now she was being dismissed like a child. But how could she help, and did she even care what became of the rogue? She picked up her basket and walked on. A moment later Verwood rejoined her, having caught his horse.

"I request that you keep this incident to yourself. In fact, it would be best if you forgot it entirely."

"I do not think I will ever forget this," she said, opening the gate for him as he mounted his horse. "I will remain silent, if that is your wish."

"Good day, Miss Talcott. And thank you again."

He urged his horse into a trot, leaving her to marvel at his sangfroid. Her own heart continued to race with the memory of his kiss and the thought that she might have witnessed his murder.

It was then that she recalled the man she'd seen in the lane and the menace she'd sensed in his presence.

"Wait! Stop!" she shouted.

But Lord Verwood was already too far to hear her.

Chapter Two

*V*erwood guided his horse down the sloping track, keeping an eye out for anything unusual. He had tried to keep his worst suspicions from Miss Talcott, but she was too intelligent not to comprehend what had just occurred.

The devil of it was, he'd no idea who wished him dead this time. Who had known his intended route? He might have mentioned it to Will Symonds, his valet—but Symonds was loyal, surely. As was Pascoe, his head groom. But there were any number of grooms, coachmen and stable boys at the Old Ship who might have overheard his plans.

Lord, he'd gotten careless! It had been about a year since anyone had tried to kill him. He thought he'd managed to settle the last of his deceased father's murky affairs. All, that is, except the matter regarding Lady Everton, which had mysteriously surfaced several months ago. Could it be Everton, her husband, acting out of jealousy? Apparently Verwood's enemy, whoever he was, had wished it to look like a riding accident. But Everton was an honorable sort, an idealistic reformer no less. Everton would more likely challenge him to a duel. Unless he thought the scandal might jeopardize his political career?

No, it wasn't Everton. Verwood cast his mind back over the past, trying to think which of father's enemies might still wish to do away with him.

Could it be related to his own past? But the scandal regarding Anne Norland was so ancient. It had all happened ten years ago, when he'd been only eighteen. His father and

George Norland had made their deal, and Verwood had gone out of the country. He'd returned to Cornwall on the occasion of his father's death, two years previously. Regarded as the scourge of the neighborhood, he'd not had any contact with the Norlands, not even Mariah and Edward, Anne's younger brother and sister, who'd been children when he and Anne had run away. No, no one threatened him there.

He frowned. If he were not the last of the Verwoods, he would suspect a distant heir, but their line was dying out. Perhaps deservedly.

Damn! He'd thought it was safe to settle down to a life of comfortable hedonism, even take a wife, perhaps. Since that ghastly night with *La Perle*, it had been more and more difficult to find a mistress that suited him. Now it seemed there was at least one more mystery to unravel before he could do any of these things.

The fog continued to rise, but still he had not seen anything that gave him a clue. He was lucky indeed that Miss Talcott had happened by. She'd looked pale, poor thing, her enormous hazel eyes so wide with concern that he couldn't resist kissing her. Just to see if it would bring the color back to her cheeks. As it had!

An unusual creature, Miss Talcott: one moment a shy wallflower, the next a veritable wildcat, especially when concerned over her friends. A disheveled angel who'd tumbled through the mists at an opportune moment. Her eyes and cheeks bright from the fresh air, her petite, delectable shape only half-hidden by her cloak, she'd made him forget his ingrained habit of avoiding straight-laced females.

Folly!

Adorable as she was, Penelope Talcott was far too upright and respectable to suit him. He'd failed with her bolder, more unconventional friends; there was no chance he would find favor with her. Besides, she disturbed his peace. Each time she looked at him with those intent hazel eyes, trying to decide whether to trust him, he felt as if she probed his very soul. No, he wanted a comfortable wife, one who would not seek to reform him. No doubt it was the close brush with death, combined with the fact that he'd parted from his last mistress several months before, that made him react so strongly to such an innocent little kiss.

Verwood forced Miss Talcott's image from his mind as he guided his horse down the Steine—Brighton's fashionable, grassy promenade, flanked by elegant houses and shops—toward the seafront and his current residence, the Old Ship Inn. It was time he made plans to discover who wished him underground. It was pure luck that Miss Talcott had saved his life this morning.

Another time he might not be so lucky.

Pen hurried past a pathetic one-armed statue of the Prince Regent and into the house in the Royal Crescent that her uncle had hired for the summer. As she climbed up to her room, sounds of argument issued from her aunt and uncle's bedchamber. Pen hated their endless bickering, but this morning it might serve to prevent a scold. She cringed as the door opened.

"Lace? Three guineas just for lace? It's unheard of! I demand you take it back!" Uncle Ralph commanded petulantly from within the bedchamber.

Aunt Mary, as round as she was short, stood in the doorway, her cap askew as she turned to face her husband.

"Not so preposterous as the sum you paid for that dreadful green coat! With those hideous buttons I cannot even bear to look at! They make you look as fat as—"

"*Fat?* How dare *you* call *me* fat? I'll have you know—"

"I am not listening to any more of this!"

Aunt Mary turned and slammed the door. Pen winced as her aunt whirled and stared at her, her expression darkening. "*Penelope!* Where have you been?"

"I was out sketching, Aunt."

"What have you done to your dress? Has anyone seen you?"

"No one of consequence." It was not a lie, Pen decided. Even her aunt was not so foolish as to consider Lord Verwood an acquaintance worth cultivating.

Aunt Mary sniffed, then called out for Susan to bring hot chocolate to the sitting room. "Come with me, Penelope."

Pen sighed and followed her aunt down the stairs.

"I don't know how you expect to ever attract an eligible gentleman if you make such a figure of yourself," said Aunt Mary, plunking herself down on the sofa.

"I am sorry," said Pen, calmly seating herself opposite.

"Sorry? When every tradesman in London and Brighton is dunning us, all you can say is you are *sorry*!"

"Perhaps if we returned home and lived more modestly—"

"Yes, and how would you find a respectable suitor in Lambourne? Good God! You're not still cherishing hopes of that dreadful curate, are you?"

Pen squared her shoulders and nodded. "Mr. Welling and I have an understanding."

"You ungrateful fool! With all the advantages your uncle and I have given you! Taking you in as our daughter, sending you to a select school, dressing you in the height of fashion. And you would throw it all away for a penniless clergyman!"

"I am sorry to be a disappointment to you, but the fact is that I do not desire to achieve the sort of match you wish for me. Nor do I have the beauty or wit to do so."

"Come, dear, you are pretty enough!" said her aunt in a softer tone. "If you would just make *some* attempt to behave like other young ladies, you could do very well."

Pen was silent. It was no use telling Aunt Mary that she did not care for a fashionable life, and that she was horrified by the expense to which her relations had gone to attempt to launch her into society. She would only seem ungrateful.

"We go to the assembly at the Old Ship tonight. Susan has added some lace to that pink satin of yours. I daresay no one will guess you have ever worn it before."

Pen inwardly groaned at the thought of the pink gown, which grew more hideous with each new embellishment. But unbecoming raiment helped ward off unwanted suitors, she reminded herself.

"Mrs. Pippacott will be there," her aunt continued, "along with that charming son of hers."

Pen suppressed another groan at the thought of Hercules Pippacott. A more stupid creature she'd never seen. But it didn't do to say so, for Mrs. Pippacott was one of her aunt's closest cronies.

"You know, Louisa Pippacott is most anxious that her son settle down with a good, sensible girl," said Aunt Mary with a significant look.

"I hope he finds one to his liking, then," said Pen. *One who will be content to live under her mother-in-law's thumb,* she added silently. *It won't be me.*

"Oh, you are being coy!" chided Aunt Mary, and began to prattle on about Mr. Pippacott's elegance and agreeable nature.

I saved a man's life today. The thought echoed through Pen's mind as she pretended to listen to Aunt Mary's insipid chatter. The thought of the attempted murder she had prevented still terrified her. Of course, she'd heard and read about such things, but she'd never been acquainted with the prospective victim. It was not that she cared for Lord Verwood, but the thought of such nameless malice was frightening.

Susan arrived with the hot chocolate, and Pen took the opportunity to slip away into her own bedchamber. She washed her face and hands, bathed her forehead with cool water, and then laid herself facedown on her bed.

She hated this life: the tradesmen's bills, the struggle to find ways to pay the servants, the petty gossip of fashionable society, Aunt Mary's matchmaking. She longed to be back in Lambourne, far from crowds, far from darkly handsome gentlemen who were targets for cold-blooded murder.

She wanted Cyril. Kind, sober, honest Cyril. So much more eligible in every real sense than that idiotic Hercules Pippacott Aunt Mary was always urging her to try to attract! Perhaps in time her relations would let her have her way. She and Cyril both hoped the current rector at Lambourne would soon retire.

She rolled over, trying to picture their life together. It was an exercise that had often brought her comfort. This time, her mind's eye refused to conjure up Cyril's mild-featured face, instead presenting her with Verwood's dark eyes under his sharply angled brows, his mobile, sensuous mouth. How that mouth had curved when he gently mocked her for tumbling in front of him, how warm his lips had felt upon hers. He had kissed her so casually, as if attempts on his life were a daily occurrence!

She swallowed her indignation and concentrated on her memories of the vine-covered parsonage at Lambourne, with its small garden. There was a sunny little slope that would be perfect for strawberries. She closed her eyes, trying to imagine herself sitting on a warm stone wall, eating strawberries fresh from the bed, sharing them with her children.

Once again the image of Lord Verwood, lying broken and bleeding, crushed by his horse, drove out everything else.

She opened her eyes as a heavy feeling stole over her heart. Would any of her dreams ever come to pass?

She thought of Catherine and Juliana and how boldly they had made plans to achieve their desires. Now that her peace was destroyed by Lord Verwood's predicament, she could no longer remain passive. Perhaps it was fate that she had intervened this morning. Perhaps she was meant to play some role in Lord Verwood's life before achieving her own dreams. But how could she possibly help? Was it dangerous to try?

Catherine might provide some insight into Lord Verwood. Though her letters glowed with happiness over her marriage and her new baby, she'd never explained what happened last summer. Perhaps Cat knew who might wish to kill Lord Verwood, and why.

Yes, she would write to Catherine.

Before Pen could do that, however, there was one other thing she had to do. She found a pencil, opened her sketchbook to a new page, and began to draw. With every sure stroke and firm line, her conviction grew that she was taking an irrevocable step toward a shadowy, uncertain future.

Pen gazed about the ballroom at the Old Ship. The ball had barely begun, but the large, elegant room in the Adam style was already warm, noisy, and crowded. Her aunt sat beside her, chatting away to her friend Mrs. Pippacott. Fortunately for Pen, Hercules Pippacott had wandered off to the card room, where she hoped he would stay the remainder of the evening.

She tried not to shift nervously in her seat. Was she a fool to think Lord Verwood might come here? He was certainly not accepted in polite society, but it was a public assembly, and she did not think the master of ceremonies would have the courage to turn away such an elegant gentleman. Rakes and rogues and even ladies with tarnished reputations were more readily accepted in Brighton than they were in London.

A stir of some sort occurred near the doorway, but when Pen looked over, she saw the crowd parting for a middle-aged couple.

"The Duke and Duchess of Whitgrave!" exclaimed Aunt Mary to her friend, and they all rose to bow as the master of ceremonies led Their Graces to seats at a convenient location for viewing the festivities.

Pen had already met the duke, her friend Catherine's father, a middle-aged, portly man with pale yellow hair receding over his ruddy face and pale blue eyes, and Cat's stepmother, thin and haughty, with rubies glistening in her hair and around her neck. Pen lowered her face as they passed. Their Graces had never thought her a suitable companion for Cat.

A minute or two after the Whitgraves passed by, another striking couple entered. Pen had seen them before: Lord Everton, a tall, upright gentleman said to be active in Whig politics, and his wife, whose dark hair, large dark eyes, and statuesque figure made her one of the acknowledged Beauties of the Brighton scene. Her gown was of cream-colored silk and flowed gracefully down her body. Long strands of pearls accented her dark hair and draped suggestively over her shapely bosom.

"Such an odd dress, don't you think?" said Mrs. Pippacott.

"What a tiny bodice! *I* should not like to be seen in such a shocking garment," said Pen's aunt.

Pen noted the daring ensemble as well, but without jealousy. Although she would part with her own pink monstrosity without a single regret, she had no wish to wear a gown that would attract so much attention. It *would* be pleasant, however, to have a gentleman look at her as adoringly as Lord Everton gazed at his wife.

Mrs. Pippacott excused herself at that point, saying she was going to find her son. Pen watched the lady leave, hoping she would fail to locate her precious Hercules. Then her heart skipped a beat. She'd been hoping to see him of course; still, it was a shock when Lord Verwood entered the room. Now, could she somehow gain his attention?

He came in and out of view as he wended his way through couples gathering for the next dance, a waltz. Older gentlemen eyed him disapprovingly, younger ones with belligerence and a tinge of envy. Mothers whispered to their daughters. The obedient ones looked coyly away as Verwood passed, while the bolder ones ogled him out of the corners of their eyes.

He was getting close to where they sat, so Pen took the chance and stood up, hoping to catch his eye. Again, she lost him in the crowd, then when she saw him again, he was looking the other way. Unthinkable to wave to him; that would draw far too much attention to her. What else could she do?

Then, as if reading her mind, he looked her way. Their gazes locked. She tried to convey an urgent message with her expression, but his own expression was polite and impersonal, so she could not tell if he understood. A few feet more, and he stopped next to the dashing Lady Everton. Of course, *she* must be the reason he had come.

Pen could not help noticing the lady's nervous expression or her husband's suspicious stance as he watched his wife accompany Verwood to the floor. For the next twenty minutes, Pen had the dubious pleasure of watching the handsome couple waltz together. The lady's smile seemed forced. Why had she agreed to dance with him, then?

And why was Verwood flirting with her? Did he regard a devoted wife as a challenge to be overcome? Pen decided she would make no further attempts to catch his attention.

She looked away from the couple and caught sight of the Whitgraves, still seated at one end of the room like royalty. The duke's face was red with outrage, and spots of angry color shone on the duchess's cheeks as well. Pen knew they resented whatever role Verwood had played in preventing Catherine's marriage to the lord of their choice.

"Oh, Penelope, here is Mr. Pippacott," said Aunt Mary in a bright tone.

She looked up, and her heart sank as she saw that Mrs. Pippacott had returned, her gangly son in tow. No one could have been less aptly named. Mr. Hercules Pippacott was tall, but so thin that no degree of tailoring could disguise his lack of manly musculature. His exaggerated collar and the obviously padded shoulders of his pale blue coat looked ridiculous, and the cherubim style of his fair hair gave him an effeminate look.

"Mith Talcott, will you do me the pleasure of dancing with me?" he lisped obediently in response to his mother's nudge.

She paused, knowing what a ridiculous picture they would present. Unfortunately, there was no way to politely refuse.

"Ah, I had thought Miss Talcott had promised *me* this dance."

Surprise immobilized Pen as she looked up at Lord Verwood. She flushed a little, knowing how shocking it would appear for her to dance with a notorious rake.

"I am sorry—" she began, looking from one man to the other.

Verwood gave Mr. Pippacott such an amused, contemptuous look that the other seemed to visibly wilt.

"If Lord Verwood has the prior claim, I shall not—I mean, I would not—" Mr. Pippacott goggled at both of them.

"I was not aware that you were acquainted," said Aunt Mary sharply.

Then Lord Verwood turned his gaze on her. Looking flustered, Aunt Mary ceased her protests.

"Why did you say you wanted to dance with me?" Pen hissed as they made their way through the crowd.

He raised his eyebrows. "I was under the impression that *you* wished to speak to *me*."

"Yes, I did, but—" she began, and fell silent again.

"Don't pretend you wished to dance with that stupid puppy!"

"I don't wish to dance with either of you."

"It is too late to change your mind now, Miss Talcott."

They took their place, and the surrounding couples eyed them curiously, the men's expressions guarded, the ladies' coy and intrigued. A buxom young lady across from them could not take her eyes off of Verwood, and it was clear they were all wondering why he'd singled Pen out to dance. She flushed, hating to be the center of so much attention.

The music started, and the first figures of the dance were too lively to permit conversation. They came together a few moments later.

"If you wish to speak of this morning's incident," he said in a low voice, his hand on hers sending an uncomfortable tingle up her arm, "I would still recommend you forget it."

They separated again, and Pen forced herself to smile as she danced with another gentleman.

"I saw someone up on the Downs before we met," she said, the next time the figure of the dance brought her together with Lord Verwood.

He looked at her sharply before releasing her.

A moment later they reached the top of the line. Good. They would have a moment to converse further.

"I have made a sketch of him," she said quickly, trying to keep her voice low as Verwood leaned closer to hear her. "I thought perhaps he was the one who had set the trap for you. Perhaps the picture would aid you in discovering his identity. If you give me your direction, I could arrange to have my maid deliver it to you."

"I am staying here in the Old Ship. Your maidservant— can she be trusted to be discreet?"

She nodded.

"Very well. I thank you for your assistance, Miss Talcott."

He smiled, as if touched by her concern.

"There is no need to thank me," she said. "I wish for no further involvement in your affairs."

He bowed slightly, as if in acknowledgment of her desires. The next couple had caught up to them, and they reentered the dance. Verwood's casual touch disturbed her. She longed to be outside, to feel cool sea breezes on her hot face, to have nothing further to do with a heedless rogue who courted death in order to dally with a married lady.

As the dance ended, Verwood took her arm to escort her back to her aunt.

Lowering his head to speak into her ear, he murmured, "Thank you, Miss Talcott."

She felt his breath on her cheek and flushed with suppressed fury as she remembered his behavior on the Downs. Her first kiss, and Verwood had robbed Cyril of the chance to share it with her. All to satisfy what must have been a casual, fleeting temptation!

"Now you have done all you can for me," he continued. "I do not think your reputation will be permanently damaged by one dance with me, but there our association must end."

"You cannot wish for that more than I do," she retorted.

He nodded, his expression hardening, and brought her back to Aunt Mary. She glared at them both, but there was a look of strain in her eyes.

"Penelope, I am dreadfully fatigued," she complained. "I am afraid we must leave. Immediately."

"I am desolated to hear it, Lady Talcott," replied Lord Verwood. "Can I be of any assistance?"

"No, thank you. You have done quite enough for us already," she said, laboriously pulling herself up from the chair. "Come, Penelope, let us go to the card room and find your uncle."

Verwood bowed and strolled off, looking perfectly at ease.

Before she and her aunt had taken more than a few steps, however, Mr. Pippacott reappeared before them.

"Miss Talcott, m-may I solicit the pleasure of the next dance?" he asked.

Pen stared at him, wondering what had prompted him to ask again.

"Of course you must dance with him," insisted Aunt Mary.

"But I thought you were fatigued, dear Aunt—"

"Nonsense, my dear. Now, go along and enjoy yourself!"

Pen sighed and allowed herself to be drawn once more toward the dance floor.

*   *   *

Verwood watched as Miss Talcott joined the dance. It came as no surprise that she wanted nothing more to do with him, though he felt an unexpected sense of regret that he'd never taste those sweet lips again. But the dandyish puppy she was dancing with was not worthy of her either! Then, looking about the room, Verwood chuckled softly to himself. Several young bucks were watching her, clearly determined to discover why he had singled out such a wall-flower. Good. Their dance together had done Miss Talcott no harm.

He gazed back toward her aunt. What a vulgar creature! And she dressed her niece so unbecomingly. Years of experience enabled him to recognize that Miss Talcott had quite a fetching little figure beneath that pink fright of a gown, but most gentlemen were not so perceptive. Unless her charms were more suitably displayed, she might never attract the husband she undoubtedly deserved. A plan began to form in his mind. Dare he meddle? But surely he owed Miss Talcott *something* for all she'd done?

He returned to Lady Talcott, who glared at him, putting him much in mind of an angry hen with her feathers ruffled.

"My apologies for disturbing you once more this evening, Lady Talcott."

"Must you speak to me?" she asked in a voice lowered so that no nearby persons could hear. "You have drawn enough attention to my niece as it is."

"Attention which appears to have attracted a previously uninterested swain."

She paused, frowning as she looked at her niece and her partner, and the other curious faces turned in her direction.

"Perhaps, but I forbid you to seek out my niece any further. A little more such attention, and she will be branded a *fast* girl, which I assure you she is not."

"I mean no harm to Miss Talcott's reputation. I promise to keep my distance henceforward . . . on one condition."

"What is your condition?" she asked, playing nervously with her fan.

"Miss Talcott must be given a new look. Her hair must be dressed high on her head. That pink gown must be given away, and any others like it. She must be attired in sea-greens, blues, straws, ambers. No rosettes, no flounces, only the simplest of ornamentation. The bodice cut lower, the skirt narrower—"

"Wider skirts are coming into fashion, and rosettes are all the rage. She will look a complete dowd!"

"Ladies care about the latest fashions; gentlemen prefer to see the female figure displayed to advantage. Miss Talcott has already had two London Seasons, if I remember correctly?"

Lady Talcott glared at him, but he could see her wavering.

"If you continue to dress your niece in those appalling garments, I positively will have to come to her rescue as she sits alone waiting for a partner."

"Oh, very well!" said Lady Talcott ungraciously.

"I thought you would see reason. I shall attend a few more assemblies to make sure my instructions have been carried out. I promise to make no further attempt to approach your niece."

"You had better not!"

"I give you my word as a gentleman," he said, conscious of the irony of the statement.

She scowled.

"Lady Talcott, I do know what I am about. Who better to know what will appeal to the male sex? Now I shall relieve you of my presence. Make sure you carry out all my instructions!"

He bowed and left her, reasonably satisfied with his evening's work. He'd taken the next step toward concluding the affair regarding Lady Everton. One more meeting and they would both be free to go their own ways.

However, he'd felt hostile eyes upon him all evening but had failed to make any progress identifying his enemy. Whether Miss Talcott's drawing would be accurate enough to be of use was questionable. Still, he was touched by her kind impulse.

He hoped his advice to her aunt would prove helpful, despite the annoying inner voice that reminded him that good intentions invariably led to disaster.

This time it would be different.

Chapter Three

*I*t had been several days since Pen had danced with Lord Verwood at the Old Ship, and in that short space she'd become the object of everyone's curiosity. Bucks who had previously ignored her now accosted her as she accompanied her aunt to the Royal Marine Library or promenaded along the seaside. In fact, she reflected as she alighted from the carriage, this very invitation to the Royal Pavilion for one of the Prince Regent's musical evenings might well be the result of the stir caused by Lord Verwood's brief interest in her.

She stared up at the exotically domed building, disquieted by its very un-Englishness as much as by the unwanted changes that had been wrought in her life since the assembly. Her anxiety grew as they passed under the roof of the octagon hall, and on into another entrance hall, all in gray and green, decorated with fantastic chinoiserie patterns.

"Just look at that marble chimneypiece! And those lanterns! Those vases! How beautiful!" exclaimed Aunt Mary. "Do you not think so, Penelope?"

"I cannot help but think of how many hundreds of thousands of pounds were spent on this place," she answered truthfully, thinking of the prince's many subjects who could barely command the necessities of life.

"You'll do well to keep those views to yourself, gel!" hissed her uncle.

"I shall endeavor not to embarrass you," she whispered, knowing it would be no use airing her views.

After being announced by one of the flunkies at the back of the hall, the Talcotts passed through the door into the Chinese Gallery, where the Prince Regent stood in the center ready to greet his guests. This was Pen's first close view of him, and she was a bit shocked to see that he was as fat and as gaudily dressed, in a peacock-blue coat and lavishly embroidered waistcoat, as in any political caricature she'd ever seen.

She sank into a deep curtsy beside her aunt, and the Prince Regent shook hands and exchanged some polite words with her aunt and uncle. During this time she observed him quietly and was surprised at his good-humored smile and friendly manner. It was hard to believe this was the same man who had behaved with such selfishness toward his wives and lovers and with such negligence for the state of his country. Then he turned to her.

"Ah, so this is your pretty little niece who has become the talk of Brighton?" he asked, confirming Pen's suspicions of why they'd been invited.

She blushed as he subjected her to a close scrutiny. Garbed in a new and daringly cut gown of pale sea green, she felt exposed, unlike her normal self.

"I am sure all of the young bucks will be breaking their hearts over you, my dear," the Regent replied with a smile.

"You are too kind, sir," she said, relieved to see that he was already preparing to talk to a new set of guests. She remembered that he was known to prefer handsome, buxom ladies, often older than himself.

Pen and her aunt and uncle joined the rest of the guests in strolling through the Gallery before the concert. Aunt Mary could do little but exclaim at the beauty of all she saw, from the luxuriant blue and pink murals, the stained-glass lanterns, the Oriental vases and figures, while Pen continued to ponder the blind extravagance of it all.

"Mith Talcott!" Hercules Pippacott exclaimed, coming toward them, his mother in tow.

No sooner than they had exchanged greetings, Mrs. Pippacott proposed that her son show Pen all the glories of the vast corridor. Uncle Ralph and Aunt Mary urged her to take his arm, so Pen steeled herself for the upcoming ordeal.

"You are looking exthessively beautiful tonight, dear Mith Talcott," he said.

She thanked him, then her heart gave a little lurch as out of the corner of her eye she espied Lord Verwood. She was surprised to see him, then remembered the Prince Regent was said to have many scandalous cronies. She also felt an overpowering sense of relief at seeing Verwood still alive and well. Apparently, she'd been deluding herself the past few days. She still cared what became of him.

"What do you think? Ith it all not very beautiful?" Pippacott claimed her attention again.

"Quite out of the ordinary," she replied diplomatically.

A brief opening in the crowd showed Pen that the Prince Regent was now welcoming Lord and Lady Everton. Lord Everton wore a determined expression; perhaps he hoped to persuade the Regent to support one of his progressive policies. Seeing the prince's expression as he looked at Lady Everton, Pen doubted politics were on his mind. It was not Lady Everton's emerald necklace that riveted the royal gaze.

Pen wished she were miles away. With both the Evertons and Lord Verwood in attendance, the evening seemed fraught with possibilities for intrigue.

Distracted, she did not notice that Pippacott had guided her through a door at the end of the Gallery until it was too late. She found herself standing in a vast drawing room, with a pink ceiling and columns in the shape of palm trees. A few candles were lit, allowing her to see the self-satisfied smile on Pippacott's face as he blocked her exit from the room.

"Let me by, please," she said, but he stubbornly stood his ground.

"Not before you have lithened to what I have to thay," he announced. "I love you. Marry me, lovely Penelope!"

"This is ridiculous. Are you drunk? Let me by!"

Still, he stood his ground. "You are too cruel! You will lithen to me, and let me tell you about the life we shall lead together!"

She said nothing. Perhaps if he spoke his piece, and she refused again, he would realize it was hopeless and let her go.

"We will honeymoon on the Continent, and when we return we shall perthuade Mama to hire a house in London. Only think about it!"

Pen's temper snapped. Heavens, the fop wished to marry her so that she might help him break free of his mama's leading-strings!

"We are wretchedly ill suited, Mr. Pippacott," she interrupted. "I prefer country life. Let us rejoin the other guests now."

She came forward, lifting her hands to push him aside. He wrapped his long arms around her, trapping her hands against his chest, and tried to kiss her. She averted her head just in time, and his lips damply brushed her temple.

"Let me go," she demanded in a low voice as she struggled to free herself. Heaven help her if they were overheard!

"No, I shall not. I will not be denied!" he said, clumsily pawing at the neck of her gown as she continued to turn her face away from him.

Her hands were still imprisoned between them, inches away from the ends of his intricately tied cravat. It gave her an idea. She reached up and grasped the folds, relaxed for an instant, then flung herself backward with all her might. Pippacott's neckcloth unraveled, and she regained her balance a few feet away, relieved to be out of his arms.

"What have you done? I'll have you know it took me three hours to achieve just the right effect!" he said, his lisp suddenly gone. "It will take ages for me to make myself presentable again!"

"Then I suppose you will have to miss the concert," she said, preparing to go around him once more.

"We shall both miss the concert," he said, triumphantly blocking her way once more. "You are compromised, and everyone shall know it!"

"Tell them what you wish; you will only make yourself ridiculous. I won't spend another instant in your presence!"

The thought of being a laughingstock brought a look of loathing to Pippacott's face. He still blocked her path, so she turned to exit the room by a door she saw in the adjacent wall. Out of the corner of her eye, she saw he was absorbed in retying his neckcloth. Good! She hoped it would take hours.

She passed swiftly through the door, hoping it led in the right direction. She burst into a huge, domed Saloon, then stopped short.

Lady Everton stood there, Lord Verwood behind her, his hands on her shoulders. Both of them were smiling.

Pen stared for a moment, feeling almost sick with revulsion and some emotion she refused to name. Their smiles faded as Verwood removed his hands from the Lady Everton's shoulders.

"M-miss Talcott, is it?" stammered Lady Everton. "This is not what it seems, I assure you. I hope you—"

"There you are, damn you!"

Pen turned her head. Lord Everton rushed across the room from a door opposite to the one she'd entered by. Lady Everton gave a frightened squeak and turned to face her husband. Lord Everton stopped, his expression furious, then stared at Pen, looking puzzled to see her.

"My friend Miss Talcott was unwise enough to slip off with this mischievous rogue," explained Lady Everton. "I—I saw them and followed to make sure they were properly chaperoned."

"Is this true?" Everton asked, staring at Pen, his hands clenched into fists. His wife looked terrified, as if he would explode into violence at any moment. Already hating herself for it, Pen decided to help avert the crisis. She nodded.

Everton gave them all a skeptical look, but he seemed aware of the impropriety of brawling in a royal palace. Pen was relieved to watch his arms drop to his sides.

"I would warn you not to become caught up in this scoundrel's games," he said to Pen. Then he turned to Verwood. "You are not to come near my wife again. Do you understand?"

"Perfectly," said Verwood. "I trust you will speak no further of this matter as regards Miss Talcott?"

"I have no wish to indulge in idle gossip," said Everton. He took his wife's arm and pulled her toward the door that Pen thought must lead back to the Gallery, leaving her and Lord Verwood standing together under the dome.

She started to follow the Evertons, but Verwood put a hand on her arm.

"Wait," he advised. "If you burst out of the room after the Evertons it will give rise to more gossip. Particularly if I am seen to be with you."

"What would you have me do? Stay here with *you*?"

"Not at all. Soon the guests will make their way toward the Music Room. Come with me. I can bring you there by another route. I will hang back, and it will merely appear that you were one of the first guests to reach the Music Room."

He took her hand and led her toward the other door, seeming quite familiar with the place. She went along, seething with disgust at his behavior.

"I must compliment you on your new gown, Miss Talcott," he said, perhaps in the hope of soothing her scorn. "You look very fetching in it."

"I hate it!"

"Good God, why?"

"Aunt Mary has already spent far too much on my apparel, and we can ill afford new gowns. Besides, this style has drawn the most odious of insults upon me."

"From young Pippacott? Is that why you burst into the Saloon so abruptly?"

She nodded.

"Oh, dear."

The rueful look on his face caused her anger to flare even higher. "Was this *your* idea, then? Is *that* what you were discussing with my aunt at the Old Ship?"

"I only wished to be helpful," he said, his apologetic tone belied by the roguish smile on his face.

"Helpful! Who gave you the right to meddle in my affairs? You cannot know anything about what is attractive to the sort of man I wish to marry. Am determined to marry!"

They passed into another vast drawing room, and Verwood quirked his eyebrow at her.

"It sounds as if you have already found him. Why have your relations not already embraced this fortunate gentleman?"

"He is in orders, and not wealthy," she replied briefly, not wishing to speak of Cyril to Verwood.

"Oh, a country curate! Very fitting, I suppose."

"Don't mock him! I wish I were with him now. I'm tired of you and this wretched place!"

"Softly, Prinny might hear you," he chided. "You must not let him hear anything but admiration for his home or his favorite town."

"I don't care. What a state England is in, with a maddened king and a Prince Regent who can't bear to think about anything *real*, but instead numbs any true feelings with food and wine and insane schemes to decorate and redecorate his pleasure palace. And like sheep, half the gentlemen in England admire and imitate his idle extravagance, wasting whatever intelligence and talents they've been given!"

He watched her with an amused, indolent smile that only stoked her fury. She stopped, turned, and glared up at him. "Well, have *you* ever shown your face in Parliament?"

"I cannot say that I have. Nor do I think my opinions would carry any weight there."

"So you will not even try. Instead you prefer to waste your time throwing kisses about and dallying with other men's w-wives!" she said, hating how her voice broke.

"It's clear I am a hopeless case," he said, his dark eyes sparkling with amusement. "Here we are. This door leads to the Music Room. Wait. Let me see if anyone is there yet."

She waited as he peeked through the door, shaking with anger but trying to compose herself.

"No one but the musicians," he said, and motioned her in.

Pen entered a room more bizarre and ornate than any before. Deep red walls, gilded dragons, and a stifling heat overwhelmed her, making her wonder if she'd descended into Hell rather than the Prince Regent's Music Room.

She found a seat in a corner, and a minute or two later her aunt and uncle entered, Mrs. Pippacott along with them. They came toward her, faces falling in disappointment to see her alone. She sighed. She would be scolded for not accepting Hercules Pippacott's proposal.

Then she saw Lord Verwood enter, accompanying a dashing widow in a hideous yellow gown, presumably his next conquest.

Perhaps this was indeed Hell. Purgatory at the very least.

Verwood flirted with Mrs. Covington while secretly scanning the room. Yes, there was Miss Talcott, sitting calmly beside her relations. Good! No one had observed her clandestine entry, and his flirtation with the voluptuous dasher beside him should divert gossip away from both Lady Everton and Miss Talcott.

Several hours of heat, Handel, and the covert brushing of Mrs. Covington's thigh against his, and he was glad to see the concert come to an end. Not without some difficulty, he extricated himself from the widow and set off for the Old Ship. In contrast to the majority of Prinny's guests, he'd decided to walk. He took a deep breath of the cool night air, so refreshing after the cloying atmosphere of the Pavilion. This evening he would exit near the stables. Over the past few days, he'd reverted to his old practice of varying his routes, in case someone at the Old Ship was tracking his movements.

Thanks to Miss Talcott and his man Symonds, he now had the name of his attacker. Symonds, having donned a disguise and memorized the image provided by Miss Talcott, had visited several local hedge-taverns and learned that the culprit was most likely one Ted Booley, a fisherman who was known to not be above seeking additional income through smuggling or the odd bit of thuggery. Symonds had not discovered who had hired Booley, but he'd learned the name of Booley's sweetheart. Soon, Verwood hoped, all would be clear.

Clouds fleeted overhead, obscuring the moon at intervals as Verwood briskly moved along Church Street, staying close to the shadows of buildings. He waited for the clouds to dim the moonlight before crossing to Portland Street. A sudden intuition caused him to glance back. Damn! It was Everton.

On reaching North Street, he turned right, ducking behind a building. Clouds had once more obscured the light, so he hurried across toward West Street. With any luck, he'd give Everton the slip, and perhaps Lady Everton would find a way to soothe her husband's jealousy.

But when Verwood reached the seafront and turned in the direction of his inn, moonlight illuminated the figure of a man who peeked out from behind a building, then just as quickly retreated again into the shadows.

Verwood waited until the clouds again hid the moon. Under the cover of darkness, he descended to the beach. He fingered his walking stick, reassured by the knowledge that it concealed a sword. Not that he actually thought he'd need it with Everton, but it was good to know he was armed.

He hoped the Evertons would be discreet about the role Miss Talcott had played in the evening's events. How angry she had been, and rightfully so, for they'd both used her shamelessly. As he walked softly along the pebbly beach, desire arose within him at the memory of how she'd looked. Utterly too tempting, her heart-shaped face with those plump, kissable lips set off by the simple arrangement of her hair, her gown skimming provocatively over delightful feminine curves.

He'd even rather enjoyed the tongue-lashing she'd given him. He hadn't seen such passion in anyone for quite some time. He hoped her country parson would appreciate her. Somehow the thought was annoying. No, he could not be jealous. Perhaps it was just—

He cursed, brought out of his reverie by a movement ahead.

A dark figure rushed upon him from behind a bathing machine. In the dim light he caught sight of an upraised cudgel. Just in time, he dodged a blow intended for his head.

Instead, it landed heavily upon his shoulder, sending pain down his arm and knocking him on his back in the sand. Unable to draw his sword, he remained prone and kicked out with all his might, knocking his attacker on his backside.

Quickly, he rose and began to draw his sword, but was grappled from behind by a new assailant. He leaned back into the second thug's chest and gave another well-placed kick at the other, who let out an unmanly howl.

All his struggles failed to release him from the strong arms holding him from behind. The other man came forward once again, his cudgel poised to deal another blow at Verwood's head. He peered into the man's blackened face for an instant, seeing in a flash the inevitable conclusion. He'd be clubbed to death and dragged to the water, where the outrushing tide would consign his body to eternity.

He wondered if Miss Talcott would grieve over him.

Chapter Four

"*H*o! Stop it, I say!" a voice rang out over the waves. The man about to strike Verwood turned his head to look back the way Verwood had come, while the other slackened his hold. Without bothering to look for the source of the voice, Verwood twisted and rolled to the ground. He grasped his walking stick and released the clasp that held the rapier hidden inside.

The ruffian holding the cudgel turned and lunged wildly for him in the darkness, spearing himself on the upraised point of Verwood's sword. With a grunt, the man fell upon him, gurgling and writhing. Verwood shoved the heavy, bloody corpse off him and saw the figure of his other attacker disappear down the beach. Damn! He'd never catch him now, and the man still faintly twitching on the sand would tell no tales.

The clouds parted, and a slender moonbeam shone down on the beach. Verwood rolled the body over and cursed softly under his breath. The face illuminated by the moonlight, the small eyes staring sightlessly up at the sky were those of Ted Booley.

Looking back the way he came, Verwood spied the figure of a tall man running toward him. Everton. He rose quickly to his feet, holding the sword out before him.

"What the devil is going on here?" asked Everton, his expression harsh as he surveyed Verwood. "Are you hurt?"

Verwood lowered the point of the sword, seeing the horror in Everton's face at seeing him drenched in the dead man's blood. Everton was either an extremely good actor, or he was sincerely shocked. Verwood was inclined to believe it was the latter.

"Bruised, no more," he replied, experimentally lifting and lowering his throbbing shoulder.

"Two on one, damn the rascals!" said Everton, looking affronted. "Why did they attack you?"

"You do not know?"

"Good God, do you think *I* hired them?"

"My apologies, Everton. I don't believe you would do such a thing."

"Do you think they set upon you to rob you? I would have thought it likely in London, but here in Brighton?" Everton paused, looking down at the corpse. "Do you know who he is?"

Verwood shook his head. Everton had no need to know. "Perhaps, as you suggest, he wished to rob me. I have to thank you for providing such a timely interruption."

"I don't wish for your gratitude. I pursued you with entirely different intentions, I assure you."

"I can imagine."

"I intend to teach you the consequences of toying with other men's wives. I demand satisfaction, sir! That is, as soon as your shoulder has healed sufficiently."

Verwood laughed at the amendment.

"Are you mad?" Everton demanded.

"Don't poker up! Would that all my enemies had your sense of honor! Truly, I've no wish to fight you."

"Are you saying you're afraid to meet me?"

"I'm saying I have more important matters to deal with, and so do you. Go back to your wife, and see if she has anything to confide to you."

"Do you think I'm stupid enough to believe her lies?" There was a hint of yearning in Everton's voice.

"I believe if you expend but half the passion you do on politics to making love to your wife, you will find there is nothing amiss with your marriage. Besides, think of the harm to your admirable career should word of a duel between us come to public notice."

"May you rot in Hell!"

"Very likely I shall," Verwood replied, relaxing slightly. From the frustration in Everton's voice, he knew his last argument had hit home. There would be no duel.

It was Dutch comfort. Somewhere, a faceless, nameless enemy waited to strike again. And still, he had no idea why.

Pen passed a restless night, assaulted by images of Lord Verwood, first lying mortally wounded on the Downs, then surrounded by gilded dragons and scandalously clad widows. Finally, she fell into a deep sleep. When she awoke, the morning was half gone, and she'd missed her chance for a walk.

Over the breakfast table, Aunt Mary scolded her for having allowed such a prize as Hercules Pippacott to slip through her fingers. Pen endured it as best she could. At last they left the lodging and made their way down the Marine Parade toward the fashionable center of town. They had just reached the Steine when a tall, fashionably dressed lady accosted them. Pen was surprised to see it was Lady Everton, followed by a liveried footman.

"My dear Lady Talcott," said Lady Everton, after they had all exchanged greetings. "May I beg the pleasure of your niece's company for an hour or so?"

"Penelope will be honored to walk with you," replied Aunt Mary, looking thrilled to be addressed so kindly by a countess.

"Aunt Mary, I had promised to help you shop," Pen objected.

"Nonsense! I would not dream of being so cruel to Lady Everton. You shall rejoin me at Donaldson's Library."

Reluctantly, Pen fell into step beside Lady Everton and watched Aunt Mary hurry on.

"Miss Talcott, you must allow me to apologize to you for the dreadful lie I told last night," said Lady Everton, after her footman discreetly dropped back a number of paces. "There is no excuse for such awful behavior, except that I *had* to prevent Everton from brawling with Lord Verwood in the Pavilion."

"Very well, I accept your apology," said Pen, hoping that would be the end of it.

"No, no, you are still angry. You do not understand—"

"You are right. I do not understand, and I don't wish to."

"You've not heard the news, then?"

"News?" Pen asked, wild fears racing through her mind.

"Oh, so you've not heard. Well, you must allow me to tell you everything."

Pen's heart slowed as she realized Lady Everton's manner was too calm for her to be announcing a murder.

"Very well," she said. "First may we stop to see a friend of mine?"

Lady Everton nodded, and they stopped at the corner of the Marine Parade and the Steine. There sat one of Brighton's most notable personages, wearing a voluminous brown dress, white apron, black cape and an old black straw bonnet. Phoebe Hessell was over a hundred years old now. Though she received a pension from the Prince Regent, she still sat in her accustomed corner on sunny days to sell gingerbread, apples, and trinkets, and to tell stories from her colorful past to anyone who would listen.

"Good morning to ye, Miss Talcott," said the old woman in response to Pen's greeting. Though blind, she'd come to recognize Pen's voice. A smile crinkled the weather-beaten, strong-featured face that lent support to her story of having, as a girl, disguised herself and enlisted in the army to be with her lover, whom she'd nursed and married after he'd been wounded.

Pen politely inquired after Phoebe's health, then introduced Lady Everton.

"Lady Everton. Yes, I've heard tell of ye," said Phoebe, unabashed. "Better keep to yer husband, dearie, rather than cause such a riot and rumpus as ye have."

"I thank you for your kind advice, Mistress Hessell," replied Lady Everton, looking amused at Phoebe's knowledge of the latest gossip. Pen wondered how she could be so carefree.

"Now, as for Miss Talcott, I have a feeling ye'll not be bearing that name for long. Just be brave and faithful to yer man, and all will be well for ye both."

Pen shivered. She didn't need courage. A country parson's wife needed to be dutiful, patient, and frugal; bravery was not a requirement. But it was not a country parson who had leapt to her mind upon the older woman's prediction. Perhaps she was going mad. It would not be surprising given all she'd endured in the week or so since she'd met Lord Verwood on the Downs.

Doing her best to hide her distress, she purchased an apple from Phoebe and put it into her reticule.

"Now, Miss Talcott, perhaps you will allow me to explain what happened last night," said Lady Everton as they walked on.

Pen nodded, no longer able to resist hearing the tale.

"Everton and I were married four years ago," began Lady Everton. "I was young and foolish and resented that Everton spent so much time writing his speeches and debating various issues. No, do not look at me so! I was never unfaithful. I merely became rather addicted to card parties. I lost a vast sum at one of them, and I was terrified that Everton would find out. Well, Lord Verwood—the current Lord Verwood's father, of course—happened to be there and offered to discreetly assist me out of my difficulties."

"Did he do so?"

Lady Everton made sure no one was in earshot before she replied.

"Yes. He took the emerald necklace Everton had given me as a wedding present and arranged to have it copied. He gave me the copy and a sum that was sufficient to pay my debts, though much less than the actual value of the stones."

Pen nodded. Thus far, the story followed along with all she had heard of the previous Lord Verwood.

"Everton never guessed the deception," continued Lady Everton. "In time, I realized that he did love me, and I learned to be less jealous of his politics and more devoted to him than ever before. You don't believe me, do you? I *do* love him!" Lady Everton's large dark eyes were so full of emotion. Pen was almost convinced.

"Every time I wore the false necklace, I was reminded of my wickedness," continued Lady Everton. "I thought I would never see the real one again, that Verwood had long since broken it up and sold the stones for a handsome profit. Then, a few weeks ago, the present Lord Verwood appeared in Brighton and accosted me at an assembly. He told me the strangest thing: that he had found the necklace somewhere on his estate, with a note attached to it saying it belonged to a 'Lady E.' I was afraid at first that he wished me to pay him to keep silent over the matter, but he assured me that he only wished to restore the necklace to its rightful owner. So I did as he advised: sent for the paste necklace from London, where it was stored for safekeeping, and wore it to the concert at the Pavilion. Verwood had just exchanged the two necklaces when you burst in upon us."

Pen did her best to hide her turmoil; she found herself wanting to believe the story.

"Why do it in such a clandestine manner, then?" she asked. "Could he not have merely delivered the necklace to you somehow?"

"I still hoped to hide my folly. You know how servants gossip! I thought it best that only Lord Verwood and I knew the truth of the matter."

Pen thought the explanation sounded reasonable—or was it just her naïveté and an irrational wish to believe Verwood innocent? But if he had behaved honorably regarding Lady Everton, might some of the other rumors against him be false as well?

"Does Lord Everton know the truth now?" she asked.

"I told him last night. He was so relieved that Verwood and I are not lovers that he was ready to forgive me anything else!"

Pen stumbled a little, weak with relief that Everton's jealousy no longer menaced Lord Verwood. He was safe, and finally she could feel at peace.

"I am so ashamed of myself for having tried to deceive him, and for bringing you into the matter," said Lady Everton. "And, of course, it was so alarming to hear of the attack on Lord Verwood last night—"

"A-attack?" Pen must have turned pale, for Lady Everton put a consoling arm around her shoulder.

"I forgot you hadn't heard! Don't fret. He is unhurt, except where they struck him on the shoulder."

"They?"

"There were two of them. He killed one of them, but the other ran away. Everton saw it all from a distance, having followed Verwood from the Pavilion."

Pen swayed a little as relief and dread swept over her in waves. Verwood had survived the attack. But if Lord Everton was not his enemy, who was?

"Should we stop? Do you need to sit down, Miss Talcott?" asked Lady Everton, sounding concerned. "You look so pale."

"No, I am perfectly well," she replied, pulling herself together.

"It is only natural to feel distraught," said Lady Everton. "It is shocking that Brighton has grown so unsafe that common thieves will set upon a gentleman, just as they might in London!"

Pen agreed, hiding her knowledge that it was not common thieves who had attacked Verwood.

"Of course," added Lady Everton with an arch smile, "you have your own reasons for finding the incident distressing."

"No, ma'am, I assure you—"

Lady Everton shook a finger at Pen. "My dear, I shan't pry, but I know you are not indifferent to Lord Verwood. I cannot blame you in the least. If I were not already madly in love with Everton, I should find Lord Verwood a most romantic figure."

"You are quite mistaken. Lord Verwood and I are acquaintances, nothing more."

"Very wise of you to say so. He is a rake, after all. But I saw you dancing together at the Old Ship, and I think he finds you very appealing!"

Pen abandoned the attempt to dissuade Lady Everton from the notion. Frustrated, she realized half of Brighton must believe her besotted with Lord Verwood. No one would understand she behaved out of Christian concern for his safety!

Soon afterward Pen rejoined her aunt, and they returned to the Royal Crescent. As Susan took their bonnets, she winked at Pen and slipped a card into her hand. Pen closed her hand around it, wondering what shocking information it might contain. As soon as she could, she slipped off to her room to examine it.

Cyril Welling, read the inscription on one side. Cyril? Here in Brighton? She turned the card over to read the note penned in small, neat letters on the back.

> *Dearest Penelope,*
>   *You may picture my disappointment in having missed you on my arrival in Brighton. I console myself with the hope that I shall see you this evening at the assembly at the Castle Inn.*
>
> *Yours ever,*
> *C. W.*

Pen stared down at the note, stunned for a moment. Why was Cyril here? For an instant she feared he must have some bad tidings, but that was ridiculous. He was probably here to tell her the current rector was retiring, the living at Lambourne was his, and that he might soon be in a position to take a wife.

New, gnawing worries destroyed her hopeful thoughts. What would Cyril think if he heard the gossip regarding her and Lord Verwood? Would he think she had been carried away by the fast society and loose morals of this fashionable resort?

Although she'd attended balls at the Castle Inn nearly every week since coming to Brighton, Pen had never been so anxious on entering the tall, red brick building. The elegant ballroom, ornamented with its delicate moldings, medallions and columns, was about half full. She followed her aunt, trying not to look about too obviously in her eagerness to find Cyril.

A hundred anxious questions raced through her head. Was he here yet? Had he heard the gossip? Would he dance with her? She glanced briefly down at her blue gown, with its neckline lowered and shorn of all its superfluous trimmings. It was no more scandalous than those of most of the ladies present. Cyril was a man, after all; he'd expressed his admiration of her character, but she hoped he would also think her pretty.

Her searching gaze suddenly met that of Lord Verwood, standing more to the center of the ballroom. For an instant his eyes flickered with warmth and recognition. Then he turned back to his companion, the widow he'd flirted with at the Pavilion. Tonight the woman was all but bursting out of a purple gown that made Pen's look positively demure. From the way the creature was plying her fan and her eyelashes, it was clear she was his newest mistress, or hoped to be. Pen turned her gaze away. At least no one would couple her name with Verwood's anymore.

Before she and her aunt had gone much farther, Pen found herself surrounded by a small circle of admirers. Out of politeness, she smiled at them but told them she was already spoken for the first dance. Her aunt gave her a suspicious look, then Pen saw Cyril appear from behind several of the young bucks.

She drank in the sight of him: his curling light brown locks, his mild blue eyes. He was dressed in staid black, as befit a man in orders, but the sober hue only enhanced his angelic looks. There was a hint of a frown on his face.

She sent her warmest smile his way and was relieved to see him smile back as he reached them.

"Good evening, Lady Talcott, Miss Talcott," he said, with a bow that nearly rivaled Lord Verwood's in grace.

Now why did that stupid comparison leap into her head? Pen thrust the thought aside, then looked to her aunt, hoping she would be polite.

"Mr. Welling." Her aunt acknowledged him with a curt nod. "I had no idea you were in Brighton."

"I am but just arrived," he replied, his dignity unshaken. "I hope that Miss Talcott will favor me with a country-dance."

"Indeed, it is Mr. Welling to whom I have promised this dance," said Pen, before anyone could interrupt.

"Very well, my dear, one dance," said her aunt with a warning look, "but you must not neglect these poor gentlemen in your eagerness to welcome an old *friend*."

Under cover of the gossip and the musicians' tuning their

instruments, she looked up at Cyril and whispered, "I cannot tell you how happy I was to see your card, and how much I have been longing to see you again."

"I too am glad to see you," he said, his expression grave.

"Why, what is the matter?" she asked, disturbed to see that Lord Verwood and his widow had joined the couples assembling for the next dance. "You are not concerned with those other gentlemen? I assure you none of them means anything to me."

"I should hope not. However, I had not expected to see you looking so—so worldly, so fashionable. You must forgive me if I look surprised, but you seem like a stranger to me."

"No, never, never! This dress was altered at my aunt's bidding, along with all my others. You do believe me?"

"Of course I do. I was merely disappointed to see my angel transformed into the image of a fashionable, heartless minx. I miss that modesty in your appearance that is more truly appealing to a man of sense and refined taste."

"I have not altered in any other way, I promise you," she said, swallowing a pang of disappointment. At least he had not questioned her about Lord Verwood. Thank goodness she would have the chance to speak to him about it before he heard some polluted, garbled version of the matter from someone else.

"I am relieved to hear it," he said, "for I have some very important news to impart to you."

"Oh, has Mr. Stoughton decided to retire, then?"

"As usual, your quickness of perception has led you to the correct conclusion, my dearest Penelope. Yes, our prayers are in a way to be answered."

"Thank God," she breathed. Oh, to be away from all this madness! It seemed too good to be true.

"I shall wait upon your uncle tomorrow," Cyril continued, and she could only give him a shaky smile as they took up positions opposite each other.

The dance began, and she had to force herself to concentrate on the figures. She felt bemused; perhaps she'd waited so long for the news that it was difficult to believe it. Far-

ther down the set a flash of purple reminded her of Verwood and his partner.

Finally, the dance came to an end. As Cyril escorted her
back toward her aunt, Pen sought the right words to warn
him of what he might hear.

"Cyril, there is something I must tell you," she began,
but broke off as they nearly ran into another couple.

"Penelope Talcott, as I live!" shrieked a plump lady with
yellow curls, on the arm of a taller gentleman who might
have appeared handsome had his expression been less
peevish. The lady had grown fatter, but Pen could still recognize Lydia Bixley, now Lady Staverton, one of Pen's
chief tormentors back at Miss Stratton's select school for
young ladies.

"Good evening, Lady Staverton," she replied, hoping to
brush through the encounter quickly.

"Oh, you cannot stand on ceremony with me! Adrian
darling, this is Penelope Talcott, one of those *dear* girls
from Miss Stratton's. You must introduce us to your new
beau, dearest!"

Cyril smiled politely, and Staverton looked completely
bored as Penelope performed the necessary introductions.

"Mr. Welling is the curate at Lambourne," she concluded.

"Oh, a curate! How perfectly delightful," said Lydia.

"Mr. Welling and I have worked together on plans for the
education of the children of our parish," said Penelope.

"How very charming. Well, Mr. Welling, I'm sure you
will suit dear Penelope so much better than the *gentleman*,
or should I say *nobleman*, with whom she has been consort-
ing of late. However, I am not surprised Lord Verwood has
become bored with you dear. He has not danced with you
tonight, has he?" Lydia tittered. "Of course, you are not
quite the sort of female to attract more than passing attention from a rake."

Cyril shot a questioning glance from Lydia back to Pen.
Restraining an unladylike urge to slap Lydia for her malice,
Pen turned to Cyril.

"Lady Staverton refers to a dance I enjoyed with Lord
Verwood at the Old Ship Inn about a week ago. He only

wished to speak to me about a mutual friend of ours, but I'm afraid some people have made more than they should of our encounter."

"I am certain Miss Talcott is above any sort of impropriety," said Cyril in such a firm voice that Lydia seemed abashed. Pen felt warmed by his quick defense.

"Oh, yes, of course. Well, Adrian dearest, I am positively dying for a waltz. You must indulge me."

"Of course, my love," Staverton slurred.

Pen sighed in relief as they walked off. Then she turned to Cyril and saw he was frowning again. Oh dear, had she made him jealous?

"*You* do not think I wish to encourage a rake, do you?" she asked.

"Not at all. However, I cannot like the fact that you have become the subject of gossip. I imagine you did not know Lord Verwood's reputation when you accepted his offer to dance, but I trust you will be more circumspect in the future."

"I have no interest in pursuing his acquaintance," she replied, stifling an irrational sense of annoyance at the command in Cyril's voice.

"I did not think so, my angel."

Again, she swallowed a guilty sense of disappointment. His tone made it clear he was *not* jealous, merely concerned for her reputation. But why should she wish him to be jealous? Cyril trusted her, and she had not the slightest partiality for Lord Verwood. If she could only be easy about his safety, she would not give the man or his kisses another thought.

Pen awoke early after a restless night. Cyril had left the ballroom early. Aunt Mary had spent the rest of the evening scolding Pen for encouraging him and warning her that her uncle would not approve of his suit.

Pen sighed, got out of bed, and went to the window to allow the sea air to cool her forehead. It was going to be another lovely, breezy day, and she had her weekly sea bathing to look forward to. Surely she would feel more optimistic afterward.

A half hour later, she and Susan were down on the beach. The wind was brisk, but the waves were not too high for the bathing machines to go out. Pen looked around for Lucy Golding, her favorite of the bathing machine attendants, a cheerful, good-natured woman who allowed Pen to bob and float as she wished and did not roughly dunk her as some of the other 'dippers' were prone to do.

This morning, Lucy rushed up to Pen with an apologetic expression, explaining that a wheel had unaccountably come off her machine. Directly behind her, another dipper Pen had never patronized presented herself.

"Maggie Brown, miss," said the stout woman, who looked to be about thirty years in age, with dark hair and large but comely features. "I'd be happy to take care of ye."

Pen smiled at Lucy, then followed the other woman to one of the brightly colored, horse-drawn wagons standing on the beach. She began to describe to Maggie how she liked to bathe, but the woman interrupted her explanation.

"I've been dipping ladies for the better part of ten years, miss. You can trust me to know how to do it right," she said with an aggrieved look.

"I meant no offense," Pen replied, wondering if she should postpone her dip until tomorrow. No, she needed it today.

She ascended the steps into the bathing machine. While the horse towed the bumping and swaying vehicle out into the waves, she removed her clothing and changed into a long flannel shift. When the machine stopped, Maggie opened the door. Pen went to the edge and looked out.

"Have we not gone out a bit farther than we should?" she asked, seeing the other bathing machines closer to shore.

"Now, don't be a coward, miss," said Maggie.

"I am not—" Pushed from behind, Pen fell into the chilly water, inadvertently taking some in before she closed her mouth. She tasted salt, her feet touched the bottom for an instant. She suppressed a spurt of panic as she realized the water was over her head. Then Maggie's strong hands grasped her shoulders. She rose above the surface, shivering and coughing.

"What are you doing?" she sputtered, trying to draw breath.

"Don't worry, miss. Trust me to know what's best," said Maggie, and thrust her back under the waves.

This time Pen was prepared. She held her breath, but the woman dunked her an instant longer than was comfortable. She would certainly not patronize Maggie Brown again.

"Stop! I wish to go back," she demanded as soon as she recovered her breath.

"Ye've paid yer money, ye'll get yer bathing," said the woman, with venom in her voice, and roughly dunked Pen once more.

"What are you doing? What have I done to you?" Pen asked, her annoyance turning to fear as she braced herself for the next dunking.

"Ye ask what ye done? Ye poked yer nose where it don't belong, that's what, my fine lady with yer fine drawings!"

Good Lord, Maggie must have some connection with the man who had tried to kill Lord Verwood. The one whose likeness she'd sketched! Pen tried to think of a reply that would not further infuriate the woman, but Maggie dipped her again. This time she held her under longer. Panic seized her, and she tried to pry Maggie's hands from her shoulders, but she was not strong enough. Her lungs began to burn, but she fought the urge to breathe, knowing all she would take in was seawater. She had to stay calm. Perhaps the woman only meant to frighten her.

Maggie lifted her again. Pen gasped, relieved to be able to draw breath.

"Stop," she pleaded as soon as she could. "You'll only bring more trouble upon yourself if you continue this way."

"What do I care? Let 'em 'ang me. My Ted is gone, dead, stabbed through the lung by that damned lord of yers!"

Horror paralyzed Pen as she heard the pure anguished hatred in Maggie's voice as she bewailed her dead lover. Struggling to hold back panic, she held her breath again as Maggie pushed her under the waves. Once again, her head ached, her lungs burned, and again she battled the overpowering urge to inhale.

Again, Maggie let her rise, and Pen choked and gasped, unable to breathe quickly enough to refill her lungs, knowing she might not survive another such dunking.

"Ted is dead, did ye hear me? Killed in the prime of 'is life. He was going to make his fortune. We were going to be *married*. Damn you! Damn you all!"

She pushed Pen under, more viciously than before. Pen struggled again to keep from breathing, all the while praying for a rescue she feared would not come. Even if Susan noticed what was happening, could anyone reach her in time?

In the chaos of the dark cold water, the burning ache in her head, throat, and lungs overwhelmed her. She knew she could hold back no longer. She would burst if she didn't breathe soon. But if she inhaled, she would surely drown.

She prayed one more fervent prayer, then dizziness overcame her and seawater rushed into her lungs.

Chapter Five

Strong arms grasped Pen from behind and pulled her up and away. Her flannel gown tore from Maggie's grip. Held up by her unseen rescuer, Pen coughed violently, struggling to clear her lungs. Her rescuer turned, interposing his body between her and Maggie, at the same time edging sideways to bring her close to the bathing machine's steps.

"Hold on," she heard him say. It was Lord Verwood.

She obeyed and clung to the bathing machine with trembling hands. The wet gown hung heavily upon her, and the breeze chilled her bare shoulder. She hadn't the strength to climb farther. She turned her head to see what was happening, and a breathless scream escaped her as she watched Maggie seize Verwood from behind and drag him down into the water with her.

Terrifying moments passed as Pen tried to make out the combatants in the roiling, splashing water. The bathing machine listed. Pen clung more tightly and saw that the incoming waves were rising, battering the machine and causing it to sway. On the other side she heard the horse begin to snort and plunge.

She turned back to see Maggie and Verwood emerge from the water, still wrestling. Pen wished she could swim; there was no way she could help. But Verwood was already winning the struggle, and several men and a few of the other dippers were swimming toward them to help. Minutes later, Maggie was held tightly between two of the men.

Verwood left the group and swam with swift strokes back to the half-flooded bathing machine.

"Are you all right?" he asked, his voice hard and anxious.

She nodded. "I—"

"Shh, don't talk. You are safe now," he said, taking her into his arms and holding her close. His chest was solid and warm, his arms strong and protective. She lacked the strength to do anything but cling to him as he shifted her, lifting her legs with one arm and wrapping the other around her shoulders. As he began to carry her toward shore, Pen heard splashes and Maggie's voice. The dipper continued to call Verwood a murderer and cry about her Ted.

"Was that the man who attacked you on the beach the other night?" she whispered.

He nodded. "Ted Booley. Yes, he was her lover. My man Symonds and I were hoping to speak to Maggie today, to see if she knew who had hired him. No doubt they have an accomplice at the Old Ship who must have discovered that your maid supplied us with Booley's picture. I only wish we had gotten here sooner and spared you this. I hate to think what would have happened had we not arrived when we did . . ."

He stopped, looking more enraged than she'd ever seen him. His breathing was harsh, and she suddenly became aware that nothing separated them but his damp shirt and her soaked, torn flannel shift. Feeling a sudden heat steal through her, she turned to look at the beach.

A small crowd had assembled there, looking morbidly curious about the drama unfolding in the waves. And there was Susan, nearly frantic with worry.

Looking back over Verwood's shoulder, Pen saw Maggie break free from her captors, who had been trying to bring her to shore. Pen shuddered, and Verwood turned to see what was going on.

Maggie swam back toward her stranded bathing machine and disappeared under the wagon. One young man followed her. After a few minutes he emerged to take a breath and then turned back to pull Maggie's body out from under the machine. Others helped them lift the corpse and carry it to the beach.

As the group drew closer, Pen saw Maggie's eyes staring up at the bright blue sky, her face contorted in a permanent expression of malice.

"Don't look," said Verwood, and pulled Pen's head firmly against his shoulder. Her head swam, and her mouth tasted vile and salty. She closed her eyes, trying not to be sick as Verwood turned to carry her back toward the beach.

As they began to emerge from the water, the breeze fanned her, causing her to tremble again with cold and horror. Verwood continued to hold her close as he stepped onto the sand and only released her when they reached Susan. For an instant Pen stood, shaking and mortified by the stares of the assembled onlookers. Susan quickly wrapped her in a blanket, then Verwood picked her up once more, asking Susan the direction of their lodgings.

"You can't carry me all that way. Your shoulder . . ." Pen protested.

"Nonsense. You're a feather. I won't let you try to walk, and you will be chilled to death if we wait for a carriage."

Too weak to protest and unable to bear the curious stares all around her, she buried her face into his chest once more. She was alive, but would she ever feel safe again?

Verwood glared at the gaping onlookers, sending them scurrying, then climbed up from the beach, holding Miss Talcott tightly in his arms. His injured shoulder protested, but he ignored the pain. It was both a relief and a penance to hold her breathing, vital form against him, knowing she might have been brutally drowned on his account. He wanted the privilege of comforting her, yet was agonizingly aware there was no way he could wipe away the horror of what she'd just endured.

When they reached the Marine Parade, he ordered her maid to run ahead and start preparing a warm bath. As he walked on in the direction of the Royal Crescent, glowering at anyone who stopped to stare at them, rage coursed through him. Rage that he and Symonds had bungled this, that they'd arrived too late to prevent the attack. That they'd failed to extract the information that would end the madness.

He'd almost been too late to save Miss Talcott, though he'd flung off his coat, pulled off his boots, and plunged into the water as soon as he'd seen what was happening. His boyhood days of swimming off Cornwall had stood him in good stead.

Miss Talcott stirred in his arms. Her eyes were closed, but he thought she was still conscious. She had stopped shivering, and her blanket-bound body had warmed against his, sending an unexpected jolt of desire through him, mixing with and heightening his helpless fury.

Miss Talcott's untried, sweet little body might have never known a man's touch. No doubt she had dreams of a tranquil, pastoral life in a country parsonage with that saintly looking rustic with whom she'd danced at the Castle Inn. And a bevy of little brats, of course, whom she'd undoubtedly love passionately despite the mischief they would cause. All she wanted might have been taken from her, simply because she'd taken pity on his worthless self.

Now she would regret her rash charity, he thought, walking faster as his rage continued to mount. People continued to stare as he walked, and a sense of failure jabbed him as he realized all Brighton would soon be humming with the story.

He'd saved Miss Talcott's life, but ruined her reputation.

"Thank you," she said, her eyes opening.

He frowned into their hazel depths. Was she being sarcastic? No, the little innocent was thanking him for saving her life! As if it was not his fault she'd ever been endangered.

"There is no need to thank me," he said, tamping down his helpless fury and resisting the urge to hold her even tighter, as if he could protect her from further harm.

Duels on the Continent and more recent attempts on his life had hardened him to the prospect of his own death. But not Miss Talcott's. Now he could not shake the feeling that there was an irresistible, malevolent force at work in his life, one that now threatened not only him but anyone who cared for him as well.

He had to shake off this rage. He needed to regain his cool composure, for without it he would never solve this mystery. He was no longer merely fighting to preserve the worthless but pleasurable life he sought for himself. He was fighting to preserve Miss Talcott's right to the life *she'd* chosen.

Even if that life did not include him.

Pen sat before the fire in her room, still wrapped in the damp blanket, waiting for Susan to finish readying the tub for her. She could hear her uncle's voice questioning Lord Verwood about what had happened.

She held her bare feet out to the fire, trying not to miss the warmth she'd felt in Lord Verwood's arms. Her aunt's voice, shrill with anxiety, could now be heard, though Pen could not quite make out the words. She could picture her relations' dismay over the scandal. Then she remembered that Cyril was to come today. Perhaps he would now be permitted to take her away. She should have felt relieved, but instead she felt oddly numb.

"Your bath is ready, miss," said Susan kindly. Pen arose, removed the blanket, and allowed Susan to peel the wet flannel gown off her. Naked, she shivered, feeling unexpectedly vulnerable, even though there was no one in the room but her loyal maidservant. For a moment she recoiled at the thought of immersing herself in the water, then forced herself to step in.

"If it's all right with you, miss, I'll leave you to soak for a few minutes," said Susan.

Pen nodded and sank deeper into the tub after the maid left, willing her muscles to relax. She was safe now, and Cyril would soon be here to help her deal with everything. Slowly, her body began to come alive again, caressed by the warm, lavender-scented water. How strange it had felt to be swept up in Lord Verwood's arms! She'd never been held so close by a man since being hugged by her father in childhood. It had felt so *safe* and yet in other ways, perilous. Being pressed against a man's firm body was far too heady a sensation to explore with anyone but a husband.

A few minutes later Susan bustled back in to wash Pen's hair. When Pen entered the sitting room an hour later, dressed and having had some tea and a biscuit in her room, Aunt Mary flung herself upon her, crying and moaning over the morning's events. Meanwhile her uncle frowned from his corner, sipping sherry.

"Oh dear, oh dear, what are we going to do? Your uncle went out earlier, and the entire town is talking about you and Lord Verwood. How *could* you get yourself into such a scrape?"

Pen stood numbly in her aunt's arms. Did neither of them care that she might have been killed? And where was Cyril?

At that moment Susan entered the room, announcing a Mr. Welling. Aunt Mary released Pen, her flabby, tear-blotched face taking on a calculating expression.

"Mr. Welling! Hmm, it was not what your uncle and I hoped for you, but perhaps it will do after all. If you're known to wed a clergyman, that should make it all more respectable. What do you think, Sir Ralph?"

"Let her marry her parson. No use expecting better now," he grunted, and took another sip of sherry.

Aunt Mary asked Susan to admit their caller, then dragged her husband up from his chair just as Cyril entered the room. His expression was grave; to Pen's dismay, he did not meet her hopeful gaze.

"My dear Mr. Welling," said Aunt Mary. "So delightful to see you! What a shame Sir Ralph and I are engaged to meet some friends in just a few minutes. I am sure my dear niece here will entertain you *and* be delighted to hear anything particular you should wish to tell her."

"But it would not be proper—" Cyril began. However, Aunt Mary had already swept herself and her husband out of the room, leaving him to stare after them. Pen watched his face with growing sense of dread. Where was the outpouring of feeling she'd been expecting? She wanted to be embraced, consoled, reassured. How could he just stand there, not even looking at her?

"Cyril, I—" she paused to lick her lips, which had gone dry. "I am so thankful you have come." She moved toward him, hands outstretched, but still he did not respond.

He reddened slightly and kept his hands to his sides.

"You—you *have* heard what happened, haven't you?" she asked.

"Yes, I have heard. I cannot help wishing your aunt, or your maid, were here to maintain propriety."

A chill spread through her at the formality of his address.

"Yes, but—but at such a time, how can you wish someone else to be present?"

"I would not wish to offend against the proprieties under any circumstances, particularly those under which we are now laboring."

"How can you speak so? Cyril, do you realize I nearly drowned this morning?"

"So I heard. I am glad such a dreadful tragedy was averted," he said, his expression tranquil.

"Is that all you can say?"

"The manner in which your life was preserved has, as I am sure you are aware, occasioned a degree of gossip that is highly disturbing to anyone who has your interests at heart," he said, avoiding her gaze.

"Yes, Lord Verwood rescued me. You—you should be grateful to him, regardless of what the scandalmongers are saying."

"Do you realize they are saying he must have been ogling you through a telescope, as I am told is the fashion among rakes? That you may have encouraged him to do so?" he asked, a touch of dismay in his voice.

"Who would believe such a thing?" she asked, stung. "*You* cannot!"

"Of course I do not," he said, his tone kind but impersonal. "I will always hold you in my memory as an example of the highest moral character a woman can have."

"In your memory?" she blurted out. "I don't understand."

He gave a deep sigh. "Sometimes divine providence leads us on a different path from that which we have planned for ourselves. I thought you would understand. I thought you believed in my work and in the sanctity of my goals."

"I thought we were going to work together to achieve them."

"Perhaps the disturbing incident of the morning has un-settled your mind. Once you have recovered, however, I am sure you will understand the sacrifice that is being asked of you, and knowing your superior nature, I am sure you will make it willingly."

"Sacrifice? Willingly?" she asked through lips that felt like wood, her mind unwilling or unable to grasp his intent.

"My angel, I am persuaded that once you have time to reflect upon the matter, you will realize that a wife whose reputation is anything but spotless can be nothing but an obstacle to all the good I wish to achieve."

"But I thought you were promised the living at Lam-bourne?"

"Yes, of course, but that is only the start. Do you think God has given me the talents He has so that I should waste them on a single, rural living?"

She stood still, her mind still recoiling from his words. He thought his talents would be wasted at Lambourne? What was his ambition then? To collect the tithes from multiple livings while his curates did all the work? Or were his goals still higher: a bishopric, perhaps?

"I thought you understood my hopes, my angel," he said in a soothing tone. "You were the ideal helpmate to assist me in achieving my goals. Now, alas, it is not possible. You are too generous of spirit not to understand—too noble to stand in my way, I am certain."

Finally, the full import of his words sank in. She nearly staggered with the weight of them. There would be no em-braces, no loving words to help her recover from the horror of what she'd just suffered.

Instead, she was going to be dismissed. Jilted. Discarded. For the sin of having nearly been murdered.

She stood for a moment, suffocated by pain, then took a deep breath. Tears would be a release, but she would not cry, not before one who had so bitterly betrayed her. She pressed back the pain, and it resurfaced as anger. Yes. Anger would serve her now.

"You sanctimonious hypocrite!" she hissed, and had the brief satisfaction of watching Cyril grow pale.

"My angel—"

"Don't call me your angel! Leave me now, or I shall summon a servant to throw you out!"

"You will not—you cannot be thinking—"

From his terrified expression, she realized he was worried about a suit for breach of promise. The pain struggled to resurface, but again, she held onto her anger like a shield.

"Do not disturb yourself," she said. "I will make certain my uncle does not start any proceedings against you. I could never marry you, you vile, miserable excuse for a man of God. Begone now!"

He took one more frightened glance at her and fled the room.

Pen watched him depart. Abruptly, her anger spiraled inward, joining the pain residing in the dark, cold knot in her center. She wrapped her arms around herself and began to pace aimlessly about the room. The rhythmic movement was soothing, keeping the anger and the pain at bay until she was strong enough to bear them.

The floor creaked, and Pen looked up to see Susan enter the room.

"Lord Verwood is here to see you, miss."

Verwood heard Miss Talcott refuse him admittance and stepped over the threshold of the room anyway. A brief glance at Miss Talcott frightened him. She was pale, and there was a frozen look in her large, usually expressive eyes. Was she ill? Had she succumbed to an inflammation of the lungs from having breathed in too much water? Why was she alone at such a time?

"Leave us now," he commanded, but the servant stood her ground, her arms crossed in front of her.

"If Miss Penelope doesn't want you here, you'll leave," she said stoutly, but her eyes were wide with fright.

"You may leave us, Susan," said Miss Talcott in a placid, weary tone he'd never heard her use before. He couldn't bear the sound any more than he could bear her unusual pallor.

"Sit down, Miss Talcott. You look ill."

He went to her and gently guided her onto the sofa. Her

lack of resistance brought renewed stabs of guilt to the conscience that had long lain dormant.

"Thank you for your concern, my lord," she said. "I am perfectly well, but I wish to be alone."

No. He couldn't leave until he saw some signs that she would recover, that he hadn't destroyed the vital, passionate creature she was at her core.

"You should not be alone now. Where are your relations? Where is that curate of yours?" he asked, taking a chair close by. Much as he would enjoy taking her in his arms, he supposed she was too devoted to her saintly suitor to welcome the gesture.

She winced at his second question, and realization dawned on him.

"The sanctimonious hypocrite," he breathed softly, then wondered why she suddenly lifted her head to stare at him. A tiny spark of anger lit her eyes, and it was a relief to see a sign of her reviving passion. Perhaps he could fan the spark into a flame.

"So he has abandoned you? I'm not surprised. You must be delighted to be rid of such a bad bargain."

She stared at him for a moment, as if to ask how he could be so callous. Then she nodded, her eyes reverting to the hopeless look that he hated.

"He never loved me," she said, still sounding tired. "He only wished to marry me because I would make a suitable wife for a clergyman."

"He sounds like a dull dog to me. Why, if he were a man, he would have drawn my cork by now." Seeing her confused look, he explained, "Made my nose bleed. After all, it was what Woodmere and Amberley both did when I was foolish enough to interfere in your friends' affairs. What any man worthy of you would do after the trouble I've caused you."

"It is not your fault. I chose to help you," she said, still in that quiet, controlled voice.

He groaned inwardly. Why did she not berate him? They would both feel better for it. Then he would be able to tell her his newly formed plan for restoring her reputation.

"But I have ruined your life, haven't I?" he asked, in a casual tone, and was rewarded with another spark in her eyes.

Still she said nothing, only sat there quietly.

He got up from the chair and took a position next to her on the sofa, deliberately allowing his knee to brush hers before she repositioned herself.

"Perhaps *you* wish to hit me, since your priggish suitor did not. I deserve it, do I not, for blighting all your hopes?"

"You are ridiculous. I disapprove of any sort of violence," she said, anger threading her voice.

"Come. You wish to hit me. Do I not deserve at least that much punishment?" he said. He leaned down, bringing his face scandalously close to hers. Close enough to hit. Or kiss. No, she was not ready for *that*.

"Please leave me now, or I *will* hit you," she said, her voice unsteady.

He could sense her passion very near the surface now.

"I don't wish to leave. You are angry, and rightfully so. Hit me," he said with a smile calculated to infuriate her.

"Stop making a game of me!" she cried.

Her eyes were brighter and the color had returned to her cheeks. Good, she was coming back to life again. She was too much the lady to hit him, but still—

A small, determined fist connected with his nose. The sharp, familiar pain was a surprise, but a most welcome one.

"Oh dear, what have I done?" she exclaimed, staring down at her fist and sounding quite like herself again.

Verwood was just congratulating himself on his strategy when he saw her shocked expression and felt a small, warm trickle of blood run down his lip.

"Well done, Miss Talcott!" He grinned as he pulled out his handkerchief to stop the flow.

"Lean back, before you stain everything in sight," she scolded, jumping up from her seat and heading toward the doorway.

"Sit down. My handkerchief will suffice. The bleeding has nearly stopped already."

She remained standing, looking adorably contrite. "I am sorry, but if you had not taunted me so—"

"There is no need to apologize." The guilt lodged in his

chest softened at the sight of the renewed color in her sweet, rounded cheeks. At the same time desire for her stirred again. What a tempting little piece she was . . .

He cleared his throat and straightened up, checking with his handkerchief to make sure the blood had stopped flowing.

"I trust *you* are feeling better now," he said, smiling up at Miss Talcott, hoping to coax an answering smile out of her.

She stared down at him for a moment, then her shoulders began to shake. For an instant he thought she was crying, but no, she was laughing, a delightful gurgle of much-needed release. Feeling his own heart lighten, he joined her, glad she had recovered enough to laugh.

Still, he was not surprised when she suddenly covered her face with her hands, her laughter giving way to sobs. An entirely natural reaction to all that had happened, and he knew how to deal with that, too.

He arose and quickly put his arms around her, thinking she would now find comfort in his embrace. Women loved to have a man hold them; he didn't know why more gentlemen didn't take advantage of that useful fact. She did not push him away. She even put her slender arms around him, so he held her, relieved that he could give her solace.

Gradually, she grew calmer but still made no signs of wishing to leave his arms. So he continued to hold her, a guilty pleasure now mingling with his nobler intentions. He was a scoundrel, no doubt, but he couldn't help enjoying the way her head nestled on his chest, the way her warm, softly curving body felt against his. As long as he kept his arms firmly and comfortingly around her back, as long as he didn't allow his hands to stray elsewhere, all would be well.

So he resisted temptation until she lifted her head from his chest to look up at him. Her eyes were huge, pupils darkened like onyxes set in aquamarines. He'd seen that dreamy expression far too many times to be mistaken. Demure little Miss Talcott felt a spark of answering desire for him. Most promising!

Then her plump lips parted, just slightly. Lord, it was just not his way to resist temptation. He lowered his face to

hers. When she did not pull away, he brushed her lips with
his. Still she did not move, so he tasted her more deeply.
Shyly, she opened to him, then impetuously began returning his kiss, pressing herself against him, mimicking the
movements of his tongue and making little moaning sounds
deep in her throat.

She was merely overwrought, he reminded himself.
She'd undergone so much terror, anger, and betrayal that
this was just another natural outlet for her passion. One he
was happy to provide. He would not take advantage of her
fragile state. Not too much, anyway.

Yet his senses screamed at him, threatening revolt. Her
breath was sweet, tasting of tea and biscuits, her scent that
of lavender soap and freshly bathed woman, her mouth a
little clumsy, eager, and delicious.

No. He could wait, despite his protesting body, which reminded him he'd not enjoyed such pleasures in far too
long.

It would be so easy to carry her to the sofa and proceed
to offer her more potent distractions from her woes.

No. It was too soon.

She clutched at him as if she were once again drowning,
and her vital, warm, sweet-smelling body drove him to distraction. Oh, how he longed to run his hand down the curve
of her back, to feel her luscious little . . .

Damn. He cursed the errant hand that had followed his
thoughts all too precisely. Miss Talcott was already pulling
away from his embrace, already staring at him from out-
raged, stormy eyes.

He was in for the devil of a scold now.

Chapter Six

"**Y**ou are despicable! Leave me. Now!" Pen's body still tingled from Verwood's caresses, but the new, intoxicating sensation only fueled her outrage. Her hands curled into fists as she backed away from him.

"My apologies, Miss Talcott. I meant no disrespect," he replied, making no attempt to either leave or follow her.

"No disrespect? To use me as you would any of your mistresses—" Her voice faltered and she shook with indignation.

"I only wished to console you."

Even as Pen told herself it was false, the sympathetic tone in Verwood's voice soothed her anger and brought the pain to the surface once more. His odiously handsome face blurred. A tear spilled onto her cheek as she thought of Maggie's attack, her uncle and aunt's reactions to the resulting scandal, and Cyril's desertion. She had never felt so alone in her life. She longed for Catherine and Juliana, but they were far away. For a moment it had seemed as if Lord Verwood was her friend, but he was only toying with her, after all.

"You cannot blame me," he continued, "for giving in to an irresistible temptation."

His voice seduced her once more, as did the cajoling expression in his brown eyes. Trying to ignore the unfortunate effect they had on her, she brushed her tears away.

"Don't look at me with those—those puppy eyes! Oh,

very well, I suppose you were only acting in accordance with your nature. I forgive you. You may leave now."

"Not yet. I will not leave until I am certain you will suffer no lasting harm from your involvement in my affairs."

"I shall do well enough without your help."

"Please, may we sit down again? At least let me tell you what I have in mind."

It occurred to Pen that he might be planning to offer for her. It was certainly what a rigidly honorable gentleman would propose, but Verwood was not a rigidly honorable gentleman. It was a preposterous idea, but what else could it be? Curiosity overcame her scruples. She nodded and sat down in a chair. She was not going to risk sharing the sofa with Lord Verwood again.

He lounged comfortably in the opposite chair.

"You know, you would have been wasted on that parson."

The languorous, amused look in his eyes brought a flaming heat to her cheeks. How wantonly she had responded to his kiss! What had possessed her?

"I do not usually—I mean, I would not normally—"

"There is no need to explain. You were overwrought. Given all that you have endured today it was understandable that you needed an outlet for your feelings. I promise I mean you no harm. You are safe now."

"I don't know if I shall ever feel safe again."

She shivered. His entire being tensed, and she knew he was angry, not with her, but with whoever had set this whole train of events in motion.

"I won't belittle what you have undergone," he said bluntly. "You may have some bad dreams, and at times fears may threaten to overwhelm you. But I promise you, your spirits will recover in time. There *will* come a day when you wake up feeling only happiness and go about your day free from fear."

She'd never heard him speak with such force, and wondered if he'd had to contend with many attempts on his own life. Did he believe his words, or did he merely hope they were true?

He moved to the sofa, taking a position closer to hers.

Although their knees did not quite touch, still she felt a cord of understanding between them. Understanding and something more potent.

"Miss Talcott, marry me. Give me the right to protect you and keep you happy."

She'd expected it, yet the simplicity of his proposal moved her somehow. As if he needed to help her as much as she longed to have someone care for her.

"Thank you," she said, a lump coming to her throat. She swallowed, pulled herself together, and continued. "It is not possible. I cannot accept your offer."

"I don't expect an answer today, my dear," he replied calmly. "I only ask that you think about it."

She shook her head. "It is a preposterous idea. We are entirely unsuited to one another."

"I know I am not so respectable a suitor as your curate. On the other hand, I'm quite certain I have a much better appreciation for your . . . spirit."

"I have no doubt of that," she said tartly. "The mere idea of our marrying is absurd. You need not make such a sacrifice."

"It would be no sacrifice, I assure you," he said, still with that wicked, lazy smile in his eyes.

"You owe me nothing. It was my choice to make that sketch for you. Regardless of the scandal, I am glad you rescued me this morning, and . . . and I know it would have been a grave mistake to marry Cyril."

"You loved him?" His gaze searched her face.

"I thought I did. Now I see that I was only happy to find someone who entered into my feelings about my aunt and uncle, who disapproved of their extravagance and their irresponsibility as much as I did. I suppose I was really in love with the rectory at Lambourne. You must think me a complete idiot!"

"No," he said with unexpected softness. "You wished for a certain sort of life. He was just not the right man."

The kindness in his voice unsettled her. "*You* are not the right man either, and you have your own troubles. Or have you forgotten that someone has been trying to kill you?"

"I did some investigation into the staff at the Old Ship

and made some interesting discoveries. I believe I am now very close to resolving the matter."

"Oh, do you know who it is, then?"

"I do not wish to say it until I am certain."

She bit her lip, annoyed but knowing it was useless to ask any more questions. "Well, even so, you are not at all the sort of man I wish to marry."

"I'm well aware of that. However, there are things I can offer you. I know you do not care for my fortune, and certainly my reputation is not what you would wish. Still, I can offer you independence from your relations, and a home of your own."

"I don't wish to be married out of pity." She frowned, knowing what he hinted at: that with no fortune, and a damaged reputation, all she could hope for was a shadowy existence as an embarrassing, unwanted inmate in her relations' household.

"The arrangement would benefit me as well. I need—" He paused, and once more, Pen heard footsteps on the threshold.

"There's a Mr. Woodmere here to see you, miss," said Susan, bright-eyed with curiosity. "Shall I show him in?"

Catherine's husband? Had he come all the way from the Lakes in response to her letter? Pen nodded.

A moment later a tall, wide-shouldered man entered the room. His broad face, framed by dark brown hair, was not precisely handsome, but ruggedly masculine for all that. His mahogany brown eyes were full of concern as he looked first at Pen, then flashed a distinct challenge toward Lord Verwood. Tension filled the air as the two men eyed one another, and Pen wondered again what had passed between them last summer.

"Mr. Woodmere," she said, rising from her seat to greet him with a smile. "I cannot believe you have come such a long way to see me. How is Catherine? And little Elinor?"

"Both are thriving. Catherine has completely recovered from the birth and sends her love," he said, his expression glowing for an instant before turning anxious again. "How are *you*, Miss Talcott? I have just heard the most alarming news."

"I am as well as can be expected," she replied.

"I am relieved to hear it," he said, his kind eyes scrutinizing her closely. "Since Catherine regards you as a sister, so do I. Know that we will help you in any way we can."

"Thank you," she replied, touched by the warmth in his voice. It seemed she did not lack for friends, after all. Then Woodmere looked back toward Verwood, and his expression hardened.

"Please, sit down, both of you," she said uneasily. "Mr. Woodmere, you have met his lordship already, I believe."

"Yes, we have had that . . . pleasure," Lord Verwood interposed, looking cautious but not hostile. He resumed his place on the sofa while Woodmere took a chair.

"Indeed we have," Woodmere said, looking thoughtful. "In fact, Miss Talcott, I have a letter for you from Catherine, regarding his lordship. If you wish you may have it now, but perhaps you will first tell me what prompted *your* letter?"

She glanced at Lord Verwood, not knowing how he would react to the knowledge that she had pried into his affairs or whether he wished Woodmere to know the truth.

"Go on, Miss Talcott. I trust Woodmere, even if he does not trust me," he said.

She gave a brief account of the attempt on Verwood's life up on the Downs. "I was quite—distressed by the incident, as you may imagine, and hoped that perhaps Catherine could shed some light on the matter," she concluded.

"Perhaps. Before you read her letter, though, I hope you will tell me what has happened since the incident on the Downs. I imagine today's attack was not unconnected to Verwood's affairs," he said, his expression grim.

Pen glanced over to Verwood, but his face betrayed nothing. She gave Woodmere a summary of the succeeding events, ending with Maggie Brown's attack and Verwood's subsequent rescue.

"Catherine spoke of a clergyman you hoped to wed," said Woodmere when she'd finished. "Has he been informed of what has happened?"

"He is in Brighton, Woodmere," Verwood answered for

her. "He knows what has happened and has decided *not* to honor his understanding with Miss Talcott."

Woodmere looked stunned for a moment. "What a lily-livered, cowardly worm!" he growled, getting up from his chair and taking a few strides about the room. "He deserves to be soundly thrashed. Where is he staying?"

The scowl on Woodmere's face gave him a piratical aspect, and his angry posture drew attention to the obvious strength of his arms, large as a blacksmith's, even encased in the sleeves of a gentleman's coat. Had she not known his anger was on her behalf, Pen might have been frightened. Instead, she found a reprehensible amusement in picturing Cyril's dismay at a confrontation with this formidable man.

"There is no need to pursue Cyril," she said, stifling a guilty regret. "I realize now how mistaken I was in him."

"He is not worthy of you, certainly." Woodmere looked back at Lord Verwood speculatively.

"Lord Verwood has offered for me already," said Pen, to forestall any questions. "I have refused his kind offer."

"And I have asked Miss Talcott to take some time to consider before coming to a decision," Verwood added.

She frowned at him, then turned back to Mr. Woodmere.

"I have another plan you may wish to consider," he said. "If you do not wish to marry Lord Verwood, and your relations make you unhappy, Catherine and I would be happy to offer you a home at Woodmere Hall."

"Thank you," she said, touched by the offer.

"You would be most welcome," Woodmere continued. "Catherine says you prefer country life, and we can certainly offer you plenty of fresh air and beautiful scenery to sketch. Although our circle of society is restricted, our friends will receive you kindly, regardless of any gossip that might reach us."

Pen's heart warmed at the suggestion. No doubt Aunt Mary and Uncle Ralph would be happy to see her go. To live by the Lakes, a region she'd only seen in pictures. To be sheltered in the loving circle of the Woodmeres' home. To be with Catherine, whom she already loved as a sister. It was tempting indeed, but she was not ready to make such a huge decision. Not yet.

She glanced over at Lord Verwood to see if he was relieved by the solution to their difficulties.

"My offer still remains open, Miss Talcott," he said with a hint of a frown. "I know Woodmere thinks me unworthy of you—as indeed I am—but I can offer you the protection of my name, such as it is, and a home to call your own. I don't mean to press you, but only beg that you think about it before you accept Woodmere's invitation."

She looked from one man to the other. She was certain Woodmere made his offer wholeheartedly, but how did Lord Verwood feel about his? She couldn't tell from his expression.

"Perhaps it is time I gave you Catherine's letter." Woodmere stood, pulling a slim sheaf of papers from his pocket. He handed her a crisp white letter from the top, holding back a number of sheets that had darkened with age.

Curious, Pen opened the letter. Yes, it was Catherine's familiar and graceful handwriting, with its long, swooping upstrokes, almost as musical as her piano playing.

Dearest Pen,
I read your letter with feelings of gravest concern.
I believe I may have some idea as to the nature of
Lord Verwood's enemy. I am sending you these other
letters to use as you see fit. If you choose to hand
them over to Lord Verwood, be assured you can do so
without harming me or Mr. Woodmere or our family.
Although I long to see you and tell you the entire
story of all that transpired last summer, I have no
time for a full account, and indeed, it is not
something I wish to set to paper. All I can do is assure
you that although Lord Verwood's actions nearly
proved disastrous, his intent was not evil. Having
made so many unwise decisions myself, I cannot find
it in me to condemn him. I believe him capable of
redemption and not completely unworthy of your
compassion, my dearest friend.

Yours always,
Catherine

Pen looked up and saw both men watching for her reaction.

"May I see the other letters?" she asked, and Mr. Woodmere handed them over.

She glanced at the topmost. The handwriting was a bit like Catherine's, but the paper had yellowed over time. It was dated 12 October, 1797, about a year before Catherine's birth. It was addressed to someone named William and signed Helen Whitgrave. Catherine's mother. Pen bent her head and perused the impassioned account of the Duke of Whitgrave's cold nature, his casual infidelity, and Her Grace's own hopeless and guilty love for her William, whoever he was. Pen's heart ached for the lonely duchess. Having met the duke herself, she was not, perhaps, as shocked as she should have been to read about this ancient *affaire*. But what did it have to do with Lord Verwood? He must have been a boy at the time.

She read the next letter and found it much like the first. She skimmed through the remainder, as they all seemed similar.

"Are you familiar with these letters?" she asked, handing them to Lord Verwood.

"He is the one who sent them to Catherine for safekeeping," said Mr. Woodmere.

"How came you to possess the papers?" she asked.

"After my father's death, I found the letters in our London residence. My father was expert at acquiring such items," said Lord Verwood with a faint expression of distaste. "I suspect that at some point he wished to offer them to the duke for a handsome sum. The duke has always been jealous of his dignity. His greatest fear is to be made a laughingstock. Perhaps if his wife had chosen another peer for her lover, it would have been tolerable to him, but it must have infuriated him when she took up with a commoner. I can only speculate, but perhaps the duke refused to pay, or my father decided it not worthwhile to pursue the matter after Lady Catherine's mother died."

"Do you think the duke is behind the attempts on your life?" asked Woodmere.

"I have reason to suspect it. Perhaps he fears I will make

the letters public. I imagine he does not know I sent them to Lady Catherine."

Woodmere nodded. "My wife and His Grace are not on close terms."

Pen was not surprised. Cat's relations with her father had always been stormy. The duke had probably never forgiven her for wishing to marry a gentleman farmer in preference to the marquess he'd chosen for her.

"But it was all so long ago," she said, confused. "Even if he believes you have the letters, why should he fear their disclosure so much that he would attempt murder? Why did he not just offer to buy them from you?"

"I have heard that His Grace has been attempting to become more influential in Tory politics," said Woodmere. "Perhaps he fears Lord Verwood will sell them to an opponent who would use them to his discredit."

"Perhaps," Verwood mused. "I have been seen speaking to Lord and Lady Everton. Lord Everton has vehemently argued a number of issues with the duke. It is well known that their political views are poles apart. If His Grace thought I planned to sell Everton the documents . . ."

"Lord Everton would not stoop to such methods," said Pen.

"Perhaps the duke judges Everton's behavior according to his own," Verwood countered.

She nodded.

"That may be the explanation," said Woodmere, frowning.

"I think we should give these letters to Lord Verwood. Do you agree?" asked Pen, looking at Woodmere.

"His Grace cannot harm us," Woodmere replied. "He does not wish this scandal reopened. He has more to lose than we do."

"Very well, then, use them as you see fit," she said to Verwood. "I for one would like to see justice done."

"Thank you for the sentiment," said Verwood with a wry smile, "but please trust me to handle the matter. 'Twere best if I did not involve us all in further scandal."

At that point, Pen's aunt and uncle walked in. They

stopped at the threshold and stared at the two men in the room, who both stood up to meet them.

"What is the meaning of this? Where is Mr. Welling? What are *you* doing here?" Aunt Mary asked shrilly, looking at Lord Verwood. Then she looked at Mr. Woodmere. "And who are *you*?"

Pen grimaced at her aunt's rudeness and performed the necessary introductions, then informed her that Cyril had left some time ago.

"What does it mean? He did offer for you, did he not?"

Pen shook her head, and her aunt put a hand against her heart, as if about to suffer a palpitation. Fortunately, Verwood spoke before she could give way to her shock.

"Sir Talcott, Lady Talcott, I hope you will give your permission for *me* to pay my addresses to Miss Talcott."

Her relations' faces underwent a startling series of transformations: from dismay, to speculation, to enthusiastic approval. Lord Verwood's shady reputation was all but forgotten; all that mattered now was his barony and his handsome fortune.

"I have refused his offer," she said quickly, hoping they would not embarrass her more by their excitement over the match.

"Refused? Nonsense! You cannot do so. What else can you hope for, after both of you have made yourselves the talk of Brighton?" asked her uncle.

"You ungrateful creature! If you do not marry Lord Verwood, we shall wash our hands of you!" continued her aunt.

"Then Lady Catherine and I are prepared to offer your niece a home where she will be valued as she deserves," said Woodmere.

"Miss Talcott must be given some time to consider her choice," said Lord Verwood. "In the meantime, I am sure I speak for Mr. Woodmere when I say that both of us will be very displeased if we hear she is being bullied in any way."

Pen didn't know how Verwood might back up his threat. But the combined force of his words and Woodmere's resolute glare were enough to cause the blood to drain from her uncle's face. Her aunt began to nervously pluck at the edge of her shawl.

There was something very comforting about being staunchly defended by two men, each so very different from the other, but each with his own sort of strength. The question was which, if either, of their offers should she accept?

Chapter Seven

*A*fter promising to visit Miss Talcott again the following morning, Verwood and Woodmere left. As soon as they were outside, Verwood turned and saw Woodmere eyeing him with approval, which was a relief. The last time they'd met, the man had knocked him down. With good cause, of course. Woodmere was one of those big men who were slow to anger, but once aroused, completely ruthless. A trait which might prove useful.

"I hope to resolve this affair soon, but if anything does happen to me, I trust you will take care of Miss Talcott," Verwood said, breaking the silence.

"You may rely on me. Do you think she will accept your offer?"

"I do not know. She seemed rather taken with your invitation."

"Do you wish to marry her? Do you care for her?"

Woodmere's eyes were uncomfortably penetrating. Verwood thought of Miss Talcott's loyalty to her friends, and the kind impulse that had urged her to help him. His body thrummed with the memory of how she'd struck him and then responded so passionately to his kiss. It was not love, of course; that was an emotion he'd long since put behind him. But as far as he was capable, he had become fond of her.

"Miss Talcott is an admirable woman, one of the best I've ever met," he replied. "I would consider myself very fortunate if she agreed to be my wife."

"If she marries you, it will be more than you deserve."

"I am well aware of that."

Woodmere's dark brows rose in skepticism. "If you make her unhappy in any way—"

"I've no intention of making her unhappy," he interrupted, nettled by Woodmere's suspicion.

"Do you realize what this means?" Woodmere asked, a growl in his deep voice. "If she marries you and you free yourself from this threat against your life, you will have been offered a God-given opportunity to make a new and better life for yourself. For Miss Talcott's sake, I hope you won't waste it."

"If I do, you'll pursue me to the gates of Hell, won't you, Woodmere?" he asked, hoping to lighten the tone.

The other man only gave him a darkling look.

They parted where the Marine Parade met the Steine, and Verwood headed on to the Old Ship, wondering if Miss Talcott would decide to make her home with the Woodmeres. She would certainly be safe there, and he would no longer have to worry about her. He should be relieved rather than annoyed, not plagued by the conviction that *he* was the one who should protect and care for her, or tormented with the desire to kiss her again and teach her even more delightful diversions.

Fool! She was going to accept Woodmere's invitation. No doubt she would be very happy in distant Cumberland, surrounded by beautiful scenery and good, respectable people. Perhaps, in that small, friendly circle, she would even attract some virtuous suitor who would appreciate her as her faithless curate had not. But would that damnably worthy suitor know how to make her tremble and moan with pleasure the way *he* had?

Verwood decided he'd best prepare for Miss Talcott's rejection. She would not be the first lady to choose a secluded haven over marriage with him. Virtuous females had always found him lacking. Why did he hope this time it would be different?

The Whitgraves' house was one of the largest on the Steine. Entering it several hours after parting from Woodmere, Verwood saw that it was also more elegantly appointed than the majority of houses to let for the summer season. Conducted to an upstairs room that contained a desk and several chairs, he entered to find the duke sitting alone. The tic in his temple, the sweaty sheen on his face, and the nervous clenching and unclenching of his hands betrayed His Grace's fear at the prospect of confronting his prospective victim. It might have been amusing had the fool not endangered Miss Talcott.

"In what way can I serve you, Lord Verwood?" asked the duke, his voice pitched a shade higher than usual.

"It is *I* who may be able to serve you, Your Grace."

"Oh—ah, in what way?" the duke asked nervously.

"I believe I may be able to restore to you some, er, property of yours which has unaccountably gone astray."

The duke stared at him for an instant, fear and a frantic hope in his eyes. Did he think Verwood was cowed enough by the murder attempts to meekly return the letters?

"I had supposed you meant to dispose of the . . . property elsewhere," the duke said cautiously.

"Why would I return misplaced property to anyone but its rightful owner?"

"Did you not intend to sell those letters to Lord Everton?"

"Why do you think so?"

"I received a—oh, does it matter? Give them to me now!"

Verwood wondered what the duke had been planning to say. Had someone planted the suspicion in the duke's mind? Or was it just the circumstance of his having paid court to Lady Everton?

"Not so quickly," he said. "First we must discuss terms. I—"

"Oh, Lord Verwood, what a pleasure to see you," came a strained feminine voice from the doorway.

Verwood turned to see the duke's second wife enter the room. Angular, hard-faced, and fashionably dressed, she looked as anxious as her husband; apparently she was privy to his plans. Verwood stood up, smiled, and swept her a bow.

"Lord Verwood has offered to restore to us certain papers which we have been missing, my love," the duke explained to his wife after they were all seated once more.

"Has he? I wonder what could have persuaded him of the wisdom of such a course?" she asked with a triumphant look.

Verwood decided to let them think they'd won—at least for a few moments. "Certain accidents have befallen me which have made me reconsider my way of life," he replied. "I should like to regain some degree of acceptance in society, and with that in mind, I wish to close out all my father's affairs."

Another motive they could understand.

"Well then, there is no reason to delay," said His Grace. "You have the letters in your possession, do you not?"

"Would I be so foolish as to bring them with me? However, I am willing to restore them to you—upon certain terms."

"You are in no position to bargain!" Her Grace protested.

"You will find my requests quite reasonable," he replied softly. "You will cease these attempts on my life, and you will assist me in one other matter. I have just offered to marry a very respectable and virtuous young lady, Miss Penelope Talcott. If she chooses to accept my offer, I wish you both to recognize us and publicly demonstrate your approval for the match. If Miss Talcott does not choose to marry me, you will nevertheless do all you can to ensure her position in society is secure despite the rumors currently circulating about her."

"Penelope Talcott!" exclaimed Her Grace. "That little nobody, the niece of a paltry baronet, with no style, no fortune, no countenance. You ask *me* to favor *her* with my attentions?"

"That is precisely what I am asking," he replied. "Perhaps you are unaware that this morning a crazed bathing-machine attendant, Maggie Brown, tried to drown Miss Talcott? And that the attack was in response to the death of her lover, Ted Booley, whom you hired to kill me?"

"You have no proof that we did such a thing!" said His Grace, shaking. "Dear God, I wish we had never—"

"Hush, fool!" interrupted his wife.

"But it was your idea—" began the duke, and was silenced by a slap on the hand from his spouse.

"We have no notion what you are talking about," she said to Verwood. "In any case, you cannot prove it."

"Perhaps you are unaware that a certain young man who has recently been employed as a waiter at the Old Ship Inn was present at the scene, and made certain Maggie Brown would not live to tell her tale. Apparently this same person has been keeping careful track of my movements, although oddly, no one seems to know where *he* was the night of the Prince Regent's party. What is most peculiar, he bears a striking resemblance to one of your footmen, whom I recall seeing when I called on you in London last year. I had been wondering for some time why he looked so familiar," he ended, on a musing tone.

"Hearsay and supposition! You cannot—" the duchess began.

"My man, Symonds, has detained this individual," he interrupted. "I imagine he may be persuaded to tell quite an interesting tale. I have also given Lord Everton a full account of what has occurred, in case any further accidents should befall me. We are both reluctant to make this affair public because of the additional distress the scandal might cause Miss Talcott. However, we will do it if necessary. Perhaps now you see the wisdom of agreeing to my terms?"

Both their graces blanched.

"Must I remind you that an innocent girl might have been killed through her chance involvement in this affair?"

Their stricken expressions confirmed his belief that they were far out of their depth and terrified at how far the situation had spun out of their control.

"We will be delighted to do what we can for dear Miss Talcott. After all, she is my stepdaughter's friend," said the duchess, nervously.

"Of course, all shall be as you wish," echoed His Grace, a querulous tone in his voice. "Now may we have the letters?"

"They shall be delivered to you within the week, once you have proven your good faith in fulfilling my conditions," he said, rising to leave. "I bid you both good day and trust you will continue to enjoy your usual good health."

With that subtle warning, he left the house, hoping he had said enough and not too much. Sometimes it was hard to know whether a threat would safeguard him or bring on further attacks. However, he sensed that the Whitgraves would cause him no more trouble. The knowledge that he was aware of their criminal intent was probably enough of a protection.

It was a relief to feel the late afternoon sunshine on his face, but as Verwood strolled down the Steine toward the water, questions continued to plague him. Why had Whitgrave been so certain that Everton was going to purchase the letters from him? Was it his few dances with Lady Everton that prompted the panic, or had someone planted the suspicion in his mind? Who could it have been?

It also seemed a strange coincidence that Lady Everton's necklace, along with the cryptic note bearing her initial, had so recently been found under a hedge in the gardens at Tregaron House. The gardens had been neglected for years, so no one could tell for certain how long it had been there. Perhaps his father had left it there; he'd often hidden such items in odd places.

The only other explanation was that someone else was involved in his father's schemes. Perhaps it was the same person who had pushed his father off that cliff, even though the event had been treated as an accident.

As he walked on, the sun and the sea breezes lifted his mood. Perhaps he was reading too much into recent events. He'd never actually found any evidence that his father had had a partner, nor had there been any common thread in any of the previous attempts on his life. As for his father's death, he thought grimly, the man had enough enemies who might have done the deed. There was no need to imagine a greedy conspirator.

Moreover, he might just have resolved the last of his father's turbid affairs. Perhaps he'd reached the end of the coil. God, he hoped so!

On reaching the seafront, he took a deep breath of the

bracing, salt-tanged air. Time to bend his mind toward more pleasant subjects. Such as Miss Talcott, and his hope that she would accept his proposal. Would he have the opportunity to taste those intoxicating lips again?

A God-given opportunity to make a better life for yourself. Woodmere's voice intruded on his thoughts. Why did the man have to make such a weighty issue of it?

Peace and pleasure. Sweet, pure pleasure. They were all he wanted, now that his life was no longer threatened, and this morning's kiss had proven that Miss Talcott might suit him far more than he would have ever predicted. Would he suit her? He'd failed every other woman that had ever been important to him. Why did he think she would be different?

Her lungs burned. Her throat ached. Her head felt as if it might burst. Ghostly hands held her in a deadly grip. Defeated, she gave in to the urge to breathe, and took in—

Air.

She opened her eyes. Gradually, dim outlines of the furniture in her small room came into focus. Her heart slowed its frantic beating as she remembered all that had happened. She sat up, wrapping her arms around her knees and pulling them close. Lord Verwood had said she might have bad dreams, but he'd also assured her they would pass. Perhaps he knew.

Pen could almost hear his voice, teasing her into hitting him. She could almost feel the warmth of his embrace, the practiced intimacy of his mouth and hands. Mortification flooded her again at the memory of how she had kissed him back, desperate for affection and reassurance. It meant no more than that, surely: her overwrought state and his desire to console her as only a rake would.

His proposal, too, was only made out of pity. She did not belong in his world; it would be a huge mistake to marry him. She would go to the Lakes and live with Catherine. Once she knew Verwood was out of danger, surely she would be able to find peace and happiness in that beautiful rural retreat. So why did she feel so restless, so uncertain?

She climbed down out of the bed and walked to her window, wondering what time it was. There was no sign of dawn yet; stars gleamed in a velvety sky, their beauty comforting her, reminding her of all the people who truly cared for her. Her parents, surely still watching over her fondly. Her friends, Juliana and Catherine, who had sent her formidable husband from the distant north to help her.

She returned to her bed, buoyed by the thought of her loved ones. The future still loomed, shadowy and uncertain, but surely if she waited for it, the right answer would come. She curled up, still exhausted by the day's tribulations, and fell into a deeper and sounder sleep than before.

She awoke feeling refreshed enough to face her relations. Her uncle was still abed, but her aunt was all too awake, giving her many tearful, accusing looks but apparently conscious of Lord Verwood's warnings not to coerce her niece. Although it was another fine day, Aunt Mary did not propose their usual excursion into the center of town. Clearly, she was too embarrassed by the current scandal to show her face. Pen made no objection; she had no desire to see anyone, either.

They had not sat together long when Lord Verwood arrived. He looked cheerful, although there was an aura of expectancy about him she did not understand. Perhaps it meant he'd managed to resolve matters with His Grace.

"Lord Verwood," said her aunt, smiling as she heaved herself off the sofa. "I shall be out of your way in a trice. I am sure there is much you and dear Penelope wish to discuss."

"I thought perhaps Miss Talcott would prefer to go out for a walk. It is a lovely day," he said with an inviting smile.

"Perhaps I should not—" Pen started, then her aunt interrupted.

"Nonsense, dear! The very thing to make you feel better. I insist you go with Lord Verwood," said her aunt with embarrassing eagerness.

Pen wavered for a moment before agreeing. She dreaded going out, but her reputation was already in shambles. No further harm could ensue from her being seen walking with Verwood, and they needed to speak after all.

A few minutes later, having donned a bonnet and

spencer, she accepted Verwood's proffered arm. As soon as they were out the door, the breeze, the cries of gulls, and the pounding of the waves sent a chill through Pen. Would she ever hear these sounds without her insides tensing with fear?

"Are you all right?" asked Verwood softly.

She bit her lip, wishing he had not guessed her weakness.

"I suppose I must become accustomed again to the sounds of the sea," she replied, forcing herself to look down on the beach, at the sunlight sparkling on the water and the gaily colored bathing machines. Her grasp on Verwood's arm must have tightened, for he raised his other hand and stroked her arm.

"You *will* conquer this," he said, his voice soothing as it blended with the other sounds.

She nodded gratefully. It was best to face her fears, and it was kind of him to support her through it. Already she was glad she had come out. Certainly it was better than fretting inside with her aunt. If she wasn't careful, though, she might come to depend on Verwood's support. That would be folly!

"So, how did you fare with—with the person we discussed yesterday?" she asked.

"We had a most satisfactory meeting," he said with a rather fierce look of victory in his eyes.

"Oh, I am glad! What happened? Are you out of danger now?"

"He and I came to a mutually acceptable agreement," he said. "Thank you for all your help."

"You are welcome," she replied, disappointed that he would not tell her more.

They crossed the Marine Parade, and Pen noticed that several persons strolling along the promenade cast curious glances their way. She lifted her chin and walked on, thinking she would never become accustomed to being the center of attention. Oddly enough, Verwood's support was a comfort. She noticed the onlookers kept a polite distance.

"They have not been plaguing you to accept my offer,

have they?" he broke the brief silence, making a small motion back toward the Royal Crescent.

"No, I believe you and Mr. Woodmere frightened them sufficiently," she said with a slight smile.

"Good. I would not wish you to be coerced into anything."

"No, but I have already decided—"

"Please don't be so hasty," he begged. "We were interrupted yesterday, and I don't think you've had time to consider seriously. Please listen to what I have to say before you make your decision. Will you do me that kindness?"

She swallowed. He was going to persist in his suit, then.

"The Woodmeres are very good people, and I've no doubt they would treat you kindly," he said in a careful tone. "But perhaps you have not considered what *I* can offer you. Independence and a home of your own."

A home of her own. Newly buried hopes stirred to life at the phrase, and she tried to ignore them.

"I do not wish to be married out of pity."

"Don't think the advantages would be purely on your side. I won't pretend I am in love with you, but I've grown to be quite fond of you. For some time now I have been wishing to find a lady who would be a pleasant wife and companion, and provide me with an heir."

An heir. A child of her own. Another dream revived, albeit in practical, aristocratic terms. At least he was not pretending to love her, as Cyril had. But how could she possibly find happiness in such a cold-blooded marriage?

"I do not think it wise for us to marry," she said. "Your entire way of life is contrary to all I hold most dear."

"If you are speaking of my father's 'business,' " he said, "I've done my best to put an end to it all. Such games are far too dangerous and uncertain."

"How could I enjoy a fortune acquired in such a manner?"

He gave a little laugh. "I should have said, uncertain in their return. Miss Talcott, my father barely managed to satisfy his vices with the proceeds of his intrigues. I inherited little from him but debts. However, in my years abroad I've managed to learn some things about commerce and the like. It is not difficult to make money when one invests wisely."

"You acquired your fortune through *investments*?"

"Far easier to believe it was through petty extortion schemes, isn't it?"

"I suppose I should know better than to listen to gossip," she said, feeling a prick of remorse.

"Oh, some of it is true enough. I *am* a rake, my dear. You will just have to reform me."

"That is ridiculous! No one can reform another person. If you wish to change your way of life, you must do it yourself."

"I shall count on you to advise me, then."

"I would not wish to attempt such a task," she said, nettled by the lazy assurance in his voice.

"Little hornet!" he said. "Very well, perhaps I can reassure you that it is not a hopeless task. I enjoy wine, but only in moderation. I like to keep my wits clear, else I'd not have survived the past few years. I don't enjoy deep play, either. My fortune makes me very comfortable; I should very much dislike losing it over a mere roll of the dice."

"Rakes indulge in other vices than drinking and gambling," she reminded him acidly.

"Yes, I've had mistresses. There was a time when I did my best to rival Don Juan, but over the past few years I have become more particular. I have no mistress at present."

"Then who was that—that lady you flirted with at the Pavilion and danced with at the Castle Inn?"

"Mrs. Covington?" He laughed. "I used her to divert attention from you and Lady Everton. Surely you don't think I found her attractive? I like my mistresses to be good-natured and intelligent, and Mrs. Covington is neither."

Pen pondered his words for a moment. She hadn't imagined that a good nature or intelligence were the most important qualities in a mistress.

"It sounds as if you *are* seeking a wife," she blurted out.

"As I said, I need an heir, and I could not support life with a stupid or quarrelsome woman. Nor do I wish for a

namby-pamby chit who would see me as some sort of By-
ronic hero."

"Is that why you pursued Catherine and Juliana, then?"

"In part," he said cautiously. "My father's schemes
caused Lady Catherine grief, and I hoped to make some
reparation. I thought she was being manipulated into marriage with Woodmere, though I learned my mistake."

"What about Juliana? What were your intentions there?"

"I had no thought but to rescue her from the attentions of
a man I felt certain was imposing on her. In hindsight, I
wonder if it was her husband, Lord Amberley, in an as-
sumed guise. He must have been in love with her, for he hit
me even harder than Woodmere did." He smiled, rubbing
his nose absentmindedly.

Pen suppressed a chuckle, then sobered as she realized
how eager she was to believe his explanations. Was she a
fool? All had ended well for Cat and Jule, who had gone on
to marry admirable and devoted husbands, but there were
rumors of a lady who had not been so lucky.

"Is there something else you wished to know?" Verwood
asked, his voice guarded, as if sensing the direction of her
thoughts.

She hesitated, feeling unsettled. She'd started the discussion with an attempt to prove how unsuited they were, and
now, to her dismay, she found herself wavering.

She pulled herself together and nodded. "There is something I must ask you before I can even consider your proposal."

He grimaced, as if in pain, then all expression seemed
wiped from his face. "I think I know what you are going to
ask. You wish to know about Anne Norland, the young lady
I am said to have seduced and abandoned."

His voice was calm, controlled; she sensed he'd been
preparing for and dreading the question.

"Can you tell me what happened?"

"I cannot."

His brusque reply startled her. She stopped and stared up
at him.

"I am sorry, I can tell you nothing," he said, a tightness
around his jaw betraying his tension.

"Nothing at all? Is she alive? Do you know where she is?" Pen could no longer help herself; the questions poured out of her.

He shook his head in mute response.

"Did you love her?"

He glanced away, then back at her. "It was a youthful infatuation, nothing to concern you," he replied, his voice still a bit rough. "I can tell you no more, only that I never meant Anne any harm."

Pen was out of her depth. How could she judge his sincerity? Only by his actions toward herself and her friends, she realized. If he had meant no harm to Catherine, perhaps there was another explanation for the earlier scandal. Why did he not trust her with it?

She searched his eyes. The rigidity of his arm under hers betrayed the effort it cost him to return her gaze. She sensed he was sincere.

"You do not believe me," he said flatly.

"I did not say that."

"Then why will you not accept my offer?"

Then it struck her: the real reason why he persisted in his suit. If Lord Verwood did not marry her, people would say he had ruined her as he had Anne Norland. No one would believe that he had done her the honor of offering for her. If he truly was innocent of wrongdoing, it was dreadful to think his name would be blackened even further because of her refusal. But what sort of life could she expect if she did marry him?

"I still do not believe we are in the least bit suited," she replied slowly.

"I would not have thought so, either," he admitted, his expression lightening a little. "After yesterday morning's kiss, I'm inclined to think otherwise."

"You know I was merely distressed, and you said yourself that you were only seeking to console me!"

"A more pleasant task I've never set myself." His roguish smile returned.

A treacherous warmth stole through her middle. "You only behaved as you would with any female."

"You wound me," he said, mock dismay in his voice.

"Give me credit for more discrimination regarding the women I choose to kiss. Or offer to marry."

"I do," she said. "You pursued both Catherine and Juliana. They are beautiful and spirited and love adventure. On the other hand, I am little and freckled, and wish only for a safe, comfortable home."

"You are more like your friends than you think. I was not in love with either of them, if that is what worries you, but I did and still do admire all of you. It's rare to meet young women of such spirit, courage, and loyalty."

She blushed a little at being included in the compliment, but mostly she was struck by his emphasis on *loyalty*. Did he have many friends? Was that, perhaps, what he truly sought?

They were well out of the area of the fashionable promenade. He stopped and turned to look directly down at her.

"As for your looks, Miss Talcott, you don't do yourself justice. Do you know your eyes are huge and entrancing, capturing every tint of sea and sky? I find your freckles delightful, like flecks of cinnamon in cream. Your hair reminds me of a sunset over the Irish Sea; I would love to see it spilling around your shoulders. As for your figure . . ."

His gaze roved boldly over her, and she found her heart beating quickly. And not unpleasantly.

"That is quite enough," she said, mortified that the heat he conjured up in her must be shining clearly in her face. "You've only convinced me that you are an expert flatterer."

"I only spoke the truth," he said, eyes dark with amusement and something more disturbing.

"You said you wished for a pleasant companion. I have hit you and I have insulted you at every opportunity."

"When playing with a kitten, one may get scratched. It is still a delightful experience, I assure you."

"You liken me to a kitten?" she asked, indignant.

He merely grinned, then sobered. "Please, Miss Talcott," he said. "You risked your life to help preserve mine. Grant me the right to repay you. If you marry me, I'll do my best to act like a man worthy of you."

Racked by doubts, she pulled away from him. He let her go, and she stared down into the foaming waves for several minutes.

She'd always known what she wished for. A home. Children of her own. A husband who loved her. Verwood, on the other hand, had said he wanted a pleasant companion and an heir. It was clear enough from his tone that he did not want love, although he did say he'd become *fond* of her. Would it be enough?

The voice of reason spoke up, reminding her that Verwood had kept entire passages of his life secret from her, his own needs and desires hidden. All except the most obvious ones, anyway. What did she know of him? Could such a man be trusted? She'd already blundered terribly by trusting Cyril, and Verwood was far more charming. He could break her heart as easily as he could snap a twig, without even realizing what he was doing.

A home. Children of her own. The inner voice kept echoing. Could she achieve these things and still protect her heart? Was there a way?

She tried to recapture the calm she'd felt at midnight, remembering all those who truly loved her and knowing that when the time came she would know what to do. She turned her head to look back at Verwood. He was watching intently and quietly, as if he knew it was time to leave her alone to decide. Something in his eyes pleaded with her nonetheless.

She turned to stare into the white clouds driving across the sky. Was it chance or divine providence that she had met Lord Verwood up on the Downs and become involved in his intrigues? Did fate still intend her to have some role in his life?

She turned back to him, shaken by the sudden, powerful conviction that it did, and that there might be more dangers and more pain in store for them both.

"Very well, my lord," she said, her voice unexpectedly steady. "I will marry you."

Chapter Eight

Surprise paralyzed Verwood for a moment. Penelope Talcott had accepted his proposal. Her expressions and even her posture radiated such doubt and distrust that he'd all but given up. Only now, overwhelmed with relief, did he realize how much he'd hoped for her acceptance. But why had her face paled under its dusting of freckles? Was she already having regrets?

"Well," he said, collecting himself and smiling, "I am entirely delighted, and I promise you—"

"No," she said, her voice low and urgent. "I don't want you to make any promises you will not wish to keep. This is to be a purely practical arrangement. There will be no need for us to sit in each others' pockets."

He stared at her in astonishment.

"Such marriages are common in aristocratic circles, are they not?" she asked in a brittle tone.

"Yes, but I did not think that was what you wanted."

"You wish for an heir, and I wish for a home and children. As long as I have those I shall be content," she said.

Brats. He should have realized. Her acceptance had nothing to do with him, after all. With an effort, he swallowed his chagrin. If she wanted brats, she would have them. As many as she wanted, daunting as the prospect was. He certainly had no precedent for the role of parenthood, but no doubt she could compensate for his shortcomings.

Perhaps fear that he would not prove a reliable provider

and father was the source of her pallor. Or even fear that he would be unfaithful. Well, she had no reason to trust him.

"What if I choose to live in your pocket?" he asked, striving to lighten her mood.

"You may do as you wish, my lord."

Clearly it would take time to win her confidence.

"Please call me Robert," he said.

"Very well. Robert," she said, sounding shy.

No one had called him by his Christian name for years. He decided he liked to hear it on her lips. Lips he would kiss again soon, he hoped. Not yet, though; clearly, she needed some time to become accustomed to their engagement.

"Thank you. Penelope," he said. "A most suitable name: that of Ulysses' wife, who remained faithful to him throughout all his years of wandering."

"During which time he consorted with all sorts of strange women, if I recall correctly," she retorted.

He chuckled, relieved at the return of her wit.

"Let us not carry the analogy too far, my dear," he begged. "Perhaps it is time we returned to your relations and gave them the news. I hope they will not embarrass us too much with their expressions of delight."

"You are not very well acquainted with my relations, are you?" she asked with a wry look, but accepted his proffered arm.

"Well enough to know that they do not consider your wishes as they should," he replied. "For that reason, I think we should discuss several practical matters as we go. For instance, how soon would you wish to be married? For myself, I should prefer it to be as soon as possible. I suppose, however, it might appear more respectable if we waited a bit, and you had time to purchase bride clothes and the like."

"I think there is so much gossip about us already that it can hardly be any worse. And I have too many new dresses as it is. I see no use in delaying."

Her arm tensed as she spoke. He knew she longed to leave Brighton and her relations, but feared the future as well.

"Very well," he replied. "I shall see what arrangements I can make. A week or so should be sufficient to procure a license and make any other necessary arrangements. Another question I should like you to think about is where you would like to make your home. I have a house in London, and Tregaron House in Cornwall. I must warn you, I am not well-liked in Cornwall. Although no charges were pressed, most people believe I seduced Anne away from her home. It might be more comfortable for you if I purchased another estate. Here in Sussex, perhaps, if you wish to remain in your native county."

"Tell me about Tregaron House," she said after a pause.

He considered his words carefully. "It is an Elizabethan manor house, not large, but said to be a good example of the architecture of the period. The structure itself is in good repair, but the interior has not changed in many years and is perhaps a trifle shabby."

"Are there gardens?"

"Yes, though they have not had sufficient attention for some time. The surrounding hedge is quite overgrown, so perhaps the hardier plants have survived the rigors of the climate," he said, allowing some of his distaste for the place to creep into his voice.

She looked up at him, frowning.

"Tregaron House is very close to the sea. A grove of trees and the hedge are all that separate it from salt and high winds," he explained, determined that she completely understand its situation.

She looked away to their left, toward where seabirds circled above the Channel while the waves continued to crash beneath, as if testing herself and her fears. He watched and listened quietly.

Unexpectedly, long-buried memories surfaced. He recalled long days spent on the cliffs and beaches, swimming, wading, playing pirates with his onetime friend Nick Dalton, observing birds, seals, dolphins, and learning all their ways. Escaping from a house—for he would not call it a home—that was filled with quiet, chilling strife.

He stifled the unwelcome images. He'd no desire to return to the scenes of his childhood. After all Penelope had already endured, she would not wish to face unfriendly neighbors and a house constantly buffeted by the sea. Surely it was best to start their life afresh and avoid reviving old specters.

"I would like to go to Tregaron," she said, as pale as when she accepted his proposal.

Damnation. Why had she chosen Tregaron? He'd allowed her to choose, and now he would have to abide by his word.

It was all Verwood could do to force a careless smile to his lips and say, "As you wish, my dear."

Over the following week, Pen struggled with a continual sense of panic, as if she were riding a runaway horse. On their return to the Royal Crescent, Lord Verwood spent several hours discussing the marriage settlements with her uncle. From the delighted expressions on her relations' faces, Pen deduced that his lordship had been most generous. The next morning, he traveled to London, where he stayed for several days to procure a license and arrange other matters of business.

Pen had little opportunity to speak with him privately on his return, both of them having received a number of invitations to fashionable private parties. They dined with the Evertons and even attended a party given by the Duke and Duchess of Whitgrave, who welcomed both Pen and Verwood with outward politeness, thus conferring public approval on their marriage. Pen could only surmise it was part of the bargain Verwood had struck with Their Graces.

Knowing their elevation to respectability would benefit their children, Pen had to be grateful. But it was a strain to be the object of so many curious eyes, knowing that many who now called their story an "affecting romance" had just days before rejoiced in making a scandal out of her misfortune. Some might even be secretly placing bets on how long it would take for Lord Verwood to tire of her.

She busied herself with letters to Catherine and Juliana and with the necessary preparations for the trip to Cornwall, for she had declined Lord Verwood's suggestion of a honeymoon. Aunt Mary bemoaned the fact that there was not time to go to London to shop for bride clothes, and consoled herself by dragging Pen to the most expensive dressmaker in Brighton, who promised to complete a wedding gown and several others in the allotted time. Here, Pen set her foot down, rejecting her aunt's fashionable but ill-considered suggestions. To her disgust, the words "Lord Verwood would not approve" worked like a charm.

Each night, she fell into an exhausted but restless sleep, although her nightmare recurred only once more. As often as she reminded herself that she and Verwood were safe, she wondered how long it would be before she truly believed it.

St. Nicholas Church was the oldest building in Brighton, its square tower a solid contrast to the fancies of the Pavilion. At its entrance, Verwood waited for Penelope and her relations and struggled with the contrary emotions that had stirred within him since she'd accepted his offer. Keen anticipation of a happy married life. Worry that history would repeat itself, and he would fail her in some way.

Then she arrived, accompanied by her relations, dressed in a beautifully fitted, low-cut ivory gown and bonnet, both trimmed simply with ribbons in a warm, spicy shade of amber that set off her coloring. She looked good enough to eat. A happy thought, were it not for her grave expression, which once again revived his unwelcome, annoying fears.

Everything was going to be well, he told himself, coming forward to greet them and take Penelope's arm. She accepted his escort passively as they entered the church and walked up to where the vicar awaited them. Already seated in the church were old Phoebe Hessel, a smile on her leathery face, several friends of the Talcotts, the Evertons, and Mr. Woodmere, his gaze soberly directed at Verwood in a clear warning to honor the solemnity of the vows he was about to utter.

Suppressing a spurt of unholy anger over Woodmere's unspoken threat, he played his part in the ceremony. He

spoke his vows clearly and emphatically, as if he could
deny Woodmere's suspicions. Or his own.

Then it was time for Penelope to repeat her vows, and a
beam of sunlight coming through one of the windows illuminated her face, solemn as she listened to the vicar.
Something of her character shone in her face, and a rush
of pure joy and anticipation assaulted Verwood almost
like a physical pain. The feeling was too sharp, too in-
tense, and probably deceptive. It was almost a relief when
the sound of Penelope's voice, tranquil and resigned,
brought him back to reality. Did she, too, doubt his good
intentions?

As he slipped the ring upon her hand, her pale face and
the coldness of her fingers rebuked him, reminding him of
all the trials and changes she'd suffered in the past few
weeks. It was too much to expect her to look forward to
their marriage as he did. Still, he longed to tease and cajole
the color back into her cheeks. That would have to wait.
They were in church, so all he could do was smile and vow
to be patient with his new bride, so their marriage would
start, not with strife and vexation and overwrought emotions, but with pleasure and delight.

Pen allowed Verwood to assist her into his traveling
chariot, then sank into the luxuriously upholstered seat
with a sigh. The wedding breakfast, held in a parlor of the
Old Ship, had seemed interminable. Why did they call it
that, anyway, she wondered in annoyance. Fashionable
ones often lasted late into the day. Her head ached, her
face hurt from trying to smile at everyone, and she wanted
nothing better than to retreat to a quiet room by herself.
And she still had to face her first evening with a new husband.

Verwood climbed into the chaise and sat down beside
her. His closeness sent her nerves screaming again. How
could he look so calm, smile so cheerfully? At least he did
not attempt to touch her as they set off.

"Does your head ache very badly?"

She looked up, surprised by his sympathetic tone.

"A little," she replied, wondering how he had known.

"If you wish, I could rub your temples."

The offer was so unexpected she did not reply. Apparently he took her silence for acquiescence, for he drew the curtains, then untied the ribbons of her bonnet and removed it. She was too tired to protest when he pulled her into his arms, pressed her head against his shoulder and began to gently rub her temple with long, dexterous fingers.

Relief spread through her as he shifted and massaged the other temple, then continued his gentle kneading up and down her neck. As her tension receded, her body began to revive and thrum with the alarming consciousness of being pressed up against him. His hand traveled down to the junction of her neck and shoulder, and she stiffened. He stopped, not moving his hand farther but continuing to lightly stroke the same spot.

"Don't look so frightened, my dear," he murmured. "I know you've had no time to become accustomed to me or to the thought of our marriage. Although I find you completely entrancing, I'm not a beast. You must tell me when you are ready for further intimacies; for now I only wish you to rest."

She relaxed a bit more. Pain continued to drain out of her shoulders as his fingers deftly probed through the fabric of her spencer and soothed any sore spots they found.

"As for tonight, I have engaged two rooms. I will always do so, for I prefer to sleep alone."

Two rooms? She knew aristocratic couples often kept to separate bedchambers. But on their honeymoon? Was this merely to set her at her ease? She turned her head to look at her husband, but in the dim interior of the coach she could not read his expression.

"This does not mean," he added in a silky tone, "that I will not visit *you* in your bedchamber whenever you say the word."

The caress in his voice caused her to tense, but he turned her so she faced away from him and began to work the knots out of her back, sending tingling sensations all the way down to her feet. She uncurled her toes in relief, realizing she'd been holding them clenched tight for some time.

She sighed and allowed him to pull her into his arms once more. He moved back up, stroking her neck and jaw and then her temples again. Where had he learned such magic? How did he know exactly what hurt and how to soothe it? Soon she gave up wondering, surrendering herself to bliss.

She woke to find herself still in Verwood's arms, feeling warm and safe, if a little confused. How long had she slept?

"This is Shoreham-by-sea. We'll stop here for the night," he said, releasing her to draw the curtains open again. "I thought it best not to try to go too far today. How are you feeling?"

"Mmmm . . . a little sleepy still," she admitted, stretching.

"I will see if everything is ready for us," he said, and climbed out.

The innkeeper and his wife bustled out from a doorway. Beyond them Pen saw the welcome face and form of Susan, who had gladly agreed to accompany Pen to Cornwall. A moment later Verwood was back at the carriage to help her out. She wobbled a little, feeling a bit dazed, and he steadied her before accompanying her to the entrance. She looked about her. The Red Lion, as the brightly painted sign proclaimed, had whitewashed walls and a thatched roof. The inn was not grand, but had a look of comfort about it.

After being greeted warmly by the hosts, Pen followed Susan up to her room to tidy herself before dinner. Her room was as comfortable as the exterior of the inn promised, its floor covered by a pretty carpet, the spacious bed spread with a sparkling white counterpane and surrounded by pristine curtains worked in a pattern of flowers. The room was cheerful and not at all ostentatious.

Her husband had said she could enjoy it alone, if she wished. She should have felt reassured; instead, a feeling of indecision pressed on her as Susan brushed out and pinned her hair back up again. Verwood—or Robert, as she should become accustomed to calling him—had been nothing but kind and patient. Was she behaving like a coward to wish to delay matters?

Still racked by uncertainty, she rejoined her husband in the private parlor he'd hired for their dinner. *Her husband*, she thought, looking at him with a growing awareness of the face and figure half the belles in Brighton had swooned over.

"I hope I've ordered what you would like," he said, motioning toward the table.

His gentle tone soothed her nerves and made her feel pampered as she had never been before. The smell of fresh bread, of fish in a simple lemon-butter sauce, the steam rising from the potatoes and the French beans reminded her that she'd eaten little that day. Her appetite miraculously revived, and she enjoyed the simple but well-prepared meal, which was served with a delicious white burgundy. Meanwhile Verwood talked of his plans for the rest of their journey, which he'd warned her would take several weeks to accomplish, particularly since the roads would become worse farther west.

"Is there any place you wish to visit during our journey?"

She thought a moment before replying. "Stonehenge. If it is not too far out of the way."

"Not at all. You are interested in antiquities, then?"

"My father was particularly fascinated by ruins and ancient monuments," she admitted. "He often took me to such places and taught me all he knew of their history. My own interest has never been quite so scholarly, though. I just like to visit such places, that is all."

She stopped, embarrassed. If she told him how such ancient places seemed to speak to her, as if the spirits of those who had lived there dwelled on in the old stones, he would think her eccentric in the greatest degree.

"Good," he said, smiling. "Now I know how to keep you entertained during our trip. There are also several ancient sites very near Tregaron."

The mention of his home brought back the vague disquiet she'd felt on making the decision to go to Cornwall. She still wondered if it was the right choice, but at the time she'd felt the same compulsion that had led her to accept his proposal, a sense that they were meant to go to Tregaron. That something awaited them there that had to be faced.

"I know," she replied, trying to shake off the uncomfortable sensation. "I believe it is not far from Tintagel?"

"Not far at all. There are also some ancient sites closer by."

He changed the subject, then the waiter reappeared to clear the remains of the meal, bringing dessert with him: a tray bearing nuts and fruit, some strawberries and a pitcher of cream. Pen could not resist a bowl of the last two items; strawberries in cream were one of her favorite summer pleasures. As she savored their ripe sweetness, she noticed her husband looking at her with a satisfied gleam in his eyes. As if he'd planned it all to set her at her ease, she mused. Why did the thought have the opposite effect?

She swallowed and tried to think, which was becoming increasingly difficult after encountering the warmth in his velvet-brown eyes. He'd behaved so kindly, prepared everything so perfectly. Almost too perfectly, as if he could guess her every fear, her every whim, her every desire. Managing her moods as adroitly as if she were a puppet and he held the strings.

"How did you know strawberries are my favorite?" she asked impulsively.

"I did not, but I am glad you are enjoying them," he said, as if committing the fact to memory. He raised a spoonful to his own lips, then his gaze wandered to hers in a way that only raised Pen's discomfort to panic.

She didn't want this intimacy, this playful seduction. He was so skilled at it, no doubt from years of practice, that it would be terribly easy to believe that he had feelings for her. Even if he intended to keep his vows, she reminded herself, it was probably not in his nature to do so. If she fell in love with him, she might easily become a heartsick, bitter creature. It was time to end this game.

She set down her spoon and rose from the table, a desperate plan forming in her mind.

"I expect you will wish me to leave you to your port now," she said.

"We need not follow that particular custom," he replied, rising as well. "If you wish to stay, we can share some more wine together, but perhaps you are tired. Did you wish to retire to your room?"

"Yes. And—and,"—she licked her lips—"I wish you would join me there. Whenever you are ready, that is."

She blushed, and chided herself for stammering.

"As you wish, my dear," he said, the silk of his voice caressing her mercilessly.

She turned and fled before her courage deserted her completely.

Chapter Nine

$\mathcal{F}$reshly shaven and attired in nothing but a dressing gown, Verwood hesitated for a minute outside his wife's door. He was not nervous, of course; it was not as if he were without experience regarding women. Then some imp inside him reminded him that he'd never had much luck with innocents. Pen was different from Anne, he reminded the imp. History would not repeat itself. His wife's pretty blush and the way she had fled the dining parlor were evidence of maidenly modesty, nothing else. He'd already managed once to get her moaning with pleasure in his arms, and that was only due to a kiss. All would be well. Better than well. It was going to be delightful.

He knocked softly on the door and hearing a low-voiced welcome, entered and locked the door behind him.

His wife sat perched on the edge of the high bed, watching him like a bird poised to flee. Poor thing, she probably had not the least notion of what was ahead. Certainly that idiotic aunt of hers could not have told her anything useful.

She wore a plain white nightrail, and her lustrous hair hung down her back in a thick braid. For an instant, anxiety pricked him. She looked so young and vulnerable. However, the thin nightrail followed the graceful curve of her hips, reassuring him that she was indeed a young woman of twenty years, fully ripe for the pleasures of the marriage bed.

"I trust they've made you comfortable here," he said, crossing the room.

"Perfectly." Her reply was slightly breathless.

He sat down beside her. The mattress gave a little beneath him, bringing their hips into contact. The scent of lavender soap and Penelope tantalized him, but he decided it was too soon to even take her in his arms. He'd kept both his emotions and his desire tightly leashed throughout the wedding, the carriage ride, and dinner. He would just have to restrain himself a little longer.

"It is quite understandable that you should be a trifle nervous," he said. "Do you understand what we are going to do?"

"Yes. Back at Lambourne, I sometimes assisted the midwife. She explained many things to me, including what— what happens between men and women."

"Good. Then you know there might be some pain at first."

"I am prepared."

"Well then," he began, a little surprised by her calm tone. "Perhaps we may start with a kiss."

"No," she said, and pulled away as he tried to put an arm around her.

No matter, he told himself, lowering his hand. She was merely being skittish. He was still master of the situation.

"Why not?" he asked gently.

"This is a practical arrangement. There is no need to pretend you are in love with me."

Damn. It was the brats again. She did not want *him*—or would not admit to herself that she did. Why did she have to make things so difficult?

"I should very much enjoy kissing you," he said, hoping to distract her from dangerous territory.

"No." This time she said it more emphatically, then slipped off the bed and turned to face him, several feet away. "I don't wish to be kissed or—or caressed."

"It is the most pleasant way, darling," he said in a reasonable tone. "I know more about this than you do."

"I am certain you do."

He cursed, wishing he could unsay his last words, feeling the situation slipping out of his control. He persevered. "I regret that my past bothers you. I cannot undo it or forget what I have learned. All I can do is be the best husband I can, which means pleasing you as well as I know how."

His words were not helping. He could see it from the frantic look in her large eyes, her agitated breathing which taunted him with the thought of what lay just beneath the white cotton. His body cried out for release, muddling his attempts to recover from his earlier blunder.

"There is no need for you to take pains to please me," she said. "Can we not just . . . proceed?"

Now his body roared its readiness to take her up on her offer. What folly that would be! If he did not proceed slowly and do things properly, she would hate him forever. Was that what she wanted?

"*No*," he said, frustrated by the increasing tension in her stance. "That is *not* my way. I cannot and will not—" He broke off, struck dumb as she fumbled at the ties at the neck of her gown. What the devil was the obstinate creature doing?

She was untying her gown. Now she was pulling the neck wide, baring smooth white shoulders. Now letting it drop to the floor, revealing a soft, slender, youthful body even more lovely than he'd imagined.

"Please. May we get on with it?" she pleaded.

Rage and desire battled within him for a moment. Then with a stifled groan, he averted his face and, finding her by feel rather than sight, picked her up. His senses pounded, making matchsticks out of his resolution to ignore the fragrant, shapely bundle in his arms.

Somehow he managed to carry her the short distance to the bed and deposit her onto the mattress, then pulled the coverlet over her, in the futile hope that hiding temptation would lessen the urge to give in.

"What are you doing?" she cried. "You are not leaving me?"

Her frenzied protest was nearly his undoing, but he retained just enough control not to slip under the coverlet with her.

"Yes, I am," he replied, struggling to keep the rage from his voice and not quite succeeding.

"You said you would do anything I wished!" The com-

bined hurt and anger in her voice halted him as he walked
to the door.

Not risking a look back, he replied, "Not if what you ask
is complete folly. We will talk tomorrow. By which time I
hope you will have recovered your senses."

It took all his remaining resolution not to slam the door.

As the door closed, Pen curled up in a ball, shaking with
anger and humiliation. She'd not only failed to execute her
plan, she'd managed to anger and disgust her husband and
make a complete and utter fool of herself. How was she
ever to look him in the face again?

Tears stung the corners of her eyes, but she held them
back as she slid out from under the covers, feeling chilled
despite the ample fire in the hearth. She retrieved her
nightdress and slipped it back over her head, the soft fabric falling around her and reminding her of her failure.
What an idiot she was to have believed Verwood when
he'd waxed poetic about her eyes, her hair, and her figure!
Small, plain, and freckled, how had she ever hoped to en-
tice him? He hadn't even been able to look at her.

She climbed back into the bed, pulled the coverlet over
herself, and curled up again. The thought of how he'd
averted his head tormented her, even while the memory of
his warm, strong arms around her body mocked her with
her own desires. For she had wanted him, had almost
yielded to his persuasions. Perhaps she should have. *Idiot!*
He'd shown her gentleness and courtesy, and she'd behaved like a lunatic. It was no wonder he was angry, and
she had no idea how to mend matters now.

She allowed her tears to fall on the crisp white pillows
until there were no more, and finally fell into a troubled
sleep.

She awoke later the next morning to the sound of
seabirds outside her window. At first she wondered why she
felt so wretched, then she remembered the past night's de-
bacle. Her heart grew even heavier. She would have to find
a way to mend the breach, even if it meant allowing Lord
Verwood to make love to her as he wished.

Otherwise, he'd soon seek consolation elsewhere, and she could not bear that. Not yet.

Thankfully, Susan asked no questions, but merely helped her into a traveling dress and informed her that his lordship awaited her in the private parlor in which they'd dined the night before.

She entered the room, dreading the encounter, but her husband, who was sipping coffee and looking over a copy of the *Times*, stood up and bade her a smiling good morning.

"I trust you slept well, my dear," he continued, his tone so calm it almost made her nervous. Surely his anger had not evaporated overnight?

"Yes, thank you," she lied.

The waiter appeared, bringing fresh coffee. She allowed him to fill a cup for her, then went to the sideboard and filled a plate at random with eggs and toast. She and Verwood both sat down at the table again, but she could not eat yet. The waiter was gone and it was time to talk about the past night. But it was so hard to find the words. How could she tell Verwood she feared he would betray her? Such an accusation might damage any good intentions he had.

"I—you must allow me to apologize for how I behaved last night," she began.

"There is no need for an apology, my dear," he said with disturbing calm. "It was a long day and you were tired and overwrought."

"Yes, yes, that was it," she blurted out, relieved by his sensible interpretation. "I am feeling much more the thing, and I can see how foolish I was. I am—I'm willing to—to do things as you wish now."

He shook his head, smiling wryly. "No, darling. I shan't make the mistake of rushing matters again. I think you need more time to become acquainted with me."

"No, I assure you, I *am* ready," she said, trying not to sound desperate.

"You will have to prove it to me, then."

"How?"

"You must kiss me. Properly. Or should I say, *im*properly."

She swallowed, eyes drawn inexorably to his lips, curved into a roguish smile. They would taste of coffee. She got up. Instantly he arose and waited quietly as she circled the table to come to stand before him. He stood completely still, neither helping nor hindering her as she awkwardly put her arms around his waist. Was this a subtle form of revenge?

He remained motionless as she balanced against him on tiptoe, heart thudding at her own boldness. Then, realizing she could not reach him and that he would not bend down, she moved her arms and twined her hands behind his head. His dark hair was silkier than she'd expected. She pulled his head down toward hers so that their mouths were mere inches apart. She tipped her head back, took in a quick, nervous gulp of air, then joined her lips to his.

The scent of cologne mingled with the aroma of coffee tantalized her senses, but still he did not make any attempt to return her kiss, let alone begin the play of tongues as he had a week ago. For a moment she leaned against his chest, pressing her lips to his, tormented by his rocklike stillness. Then she dropped back onto her heels, flushing, and looked up at him questioningly.

"That was very sweet, darling," he said, gently removing her hands from around his neck. "But you are clearly not ready yet. I see I shall have to be patient a while longer."

Her cheeks burned with mortification.

"How can you make such a game of me?" she pleaded.

"It is a game well worth playing, my dear. When you are ready, you will enjoy it very much. Until then, I must resign myself to being tormented by the image you presented last night."

So he *had* looked at her. And found pleasure in the sight. If she blushed any harder, Pen thought, her skin would match her hair. To cover her embarrassment, she returned to her place at the table and tried to eat. She scarcely tasted the food, conscious of her husband's lazy smile as he proceeded to finish his own breakfast.

Verwood watched his bride's confusion, congratulating himself on having adroitly handled a tricky situation. Last night he had allowed his eagerness to bed her to overrule his judgment. He'd not make the same mistake again, although her shy attempt to seduce him just now had rigorously tried his control.

He would have to be patient. Her first time would mean a great deal to her, and he wanted it to be perfect. Though her pretty blush proved she was beginning to desire him, she was still hesitant. She probably needed to feel at least a little in love in order to properly enjoy the experience.

He would have been content with mere friendly affection from her, being incapable of anything stronger himself. He hadn't been in love with anyone since Anne, and in hindsight even that had been a mere calf-love. Now he could only hope to arouse the warm passions he sensed Pen needed to feel for a husband, and pray she would not be wounded by his inability to love her in return. He would not lie to her, but he would do everything else in his power to make her feel cherished.

Later she might become engrossed in children and domestic concerns. She might even wish to be rid of him. They might decide to part company, as many completely respectable couples within the *ton* were wont to do. That would be her decision, however. He had vowed to be a good husband to her and would remain at her side as long as she wanted him.

And he hoped she would want him. Soon.

Pen took her seat in the carriage, alone, since Verwood had hired a horse to ride for the first stage. Apparently, it was his ingrained habit to ride each morning, and for the present she was glad to be alone with her thoughts. She watched him through the window, seeing him easily controlling the antics of the fresh young horse that had been brought out for him. Although he seemed perfectly secure in the saddle, Pen felt a stab of anxiety. Perhaps it was due to the earlier attempts on his life, but she couldn't help worrying that the horse might have been tampered with, wondering who might know their projected route and what might happen to her husband out on the open road.

No, she was being foolish. They were both safe now.

As it turned out, the following hour passed uneventfully,

and when they stopped to change horses, Verwood climbed
into the carriage, looking relaxed, cheerful, and a trifle
dusty. So why did her mind keep dwelling on all the attempted murders?

"I hope the smell of horseflesh does not offend you, my
dear," he said apologetically.

"Not at all. I love horses. All sorts of animals, in fact."
She sighed a little.

"You have no pets that I know of," said Verwood, quirking an eyebrow at her.

"Uncle Ralph is not a sportsman, so he keeps no dogs. I
should have liked to have a cat at least, but Aunt Mary says
they scratch up furniture."

He laughed. "I have no objection to any pet you should
like to adopt. I can't think of a piece of furniture at Tregaron which I care about."

"Oh, cats can be trained not to be destructive. We had
several at the vicarage when I was a girl."

"You may have as many as you like. Dogs, too. Perhaps,
like the Duchess of York, you would like to form a menagerie,
complete with monkeys and macaws and ostriches and kangaroos."

"Kangaroos?" she said, giggling.

"I have seen them myself," he assured her.

"I promise you I shall be content with more common-
place creatures as pets."

He laughed again, and she found herself relaxing.

"That is a relief," he said. "Do you ride?"

"Not for a long time. I used to ride the cob that drew our
gig at the vicarage, but I have not been on a horse since—
since I was sent to Miss Stratton's school," she ended, not
sure she wished to speak of her parents' death.

"When we are home, I shall have to look about for a suitable mount for you," he said, politely ignoring her pause.

"That would be delightful."

"Perhaps you will join me on my morning rides."

"If you wish," she replied. Was his offer made out of politeness, or did he really wish for her company? She remembered what he'd said about loyalty, and wondered
again if what he really sought was a friend.

"We shall stop in Chichester tonight," he said. "Perhaps you would like to visit the Cathedral tomorrow."

"My parents took me there when I was a child, but I would be happy to see it again."

"Tell me what they were like, your parents," he said softly.

She tilted her head to look at him better. Was he merely making conversation or did he wish to know? It had been so long since anyone had cared about her past.

"My uncle and aunt—and I suppose most people—called them unworldly," she mused. "They were completely devoted to one another and to me. They used to take me walking with them on the Downs. Papa would tell me all about the Saxon burial mounds and Roman remains, and Mama taught me the names of all the wildflowers. Her favorites were the tiny orchids. I was fascinated with them, especially the ones that looked like bees." She paused. "I am sorry, this must sound incredibly dull to you."

"No," he said slowly. "It sounds like a charming life. How did your parents die?"

She realized she'd never talked about this much, not even with Catherine or Juliana.

"Papa succumbed to an inflammation of the lungs one winter. Mama and I nursed him as carefully as we could, but . . ." She shook her head slightly, realizing there was no need to explain further.

"After that, Mama was not strong. Her heart was weak from her having had scarlet fever as a child. The shock of losing Papa was too great for her. Afterward, I went to live with Uncle Ralph and Aunt Mary. They sent me to Miss Stratton's school, hoping I would make some useful connections there."

"It was at Miss Stratton's that you met your friends Juliana and Lady Catherine?"

She smiled. "Yes. I was so miserable, and so out of place, but they took me under their wings and defended me against some of the bigger girls who enjoyed trying to make my life a misery. I will always be grateful for that."

"I suppose you miss them, too."

She sighed and nodded.

"I doubt if I am welcome in any of their households, but certainly you should feel free to visit them when you wish and invite them to any of our homes."

"Thank you. I should love to see Catherine and her dear baby sometime. And of course Juliana and Lord Amberley, when they return from the Continent."

"Have you ever thought of traveling there yourself?"

"Catherine and Juliana talked of it so much I could hardly help but think about it."

"Did *you* ever wish to go?"

"No, all I have ever wanted was a home." She hoped he was not too disappointed. Perhaps he was feeling wanderlust. It occurred to her that being rich and having traveled extensively himself, he would be the perfect companion to guide her to places she'd never been. It was an unexpected glimpse into a life she'd not planned to lead.

"I have seen most of the Continent. I would only enjoy going if I could have the pleasure of showing you the sights."

She frowned a little, wondering if he still longed to travel. Or was he actually prepared to settle down with her?

He changed the subject, asking her more questions about her childhood and her likes and dislikes. It was only when they reached the next inn, where he left her briefly to speak to his groom, Pascoe, that she realized just how adroitly he had guided their conversation.

Would she ever fathom this strange man she'd married? He behaved as if he truly wished for the same sort of marriage she had always longed for, arousing all sorts of fragile hopes in her breast. Yet he revealed so little of himself. How could their marriage succeed without openness and trust?

She would have to be patient. A long journey still stretched before them. Surely as they became more accustomed to one another, she would find opportune moments to learn why he had erected such a smooth, polite barrier around his innermost self. Only then would she allow herself to truly hope.

*   *   *

Tall grasses whispered in the breeze; clouds tumbled by slowly in an azure sky. Returning his gaze to the immense boulders arrayed upon the high, grassy plain, Verwood reflected they could not have asked for a better day to visit Stonehenge.

He turned his gaze toward an even pleasanter sight: Pen wearing a sprigged cotton gown and a straw bonnet, rambling about the stones, stopping occasionally to touch them. He deliberately hung back, seeing that the odd assortment of rocks held such a fascination for her. He amused himself watching the breeze play with her gown, pushing it against her body and outlining the delicious curves of her hip and thigh, then changing direction to lift her hem and reveal shapely ankles.

Pen turned, smiled, and beckoned him closer.

"I trust you are enjoying yourself," he said, joining her in the center of the stone circle.

"Very much. I hope you are not too dreadfully bored."

"Not at all," he said, taking her arm in his. As they strolled toward the outside of the circle, he reflected that he had not been at all bored in the past few days. It was a joy merely to walk with her, arms companionably linked, and share her enthusiasm as she drank in the surrounding sights.

"What an immense effort it must have been to transport and erect all these stones. I wonder what purpose they really had?" she mused, turning to gaze at one of the larger megaliths.

"I can't imagine why anyone would go to such lengths, but if gazing on all this gives you pleasure, I'm glad they did."

She let out a delightful chuckle. Soon they reached the thick carriage blanket, where her chalks and sketchpad awaited. She sat down to draw, and he lay on his back beside her, relaxing as he watched the clouds drift by and stealing occasional glimpses of her absorbed expression as she sketched a view of the stones.

"You know, Robert," she said, rousing him from his reverie, "you have asked me so many things about my past, but there is so much you have not told me about yours."

"Most of it is not worth telling." He raised himself up on one elbow, wishing he had not responded so curtly.

"I can see you don't wish me to pry," she said with a little lift of her chin, "but surely there are *some* things you can tell me."

He forced a smile to his face, wishing they could indulge in more pleasurable and less dangerous pursuits than talking. He would have to humor her. "What is it you wish to know?"

"Well, what was your father like? I know you despise the schemes he used to make money, but what was he like as a parent?"

"Indulgent, when he took the trouble. He helped me after the scandal with Anne, and packed me off to the Continent, where the proceedings from his intrigues kept me in funds and very well entertained," he said, remembering the several wild, debauched years he'd spent afterward. "I have no complaints."

There was a grave, pitying look in her eyes, and he wished he hadn't let his detestation for his sire show quite so clearly.

"How did he die?" she asked.

He paused. "He fell off a cliff near Tregaron. It was said to have been an accident."

"You do not believe that." It was a statement, not a question.

"No. Perhaps it was the victim of one of his schemes. Shall we talk of something more pleasant, perhaps?"

"You said yourself that I must become better acquainted with you," she said with a small shake of her head. "How can I do that if you tell me nothing about yourself?"

Damn. Earning the right to tumble his wife was proving to be quite difficult work. Looking at her lithe young form sitting beside him, Verwood decided it would be worth the effort.

"I suppose you cannot," he admitted. "What else do you wish to know?"

"What was your mother like?"

"Virtuous," he replied. "I was a great disappointment to her. She died a few months after my father."

Pen's eyes widened.

"There was no foul play involved. Like your father, she contracted an inflammation of the lungs from which she never recovered," he explained, rigidly closing his mind to the unwelcome memory of those months.

He hoped Pen would be content with that. After she gazed at him again with those solemn eyes, she began to ask him other questions about his childhood. Relieved that she had respected his desire not to speak further of his parents, he told her something of his boyhood and of the cliffs and beaches of Cornwall.

"Do you still have any friends there?"

He sighed. Did she have to pry open every ancient wound? "None since Anne disappeared."

"You *did* have friends there at one time?" she asked softly.

"A few. It is a sparsely populated corner of the country," he replied. "There were not many children of my age to be playmates. Anne was one, and Nicholas Dalton was another. Nick never forgave me for not telling him what had become of Anne."

Now there was a distinct pity in Pen's eyes. This would not do. He could deal with almost anything but pity.

"Do not look so distressed, my dear," he said. "I assure you I found other amusements after leaving Tregaron."

She looked away then, and he was sure he'd blundered. She probably had a fair idea of the sort of vices he'd indulged in after the scandal. When she turned back, however, he thought he saw a hint of moisture around the corners of her eyes. An instant later her face was tranquil again, and she began to ask him about some of the places he'd visited.

Relieved, he answered her questions. Anything to keep her from learning how grievously he had disappointed the women who had been most important in his life. He could not have *her* doubting his conviction that this time he would not fail. His own mind already echoed the old adage about good intentions.

And the road to Hell.

Chapter Ten

"This will only take a few minutes," Pen promised Verwood. He posed languidly before the ruins of Corfe Castle, one foot placed on a fallen stone, a lazy, roguish smile on his face. She'd asked him to do so, telling him she wanted a human figure to bring perspective to the picture, but now she wondered if it was such a wise idea.

She bent to her sketchbook and quickly penciled in the keep and the Purbeck hills beyond, dreamlike and muted in the haze of the sultry day. She looked up, then began sketching in the outlines of her husband: his head, the torso with its wide shoulders tapering to slim hips. She glanced up again and paused, contemplating the curve of his thigh, boldly exposed through the leg of his riding breeches. No, this was not a good idea at all, but now that she'd started she would have to finish. At least the brim of her bonnet shaded her face from his perceptive gaze.

She added detail to the outlines of the keep, then was drawn helplessly back to Verwood's image, where her pencil somehow captured the bold curve of his limbs. It was no wonder the chambermaids at every inn ogled him shamelessly, though so far as she knew, he'd not succumbed to any of their lures. Indeed, he'd been the perfect attentive husband.

She quickly added some hints of vegetation to the open hills, thinking over the past few days. After veering north to Salisbury, he'd brought them back south to Corfe Castle, just a few miles from the sea. Below them stood the pretty village of the same name, constructed largely of the rubble left after the castle was destroyed by Parliamentarians in the seventeenth century. Little though she'd traveled, she could tell he was taking them to Cornwall by an extremely indirect route. Did he dread going home? Or was it merely that he was trying to make their journey into a proper honeymoon?

She completed the details of the keep and returned to the portion of the sketch that remained ironically blank: Verwood's face. She hesitated, although she'd longed to capture it. Then she began filling in his strongly marked features: the swooping brows, the arrogant nose, the lips that had beckoned her more than once since her feeble attempt to kiss him at the Red Lion.

She'd not gotten up the courage to try again.

Licking her own lips, she looked back up to see his eyes gleaming at her. Eyes of such a dark brown they were almost black, whose expressions she was just beginning to learn to read. After her one attempt at Stonehenge, she'd stopped trying to discuss his past directly. It was clear he was not comfortable with the strong emotions those memories evoked.

Still, she'd gleaned a few things from their discussion. She sensed his parents' marriage had not been a happy one. She could tell their discord had tainted his childhood, and that he suppressed pain and anger over the scandal that had driven him from his home. That in itself added to her conviction that he had been wronged somehow.

Looking up and seeing Verwood still patiently posing for her, she decided to set her worries aside. The revelations she sought might come in time.

"Thank you. I have quite finished now," she said, putting down her pencil.

He returned to where she sat and helped her up, his touch warming her even more than the midsummer sun overhead. He took the sketchbook from her and looked down at it. She blushed a little. Did the picture betray how attractive she found him?

"A most flattering likeness, my dear," he said, the silk back in his voice.

She blushed harder, looking down at the traitorous sketch.

"Shall we go on?" she asked nervously.

He nodded. Arms linked, they continued the circuit of the ruins. A warm breeze fluttered the ribbons of her bonnet, doing nothing to cool her, then stilled again, so that the only sound that could be heard was the humming of insects in the grass and wildflowers on the steep slopes surrounding the castle.

They passed what Verwood told her was the North Tower, then walked by several more towers, walking slowly in a wide curve until they passed through the Southwest Gatehouse. They stopped for a moment to take in the view of the village below, but Pen found her eyes drawn to her husband instead.

He looked so carefree, so much happier than she'd ever seen him. Sudden emotion caught in her throat as she realized how much peace and pleasant companionship meant to him. Of course, there were other things he wanted from her, though he'd been more than patient, only teasing her occasionally with his eyes.

She continued to watch him as he went closer to the edge.

Then she cried out, seeing the rubble slide away under his feet. Within an instant he'd disappeared. A cloud of dust rose to take his place.

Dear God, let him not be hurt. She prayed, heart pounding as she ran to the edge. She let out a sigh, seeing him crawling back up the steep slope, covered with dust and with a trickle of blood down one cheek.

"Here, let me help you," she said, reaching a hand out over the remaining stones to help him up. As she pulled him over the edge, she fell on the soft turf within the wall, Verwood beside her.

"Are you hurt badly?" she asked, sitting back up.

He raised himself up and shook his head, still trying to recapture his breath after the exertion of the climb. For a moment she stared, unused to seeing his face dirty. Then she reached into his pocket for his handkerchief and wiped the blood from the cut on his cheek. Their eyes met, and the warmth of the sun and the chorus of insects closed in around them like a protective cocoon.

He leaned toward her, took her in his arms and kissed her, gently at first, then exploring her mouth with ever-increasing hunger. As in a dream, she wrapped her arms around him and feverishly returned his kiss, opening, welcoming, begging him to satisfy desires she dared not speak.

An eternity—or perhaps a few minutes—later, he released her. She sat back, heat flaring in her cheeks. What if someone had seen them, kissing like a pair of villagers in the grass?

"I feel much better now," he said with an apologetic grin, looking rather like a schoolboy caught in a prank.

"I can see that," she said, trying to sound prim and failing. Could he tell how she longed for another kiss?

"Your kisses must have restorative powers."

She looked back toward the village and saw a party of travelers approaching the gatehouse.

"I think it is time we return to the carriage," she said unsteadily.

He nodded, and they made their way back to the gatehouse that led out of the ruins. She looked over the crumbling wall as they went. Though it was not a sheer drop, her husband might easily have broken a limb in his fall, or one of the stones could have struck him a serious, even fatal, blow to the head.

"That *was* an accident, was it not?" she faltered.

"Of course, my dear," he said.

He smiled as if touched by her concern, and her heart twisted with an ache that was frightening in its intensity. She might never have learned what sort of husband he was going to be, and now all her hesitation and objections seemed selfish and cowardly. *I love him*, she thought, with a clarity as brilliant as the sun overhead. *I love him. It is enough.*

Her husband was unusually quiet as they walked back to the inn. Perhaps he wondered if he had overstepped her boundaries by kissing her. For now, Pen was glad of his silence. She yearned to voice her passion to him but sensed he was not ready to hear such strong sentiments, much less return them. Would he ever be?

Love could not be measured or compared, she reminded herself. It was strong in itself.

Half an hour later, after she'd tended more carefully to his cut, they climbed back into the carriage for the next stage of their journey. Verwood gazed thoughtfully out the window while she gathered her resolution.

"Robert," she said to regain his attention and realized his name came more easily to her lips now.

He turned back to her, looking wary. Was he expecting to be scolded for kissing her?

"I wanted to say—that is, I think—" She paused to compose herself. "I think it is time to end this foolishness."

"You do?" he asked in a cautious, controlled voice, and she realized she'd made a jumble of it.

"What I mean is," she said, licking her lips, "I should very much like to kiss you."

He sighed softly, then a delighted smile overspread his face. He drew the curtains closed and sat back, saying, "I am entirely at your disposal, my dear."

She swallowed, realizing he still wished her to take the initiative. She sidled over, closing the scant inches of seat that had separated them, then turned, putting her arms around him as best she could. This time he obliged her by lowering his head. It was easier than she'd expected to brush his lips lightly with her own, then return for a deeper, more satisfying kiss. She lifted a hand to twine into his hair and boldly began the play of tongues he'd taught her before. Now he kissed her back hungrily, as he'd done at the castle.

With a groan he released her mouth, then lifted her onto his lap. Senses swimming, she gasped as his lips roved from her mouth to her cheek, to nibble, amazingly, on her ear, then traced a slow path down her throat. She let out a shocked protest as he unfastened the front of her spencer.

"Hush, love," he murmured. "Your first time shall not be in a carriage. I only mean to give you a taste of the pleasures ahead. Trust me."

She leaned back into his arms, trembling more with anticipation than fear, and allowed him to remove her spencer. Her breathing grew more frenzied as he deftly loosened and pulled down her bodice. Intoxicated with pleasure, she allowed him to trail kisses and caresses all over her. She let out a moan when he shifted her in his lap, holding her waist firmly with one hand against the swaying of the carriage while tracing the inside of her leg with the other.

It was wicked, what he was doing. But not evil. It felt beautiful and right. Dear God, she loved him! What did it matter where he had learned this magic, or what he might think of her for yielding to it? It was enough to be with him in the intimately darkened carriage, to lose herself in the smell of him, the sound of his breathing, the heat of his kisses, the rapture of his velvety, spiraling caresses.

To imagine that he loved her.

For the second time, Verwood hesitated before the door of Pen's bedchamber. Good God, this time he really did feel like a nervous bridegroom! What ailed him? She was ready for him. This time it wasn't just about begetting children; she'd come to care for him, at least a little. Nothing else could explain her sweet anxiety over his accident at Corfe or her passionate response to his kisses in the carriage. Just the memory caused his body to tighten in expectation.

He raised his hand toward the door, then lowered it again, remembering how Pen's demeanor had changed since their arrival at Abbotsbury and the Ilchester Arms. She'd awoken from a passion-sated sleep and smiled, but said little. Throughout a choice dinner and a leisurely walk to Chesil Beach to watch the swans, she'd seemed subdued, though not, he hoped, unhappy. He hadn't known what to make of her mood but dared not question it. Things were going well.

Perhaps too well, the imp in his mind taunted him.

He silenced the imp and resolutely touched the door. The mere sound of Pen's voice, softly welcoming him in, caused his blood to race.

Slowly, he told himself as he crossed the threshold. This night was important to her; it would be the height of folly to rush things.

She stood, half turned away from him, taking in the sunset through her window. Rays of crimson and gold streamed in, bathing her in their hot light. As on that other disastrous night, she wore her simple white nightrail, but this time her hair spilled loose in molten, red-gold waves down her back. Did she remember what he'd said about wanting to see it thus?

His desire mounted, taking him by surprise. He took a few swift strides into the room before stopping. Lord, would he be able to restrain himself enough to give her the experience she deserved?

She turned, her body shining through the sheer white cotton. She gazed at him, her face glowing in the fiery light, her eyes huge, dark, and solemn, reminding him of the magnitude of her trust in him, beseeching him not to betray it. She loved him, or at least imagined she did; would he bring her pain when all she deserved was the sweetest of pleasure?

God, he'd never wanted a woman so badly and at the same time been so fearful of blundering.

She took a cautious step toward him, out of the fading rays of the sunlight and into the mellower glow cast by the candelabra near the bed. Then she sighed and flew across the room into his arms, and he had nothing to do but gather her soft, fragrant form close. Small, warm hands twined behind his neck, pulling his face down for a sultry kiss that stoked his desire to near-madness.

"Pen," he said hoarsely, drawing back a minute later. He must not allow her to tempt him into foolish haste.

"Make love to me, Robert," she said, her face miraculously shining with a hunger that mirrored his own.

He groaned and shrugged off his dressing gown, achingly, pleasurably conscious of her wide-eyed gaze. His dressing gown barely reached the floor, and she was already untying the laces at the neck of her nightrail, pulling it down off her shoulders and allowing it to fall to the floor. She swallowed and her breathing quickened, but she continued to gaze at him bravely, making no attempt to cover herself.

For a moment he reveled helplessly in the sight, more

beautiful, more tempting even than he remembered. Then she cast herself upon his chest again. He closed his arms around her as she kissed him fiercely, the smell of her soap, the feel of her freshly bathed, velvety skin nearly shattering his restraint.

Slowly. Still holding her tight, he broke the kiss. The bed beckoned, its coverlet drawn back, and he could not resist carrying his wife and setting her gently upon it before sliding in beside her and pulling her close again. She was no longer warm; she was aflame, waves of glorious sunset hair tumbling around her, her mouth parted in welcome.

Slowly, slowly.

He kissed her again, then gradually pressed kisses down her neck, into the hollow of her throat, then down to her breasts, striving to please her while holding his own body's demands at bay. Intoxicating little sounds like the cooing of a dove overwhelmed him; small, slender fingers twirled through his hair, then ran down his arms, his back, and shyly stroked the hair on his chest.

Slowly, slowly, slowly.

"Please, Robert . . ." she begged for more, and he caressed her as he'd done before in the carriage. After a few tortured, frantic cries she embraced him with both arms and pulled as if she were strong enough to draw him on top of her, and somehow, he found himself there.

He stilled, trying to remind himself of the importance of the moment, of how wrong it would be to rush, but she was ready, inviting, entreating him, and he could bear it no longer. He gave in to her pleading, and she cried out. Fear and guilt stabbed him, then she pulled him closer, arching against him, calling his name. Relief swept over him as he realized she was in a state of arousal beyond pain and regret. Already some glorious instinct drove her to seek a rhythm between them, and he helped her to find it, regaining a scant measure of control in attempting to prolong the pleasure.

A blissful interval later she cried out again, as if succumbing to passions long restrained. Wildly, helplessly, he allowed himself to be consumed in the same fire, losing himself within her. Hoping he'd never be found again.

*   *   *

Verwood held Pen in his arms, watching as the sunset faded and stars began to twinkle in an indigo sky. Spent by passion, she slept curled up against him like a kitten, her body warm and pliant, her breathing slow and peaceful.

He could not recall the last time he'd so immersed himself in lovemaking, when the act had taken on such a blinding intensity. Perhaps it was because he'd never endured so long an interval between lovers. Perhaps it was because none of his mistresses, willing as they were, had ever shown him the innocent, unrestrained passion Pen had.

If only she did not fall out of love with him too soon.

He gently disengaged himself, sat up, and looked down at her face, still softly illuminated by the candlelight, freckle-dusted cheeks innocently rounded, reddish-brown lashes resting gently upon them. Her luscious body, slender and plump in all the right places. Infinitely appealing.

It was tempting to stay. He could search all England and not find a woman so sweet, so good to her very core. If his stubborn body could not be coaxed into sleep beside Pen, he would be a hopeless case indeed.

Longingly, he eyed the empty spot beside her, but doubts held him immobile. He'd suffered this particular inability for over a year, ever since that doxy who called herself *La Perle* had tried to kill him. It was just one of several attacks on his life during that period, and he hadn't thought it affected him much. But even his last mistress, a comic actress without a cruel bone in her body, had quite failed to cure him of his inability to rest peacefully in bed with a woman.

He looked back toward his slumbering wife. Surely it would be different with *her*. And would it be so terrible if sleep was elusive, if he just spent the night watching her, as the candles guttered and moonlight illuminated her dreaming face?

It would prove that things were *not* different. No, it was far too soon to try this. If he wanted to make the rest of their honeymoon as rapturous as this night, he needed sleep.

Quietly he slipped from the bed, donned his dressing gown, and padded across the room to the doorway. He stopped to look back at Pen, and guilt pierced him. Would she regret having taken this step with him? Would she be hurt that he had left her alone?

Fool! He'd allowed himself to become so inflamed with desire that he'd forgotten to provide himself with even a note or a flower or anything to reassure her when she awoke. There was time, however. Very likely she would sleep late into the morning. He could get some sleep himself and still have time to find some feeble token of his gratitude for the precious gift she'd given him.

Pen sat up in the dark, heart pounding with sudden panic. She was alone. Where was Robert? He'd held her in his arms just moments ago, and now the bed was cold beside her.

Fear for his safety gripped her for an instant, then she realized the candles had all guttered, or been snuffed out, and moonlight shone through the window. It was late, and he'd merely gone back to his own bed to sleep.

She sank back onto the bed, disappointment replacing her fear. He'd said he preferred to sleep alone, but she'd imagined this night at least would be different. After he'd brought her to delirious heights of pleasure, he'd held her in his arms like a treasure. She hadn't thought he would leave her.

She allowed a few tears to spill onto the pillow, then curled up, tucking the coverlet around her more closely. Perhaps he was shocked by her brazen behavior, although he'd seemed to enjoy it at the time. She couldn't tell him that this was her way of showing her love for him, the only way she thought he'd find acceptable. He had never asked for her love.

Another tear slipped out of the corner of her eye, and she hastily wiped it with a corner of the sheet. There was no use crying. No use questioning him, or clinging, or begging him to keep her in his arms. He wanted friendship, not strong emotions. All she could do was to continue as she'd begun and pray for the strength to bear it if he never learned to love her back.

She glanced back toward the window. The stars twinkling outside comforted her with their beauty, as if whispering that Robert's fondness for her might deepen into a lasting passion someday. Clinging to the hope, she allowed it to lull her back to sleep.

Tiny, soft fists seemed to pummel the bed; sunlight filtered through Pen's closed eyelids, and the smell of hot chocolate teased her nostrils. The soft thumping sounds came closer; something tickled her face, then withdrew.

She opened her eyes and looked into the jewellike pale green eyes of a tiny tiger, its striped body held gently and securely between two long-fingered, carefully manicured masculine hands. Robert sat beside the bed, holding a ginger kitten a few inches away from her face. He was clean-shaven, wearing his dark blue dressing gown and a look of boyish anticipation.

"Good morning, Pen," he said softly. "Do you like her?"

Warmth and relief welled up inside her at his smile, teasing but also touchingly earnest.

"She is enchanting," she said, lifting herself onto one elbow, then blushing as the coverlet slid off her shoulder.

"She is yours," he replied, his smile deepening.

"Thank you." Knowing Robert's eyes were upon her, she made no move to cover herself and instead reached a hand out toward the kitten. Whiskers tickled her as the kitten sniffed her hand, then allowed Pen to scratch her neck and stroke her back.

"What shall we call her?"

She thought for a moment, continuing to play with the kitten. "Circe, I think."

He chuckled. "So, Penelope, have you already tired of your Ulysses' attentions, that you are willing to share them with this charming enchantress?" he asked, his hands brushing hers as they both caressed the purring kitten. "Delightful as she is, you must know her attractions pale against yours."

Circe abruptly tired of being petted and began to gambol about the bed, leaving Pen to blush again under her husband's steady, appreciative gaze. No, he had not been shocked by her behavior last night; he had enjoyed it.

"How do you feel?" he asked delicately.

Wonderful. Rapturous. But such heated responses might unnerve him.

"Very well," she said, and gave him a reassuring smile.

"Would you care for hot chocolate? Or a roll, perhaps?"

She noticed the tray behind him, touched again by his efforts to make the morning special for her. Her stomach gurgled and she nodded. He motioned for her to remain in bed and brought the steaming, fragrant cup to her. As she drank the rich, potent chocolate, he laid a saucer of cream on the floor for Circe. Then he brought Pen a roll and fed it to her, grinning wickedly, no doubt well aware of the way his gallant attentions aroused a different sort of hunger within her.

After popping the last bit of the roll into her mouth, he wiped her lips and leaned forward to kiss her. A tear sprang to her eye, but she held it back, willingly losing herself in his fervent embrace, and his kiss, potent and tasting of chocolate.

The future would take care of itself; the present was joy enough.

Chapter Eleven

$\mathcal{P}$en's stomach fluttered as she saw the signpost to Tregaron. It would not be long now. She turned to look at her husband. He was doing his best to appear indifferent as they approached his childhood home, but she could sense his tension. She stifled a sigh. Their honeymoon was coming to an end.

The day after their marriage had truly begun, they had only gone as far as the King's Arms in Dorchester. After that, the journey had continued at an even more leisurely pace than before. Pen had lost herself in Robert's attentions: stolen kisses in secluded groves, fevered caresses in the carriage, passionate lovemaking every night that nearly reconciled her to waking alone every morning.

They had stopped in Exeter, where they stayed at the excellent New London Inn and attended services at the cathedral. Soon afterward, Pen had discovered that her womanly courses had come upon her. Though disappointed, she'd been comforted that Robert continued to join her every evening for a cozy chat followed by slow, thorough kisses that reassured her of his unabated ardor.

"We'll be in the village in a few more minutes," Robert announced, interrupting her thoughts.

Pen forced her expression to remain tranquil, though the coolness of his tone did nothing to steady her nerves. He did not seem like the same man she'd strolled with so happily through a fair in Bodmin just a few days before. He'd bought her a lovely dun mare, of a type he informed her was called a *goonhilly*. Pen was delighted with Melior, whose name, Robert told her, meant honey in the ancient Cornish tongue. It had seemed so appropriate at the time.

But when they'd reached the eerie, barren waste of Bodmin Moor, Pen had sensed a disquieting change in her husband. Though scrupulously attentive to her needs and even more fervent in his lovemaking, he talked and smiled less. In fact, he seemed more like the Lord Verwood she'd known before the wedding: suave, polite and uncommunicative. The carefree, playful Robert of their honeymoon seemed to be slipping away from her.

The carriage slowed, and they entered the village of Tregaron. Pen gazed about at the stone cottages, the inn, and the assembled villagers. Apparently most of the local populace, alerted by the fact that the coach containing their luggage and servants had passed through earlier, had found some excuse to watch as she and Robert passed. In the many eyes that followed them, she read not only curiosity, but fear, suspicion, and downright loathing.

Through the corner of her eye, she could see Robert lounging against the seat as if unaware of all the sullen looks directed at him. Perhaps the villagers were fooled. She knew from the set of his jaw and a flicker in his eyes that this was not easy for him, either.

As they left the village and entered the coastal road that led to Tregaron House, she breathed a bit more easily. She still wondered if coming here was a mistake.

Soon the carriage turned off the lane onto a drive through a grove of elms. The house came into view, and for a few moments Pen was rapt in contemplation of her new home. Built of local stone, the ancient facade was set with countless panes of glass that reflected the westering sun and topped with gables in a curious but graceful pattern of scrolls and curves. The surrounding lawn and shrubs showed signs of recent trimming and pruning.

"Why, it is lovely," she breathed.

"It is supposed to be a fine example of Elizabethan architecture," said Robert, as if quoting from a guidebook. How could he speak so coldly about such a beautiful place?

They alighted at the entrance, and he took her arm and

accompanied her into the Hall. It was a magnificent room rising two floors high, lit by one of the tall, many-paned windows and surmounted with an elaborate plaster ceiling decorated with fantastic images of plants and animals. She would have to examine it more closely later. Now it was time to meet the staff.

An elderly couple stood slightly to the fore of the row of servants. They must be the Symondes, Will Symonds's parents, who had served the Verwood family for years, rising to the respective positions of butler and housekeeper. The pair had watched her husband grow up, and their son had become his valet; Pen watched anxiously to learn their reactions to his return home.

"Welcome home, my lord, my lady," said Symonds, bowing, while his wife bobbed them a curtsy.

While they looked at Robert, Pen was reassured by the motherly gleam in Mrs. Symonds's eye. The housekeeper clearly cared for Robert. When Mrs. Symonds turned her gaze toward Pen, Pen saw she looked nervous. It was only natural she should be wondering what her new mistress would be like.

"I am delighted to meet you both," Pen said in reply to their greetings and smiled. She knew her face and manner were being carefully scrutinized by all present.

Mrs. Symonds relaxed slightly as she introduced the rest of the staff. Pen studied their faces carefully, knowing that most of them were recently hired to supplement the skeleton staff that had maintained the house for the past few years. She hoped they would work together well. Most seemed honest and eager to please, though she read fear in some eyes as they gazed on their new master. Perhaps the local villagers had warned their children to beware of the Verwoods.

She also couldn't help noticing sidelong glances from several of the housemaids directed toward her husband and then toward her. She was becoming accustomed to the way most women reacted to her husband's masculine appeal. No doubt they were already wondering why he had taken such a small and insignificant-looking creature to wife, and either hoping or fearing that he would decide to seek their favors instead. Mercifully, Robert seemed oblivious to their coy looks.

"Shall I take you to your chamber, my lady?" asked Mrs. Symonds, after all the introductions had been completed. "Or perhaps you would like some refreshment after your journey?"

"I would like some tea very much, Mrs. Symonds. Afterward I should like you to take me on a tour of the house and explain all your arrangements to me. Then," she added, conscious of a slight frown on her husband's face, "perhaps his lordship will show me the gardens."

The plan having been decided, she and Robert mounted the staircase to the second floor. Mrs. Symonds took her to her bedchamber, where Susan smiled and greeted her cheerfully, saying she had already unpacked most of her clothing.

Pen took in the room with delight. Its square ceiling was divided by beams into four more squares, the whole decorated in pristine white plasterwork in patterns of flowers and shells. The large stone hearth was surrounded by more of the same beautiful plasterwork, and a large, dark, and richly carved four-poster dominated the room. The rest of the furnishings were too delicate. Gilded and covered in pale colors that would have fit perfectly in a Palladian villa, they were completely out of tune with the Elizabethan spirit of the house.

A half hour later, having changed out of her dusty clothes and had her hair freshly pinned up, she followed Susan to the drawing room, where Mrs. Symonds awaited with tea and scones. As Robert had gone to the library to write some letters, Pen asked Mrs. Symonds to join her for tea, hoping the friendly gesture would help win her the housekeeper's confidence.

"I hope everything meets your satisfaction, my lady," said Mrs. Symonds, anxiously watching as Pen looked about the room.

It was handsome and spacious, with linenfold paneling and a large bay window, but like Pen's bedchamber, decorated with incongruously pale and modern furnishings.

"I can see you have done an excellent job taking care of everything, Mrs. Symonds," she said, surveying the gleaming woodwork. "However, I think brighter colors and antique furniture would be more in keeping with the period of the house."

"Indeed, ma'am, his lordship's mother had many of the original furnishings put away in one of the attics. Perhaps another day you would like to see them."

"Thank you, I would," she said eagerly, glad to see she had coaxed a smile out of the housekeeper.

Mrs. Symonds cleared her throat and spoke again. "If I may be so bold as to ask, my lady, perhaps you can tell me how long you and his lordship plan to stay here."

Pen looked into Mrs. Symonds's lined face and realized she was on treacherous ground. The previous Lord and Lady Verwood had led separate lives. In Pen's experience, unhappy couples tended to have unhappy households. It was natural for Mrs. Symonds to wonder whether history was going to repeat itself. With an inner chill, Pen realized that she was not sure either.

"I cannot say exactly what our plans are," she said after a pause. "I hope we shall stay here until the spring, when perhaps Lord Verwood will wish to go to London. I assure you, however, that it is my earnest wish to make this a comfortable and happy household."

"I promise I shall do all that is in my power to assist you, my lady," said Mrs. Symonds, a look of hope dawning in her eyes.

Pen was warmed by her words and decided to allow the woman at least partly into her confidence. "Mrs. Symonds, perhaps your son has explained to you the circumstances of my marriage to Lord Verwood."

"He has," Mrs. Symonds replied gravely.

Pen could see that she knew the entire story, or very nearly all of it. "Then you know how very grateful we both are for your son's assistance to Lord Verwood."

Mrs. Symonds nodded, and this time her face crumpled with relief. "Thank God they are both home . . . safe," she said, and a tear spilled from a corner of her eye.

"I believe your son and my husband were playmates once," Pen said gently.

"Yes," said Mrs. Symonds, drying her eyes. "Her ladyship did not approve, however, so it was found necessary to separate the boys."

"What was she like? Lady Verwood?"

"She was . . . proud," said the housekeeper. "With good right, I suppose. She was the daughter of an earl and thought she'd lowered herself to marry Master Robert's father, for all he was one of the handsomest beaux in London at the time."

"What was she like—as a mother?"

The housekeeper paused, as if fearful of saying too much. "She was . . . an exacting woman. She had high expectations of Master Robert's behavior. Ones which, if I may make so bold, no young boy could fulfill, much as he might try."

Pen found herself digging her nails into her palms. Had Lady Verwood scolded him for playing on the cliffs and beaches, for coming home wet or dirty, as boys do? Had she chastised him for finding playmates where he could, among the servants' and villagers' children? Had she perhaps sneered at the other two local families of consequence, the Norlands and the Daltons, perhaps even setting the stage for the scandal with Anne Norland?

Looking into Mrs. Symonds's brooding face, Pen instinctively sensed that Lady Verwood had resented any influence the good-hearted housekeeper might have had on her son. She might have even threatened her position for it. What an intolerable situation it must have been for all of them and, worst of all, for Robert.

"Her marriage was not a happy one, was it?" she asked, probing further. "That can be difficult for a child."

"No, it was not happy."

Something in the housekeeper's tone alarmed Pen. She swallowed, her mouth dry with a sudden, lurid suspicion. Robert had suggested his father had been killed by some intended victim of his schemes, but did he truly believe that? Was it possible that Lady Verwood had pushed him off that cliff? It was almost too horrible to contemplate.

She pulled herself together. She'd come here rashly, not realizing what challenges their marriage faced, but it would not do to give in now.

"Are you feeling ill, my lady?" Mrs. Symonds watched her with kind, anxious eyes.

Perhaps the housekeeper thought she was in the family way?

"No, I am quite well," she replied, forcing a smile. "I should like to see the rest of the house now."

"Very well, ma'am, but . . . there is something else I should like to say to you," said Mrs. Symonds.

She paused, and Pen knew she was choosing her words carefully.

"I would like to reassure you that Cook inspects every-thing that comes into our kitchen, and we shall both be very careful that all food and drink that is brought to your table is properly prepared."

The words were said in an entirely calm manner, but they sent a chill through Pen. So Will Symonds *had* told his mother about the earlier attempts on Robert's life.

"I understand. Thank you," she said, grateful but praying there was no need for such vigilance.

They arose and Pen followed Mrs. Symonds, who showed her the dining room, the library, the stillroom, and the kitchen. By the end of the tour, she was convinced the woman was not only highly competent in her role, but might prove an important ally.

She made her way back toward the Hall, where she was to meet Robert. He had not arrived, so she took some time to admire the beautiful plaster ceiling. Then she strolled around to examine the pictures hanging on the walls, stop-ping by a portrait of a couple in the garb of thirty years ago. Aside from his wig, the young man looked very like her husband, having the same strong, regular features and easy stance. Perhaps it was the artist's fault, but the lady was less attractive, despite the jewels around her neck and the expensive lace at her bosom. She looked proud. Proud and jealous.

Pen turned, hearing footsteps, and saw her husband at the bottom of the staircase. There was a look of taut excitement in his stance, and she wondered what caused it. He frowned as he noticed what she was looking at.

"If you were wondering, you are gazing at a portrait of

my parents," he said without a trace of emotion in his voice.

She felt as if she'd been caught eavesdropping. Was it wrong of her to wish to learn more about him?

"Does the picture displease you? We could arrange to have it moved elsewhere," she said mildly.

"Do as you wish, my dear."

Burn it if you like. It was almost as if she'd heard the words. She stared at him, but he seemed preoccupied with other thoughts.

"I will think about it, then," she said, taking the arm he offered and accompanying him through the Hall and down a passage toward a door at the back of the house. "I am certain I shall enjoy looking through the attics. Mrs. Symonds says much of the furniture that was original to the house is still there. I think a more antique style would suit it better. With all the white plaster and dark woodwork, I think we need to add some stronger colors."

"I'm sure your taste is impeccable."

She bit her lip at his absent tone, but decided to look about the gardens now that they had come out of doors. In contrast to the house, they had a lonely, unkempt feeling, as if no one had cared about them for years.

"I can see there is much work to be done here," she said, gazing at the high rough hedges and geometric beds filled with weeds, mentally populating them with fanciful topiaries and colorful flowers.

"You may engage as many gardeners as you need," he replied, "even hire a designer. Divert a stream, uproot the trees, create a picturesque landscape in the manner of Capability Brown. Turn the place inside out, if you wish."

His tone was still suave, but she sensed his resentment. Whether it was directed at the place, or at her, or both, she did not know, but she was not going to tolerate it any longer.

She pulled free of his grasp and stamped her foot.

"Don't mock me! If you are angry with me for choosing to come here, it is quite your own fault. You never told me how you hated the place, and left the choice to me."

He looked stunned by her outburst. "My dear, I never said—"

"No, you never said. You never do say what it is you want, so you cannot blame me if I don't choose according to your wishes. Tregaron is a lovely old house, and I'm sure it has seen its share of joys and tragedies. I think we could be happy here, but if you are set against it, by all means let us find another place to live!"

He turned away, and she waited, shaking with anger and fear that he might not want to make a home with her anywhere, that they would never recover the brief harmony of their honeymoon.

He turned back to her, looking unusually strained, almost as if her tirade had frightened him.

"I am sorry, darling," he said in a low voice. "I've been a beast. I'm afraid this house does not hold many happy memories for me."

"Perhaps we will be happier elsewhere."

"No," he said, a fierce light in his eyes. "If you like Tregaron, we'll stay here. Perhaps I'll like it better once you've finished with it."

"Perhaps we'll make some happier memories of our own," she suggested. "However, you must promise me that in the future you will always tell me your preferences."

"Very well. I'll tell you what I wish for now."

She looked at him inquiringly.

"A kiss," he said, and pulled her to him, grinning.

She gave a little sigh and complied, relief flooding through her. Verwood had gone and Robert remained, warmly kissing her, his hands roving mischievously about her person.

"I thought you were going to show me the grounds," she protested, laughing.

"Very well, little hornet, but we are almost at the end of them."

"Then perhaps you will show me some of the places you played as a child," she said. She hoped it would be a healing thing for him to do.

Then she wondered if she had erred. His father had died near those very places.

He nodded and offered her his arm again. They passed through a gate in the hedge and toward the grove of elms that surrounded the house. Despite how he had kissed her, there was still an unusual tautness in his carriage. He'd never shown such mercurial mood changes before; coming home had clearly stirred up strong emotions in him.

"I have just learned something you should perhaps know," he said as they passed under the trees.

He paused as if to think, and she struggled to contain her anxiety. He seemed on the verge of some sort of revelation.

"George Norland died a few months ago."

"Anne's father?"

He nodded. She could not tell if he felt remorse or relief at the news.

"How did he die?" she asked, hoping to draw more out of him.

"It was his heart. It was a surprise to me, for I believed him to be a healthy man in his fifties. Apparently his heart has been causing his family concern over the past few years."

She exhaled. At least Norland had died of natural causes.

"So who is left at Norland Manor now?" she asked. "I believe you told me Mrs. Norland died years ago. Anne had a brother and sister, did she not?"

"Yes, Mariah and Edward. Both were children when Anne left Cornwall. Mariah has since married Sir Charles Grayshott and returned home to Norland Manor after his death. Edward is much younger. His mother bore him late in her life and was not strong enough to recover from his birth."

"So many losses," murmured Pen. "So now it is just the two of them remaining. I hope they are a comfort to each other."

She ventured to look up at Robert. He was watching her with a strange look of yearning and indecision.

"I have written to Anne," he announced after a moment.

She stopped walking, stunned at the sudden revelation.

"She is alive, then? And you know where she is?" she asked, her voice shaking. "Why did you not say so before?"

"I promised Anne not to divulge her situation to anyone,"

he replied, turning to face her. "But I believe George Norland's death changes everything."

"Will you tell me what happened?"

"I am still breaking my promise to Anne, but I think she would not mind my telling *you*," he said, looking uncertain.

"You know I will be discreet," she said, longing for his trust.

He nodded. She leaned against one of the elms, as if it could support her through the tale.

"Anne and I did leave Cornwall together," he began. "Her father had arranged for her to marry Sir Charles Grayshott, and she did not wish for the marriage, since Sir Charles was so much older. I thought myself in love with her. When she asked me to help her escape the marriage, I was more than willing to do so."

"Why did you not marry her?" she asked gently.

"She refused me."

She sensed pain behind his blunt words.

"So where did you go? What did you do?"

"I took her all the way to Gretna Green, thinking I might convince her to marry me there. When she continued to refuse me, I left her in Edinburgh, with the grandmother of a friend I'd met at Oxford. That was the last time I saw Anne. We have not communicated since."

"Why would she wish to cut herself off so entirely from her family?"

He hesitated, then looked at her directly. She realized the effort it cost him to speak of it. "She had bruises on her face, Pen. Norland must have beaten her for defying his wishes."

Her heart ached for the unknown girl. No wonder Anne had not wanted to risk being under her father's power again. And Robert had kept her secret all these years. Pen's eyes filled with tears of pity; she went to him and put her arms around him.

"Don't make a hero of me, I beg you," he said in a voice of self-loathing, standing rigid within her embrace. "Anne was like a wounded creature, a ghost of her former self, and nothing I did seemed to help. So I gave up. I returned home, my father paid Norland not to press charges, and I set off for Italy, where I embarked on every sort of vice and debauchery."

She hugged him closer and to her relief, he embraced her back, as if drawing strength from her.

"When Anne returns, your name will be cleared," she said. "You must tell Mariah and Edward what happened."

He shook his head. "Not yet. I have no idea if Anne is still with Mrs. Ross, or even if she is still alive. Mariah and Edward were children when Anne ran away, and they were told she had died. Think of their sorrow if we raise their hopes and Anne does not return."

And if Anne could not be found, it would make matters worse, Pen realized. People would say Robert had made up the tale.

"I understand," she said. "I can't help wishing there was something more we could do than just wait."

"Nothing but to go on as best we can," he replied.

They walked on, crossing the lane to the open area bordering the shoreline. Rather than take her directly toward the water, Robert led her across the meadows. The rhythmic soughing of waves mingled with the sound of tall grasses swaying in a salty breeze were soothing and invigorating at the same time. They climbed up a slight rise and encountered a strange grouping of large stones near the top.

Robert turned toward her, smiling as he gestured toward the ancient stones.

"I told you Tregaron was surrounded by antiquities," he said. "I hope you are pleased."

"What is it? I have not seen the like," she said, eyeing the impressive arrangement of stones, three huge uprights bearing a truly enormous capstone.

"It is a burial site, called a *quoit*, or *dolmen*," he said.

She touched one of the stones and closed her eyes. It was cold under her hand but somehow alive with memories. A wordless, timeless monument to people long dead. Robert allowed her to stroll about it as long as she wished, and when she had seen her fill, he took her further along the same field.

"There is another site here of interest. Nick and I often

used it when we wished to escape our lessons," he said with a slightly wry look.

She remembered what he'd said about Nicholas Dalton. Did he long for the old friendship to be revived?

She followed him until they reached a large opening in the ground, surrounded and reinforced by large stones.

"There is a long underground chamber here, called a *fogou*," he explained. "No one is certain how it was used, whether for burial or storage or defense. Shall we go in?"

She nodded. He had to bend over to fit through the sloping tunnel-like opening, but she was short enough to enter more easily. By the dim light from the entrance they descended into a wider, central chamber of some sort. It was cold, but the floor was flat and clear of the sort of debris she might have expected in such a place.

"It almost seems as if it is still in use," she said.

"Perhaps children still come here sometimes. Or trysting lovers."

It was too dark to see his face, but she knew the warm, suggestive tone in his voice. He pulled her into his arms, but she stiffened, a sense of unease coming over her, like a premonition of danger.

"Is something wrong?" he asked sharply.

"No," she lied, not wishing to upset him. "Perhaps it is just the darkness, the feeling of being . . . trapped."

"Let us go, then," he said, putting an arm around her shoulders. He led her forward, and she was puzzled until she saw sunlight streaming through another opening some thirty feet from where they'd entered. So the *fogou* had two entrances.

Back in the bright sunlight, she felt foolish for having panicked, but she still found the place disturbing.

She noticed Robert looking out at the cliff edge to the north of where they stood, his face grim. Without even asking, she sensed that that was where his father had met his end. She looked the other way and saw the beginning of a rough path sloping down from the meadow along the edge.

"Is that a path? Where does it lead?"

"Come along, I will show you," he said, his expression lightening.

He took her arm again and led her down what proved to be a fairly broad though rocky path, carved along the sloping shoreline. Waves crashed on jagged rocks below, and out over the water a cormorant flew with slow, powerful wing beats. Salt tanged the air, and she drew in deep lungfuls of it. It was a rough, wild, lonely place. However, she felt no threat here as she had in the *fogou*.

"What do you think? Quite different from the Sussex coast, isn't it?" Robert asked, quirking a gracefully arched eyebrow at her.

"Quite romantic. I shall have to bring my sketchbook with me next time."

He smiled, then they walked on in companionable silence. She reflected that it was no accident that he had brought her to Cornwall along a coastal route. She had quite lost the fear of the sea she'd learned in Brighton. Almost, anyway.

They came over a rise, and Pen saw another path branch off from the main one, descending through tufts of gorse and other shrubs and disappearing over a lower shelf.

"There is a beach down there, where I learned to swim," he said, following her gaze. "Shall we take a look?"

She nodded and followed him to a small, sandy cove surrounded on three sides by cliffs that helped to break the wind. The waves even swelled more gently within the sheltered area, gleaming in the late afternoon sunlight.

"Perhaps one day you and I can bathe here together," said Robert as they stood looking at the waves.

"I—I will be quite content to just enjoy looking at the sea. I don't wish to ever go in it again."

"You used to enjoy sea bathing, did you not?"

"Yes, but I do not miss it now."

"I would love to teach you to swim. I promise I would keep you perfectly safe."

She bit her lip. This seemed important to him. Perhaps he still felt guilty that he hadn't prevented Maggie Brown's attack, or perhaps he really thought she would enjoy swimming. If she conquered this fear, would it help him face some of his own? But could she bear to immerse herself in anything larger than a bathtub?

"Perhaps," she wavered.

"Shall we go now?" he asked, looking eager as a lad.

"I have no bathing costume," she objected.

"Then you must do without," he said, his dark eyes full of mischief.

"That would be highly improper."

"It is a very secluded beach. You could not even see it from above, could you?"

She shook her head, feeling the heat rush to her face. He pulled her into his arms, kissing her hungrily. A few minutes later he started undressing, all the while coaxing and cajoling her until she followed suit. Then he plunged into the water, and she cautiously waded in after him, crying out with mingled fear and cold. He returned and took her in his arms, covering her with salty kisses, warming her with his embrace, swirling her ever deeper into the sparkling water until all her fears receded, and only joy remained.

After their delightful interlude, Verwood helped Pen up the steep ascent from the beach. Her glorious hair was still damp, and she looked tired but thoroughly contented. He was still amazed and overjoyed at how easily he'd managed to persuade her to shed both her clothes and her fears.

When they reached the upper path, a look of pure delight crossed her face.

"Are those dolphins?" she asked, pointing below them.

He nodded, relishing the childlike fascination in her wide eyes as she watched the graceful creatures frolic about, the setting sun gilding their backs as they leapt above the swells. How long had it been since he'd felt anything so intensely himself?

Now he found himself sharing her pleasure, reliving how he had felt the first time he'd seen the beautiful creatures. Such moments—blinding, uncomfortable, almost painful in their intensity—had assaulted him more and more often the longer he was married to Pen. Moments that hearkened back to childhood, when every morning had held a sense of promise rather than the threat of failure and rejection. When he'd been naively open to both pleasure and pain. And to a fragile, terrifying feeling he was only beginning to accept once more.

Hope.

Chapter Twelve

*T*he smell of hot chocolate awakened Pen, along with Susan's voice bidding her good morning. She stretched luxuriously, remembering the lovemaking that had ended her difficult but promising first day at Tregaron. Then she heard muffled footsteps outside and realized Robert was quietly going by.

"Oh, bother," she said. "I had hoped to go riding with his lordship. I forgot to mention it to him last night."

"If we hurry, you can catch up to him," suggested Susan.

Fifteen minutes later, hastily attired in her riding habit, Pen hurried out to the stables, only to see Robert riding off on his favorite bay. Longing to be with him, she ordered a groom to saddle Melior, which he did in short order.

"She's a bit fresh. Shall I come along?" asked the groom.

She shook her head, preferring to be alone with Robert. Although it had been some time since she'd ridden, she expected no trouble with the well-mannered mare. The groom helped her mount, and she quickly set off down the drive in the same direction Robert had taken. Blending with her eagerness to see him was a growing unease, a feeling that he needed her somehow.

The little mare seemed to sense her anxiety and readily sprang into a canter. Pen slowed her to cross the road, then passed through the open gate onto the meadow along the shore, her instincts leading her toward the ancient sites they'd visited the previous day. She urged the mare into a canter again, and they quickly approached the dolmen,

Melior's hooves making little noise on the dewy turf. She slowed, hearing voices on the other side of the monument.

"I am sorry, but I can tell you no more," she heard Robert say.

"Cannot? Or will not?" a higher-pitched masculine voice demanded. "Damn you, Verwood, you'll tell me what became of my sister, or I'll send you to Hell where you belong!"

A shot rang out.

Pen urged her mare forward, her heart racing with fear.

She rounded the dolmen and saw her husband sitting his horse calmly, mercifully upright and unharmed. Facing him and pointing a pistol at him was a fair-haired youth who looked to be about seventeen years of age. Neither noticed Pen.

"I have one more bullet, Verwood," said the youth. "Next time I won't shoot wide. Make your choice. Tell me the truth about Anne, or prepare to meet the devil!"

Pen listened, terrified, realizing this must be Anne's brother Edward. Would it help Robert if she made her presence known?

"I've told you all I can," Robert said in a placating tone. "Anne was alive and well when last I saw her, and I've sent word to her advising her to come back to Norland Manor, or at least write to you."

"I don't believe you! Why would you write to her *now*? If she is well, why has she stayed away these ten years?"

Pen waited, afraid even to breathe. She could tell Robert was trying to decide how much of the tale to tell. The truth might infuriate the lad.

"Your father wished her to marry Sir Charles Grayshott, and she did not care for the match," Robert replied, maintaining his calm, reasonable demeanor.

"That's rubbish! Papa would never have forced her into anything. If your story is true, why didn't *you* marry her?"

"She refused me." A grim note entered Robert's voice.

Pen saw the anger mount in Edward Norland's face and made a quick decision. She spurred Melior forward into a fast trot.

"Why wouldn't she marry you? I think it's all a lie you've concocted to escape what you—"

Edward broke off and stared at Pen as she quickly positioned herself in front of Robert.

"Pen, move out of the way!" Robert shouted, horrified.

Out of the corner of her eye, she saw him spur his horse forward, as if to nudge her and Melior out of the line of fire. Seeing Edward's distraught expression and the way his hand shook, she maintained her position. Her efforts were paying off; he seemed to be wavering.

"Damn you, Pen, get out of the way!" Robert repeated.

She ignored his angry command and instead looked Edward soberly in the eye.

"You don't wish to shoot me," she said softly. "I do not think you wish to deal with the consequences of shooting my husband either. Please lower your gun and let us talk."

He stared from her to Robert then back again, visibly shaken but unwilling to give up. A silence so complete that Pen could hear her own breathing was suddenly broken by the muffled sound of more hoofbeats coming their way. Pen turned her head and saw another rider join them, a fair-haired lady in a black habit.

"Hand me the gun, Edward," the lady ordered in a voice that brooked no disobedience.

Pen let out a sigh as the youth passed the pistol over to the lady, whom she guessed to be his sister Mariah, Lady Grayshott. The lady rode forward, and Pen noticed how closely she resembled the youth. Of medium height, she was incredibly beautiful, her eyes blue-gray, her lips mauve, her face perfectly sculpted, her hair so fair it was nearly white. She looked ethereal in her somber riding habit. Although she was clearly older than Edward, it was difficult to judge her age.

"Go home, Edward. I will make everything right," she said in that same authoritative tone.

"But, Mariah, Verwood has—"

"Go home," she repeated, cutting off his protest.

Pen was relieved to see the lad hang his head and ride off, muttering. His sister certainly had an aura of command.

"Thank you," said Robert. He gave Pen a sidelong

glance, his lips tight and his eyes flashing with what she knew was anger over her disobedience. Then he positioned his horse so they both faced the other lady.

"Lord Verwood," said the woman in a milder tone, gazing at him intently. "I suppose you do not remember *me*."

"I remember you, Mariah," he said gently. "Or should I say, Lady Grayshott. Thank you again for your timely intervention."

"I had to stop him. I don't wish to see Edward convicted of murder," the lady replied, her voice breaking. "I will see that he does not trouble you again."

"How can you be so certain? He just tried to shoot my husband!" said Pen.

"My apologies, Lady Verwood," said Lady Grayshott, turning to scrutinize Pen. "I must beg your leniency on Edward's behalf. He was very devoted to Anne, who stood as something of a mother to him since our own mother died soon after his birth. When Anne disappeared ten years ago, he was told she had died. It was only upon our father's recent death that he learned of Lord Verwood's possible involvement in the affair."

"I will tell you what I told him," said Robert. "I have sent word to Anne and hope she will return, or at least write."

Lady Grayshott's eyes flickered, whether in shock, relief, or incredulity Pen could not be sure.

"This is certainly unexpected," she said slowly. "If true, this is wondrous news. Oh, to see my dear sister again . . ."

"I realize that neither you nor Edward have any reason to believe me," Robert continued in a diplomatic manner. "I cannot promise that we will hear from Anne. It has been almost ten years since I last saw her."

"I for one am not inclined to act hastily. I am sure the truth of the matter will come out," said Lady Grayshott in a measured voice that gave no clue to her thoughts. "In the meantime you may trust me to manage Edward."

"I hope you will be able to do so," said Robert. "I want no quarrel with him, or any in your family."

"I see we understand each other," replied Lady Grayshott with a small smile, then turned to look at Pen. "I should like to call upon you soon, Lady Verwood, if you would be so kind as to receive me."

"I would be happy to do so," Pen replied, disturbed by the lady's unnaturally calm demeanor.

"You are most gracious," declared Lady Grayshott. "Now, I must return home and have a word with Edward."

She turned her horse and cantered off in the direction her brother had taken.

Pen slumped in the saddle, trembling with delayed shock over what she had just done. Had she really just faced a loaded gun? But Robert was still alive, and that was all that truly mattered. She turned toward him, wondering how deeply the incident had affected him, eager to feast her eyes on his beloved face and offer any comfort he might need.

Verwood turned to his wife and saw her watching him with the most generous, loving expression he'd ever beheld. Good Lord, she was still worrying about *him*. Didn't the little fool know she might have been killed?

"Don't ever do such a thing again!" he shouted roughly as soon as Mariah was out of earshot. "Come. Let us go home now."

He turned his horse and heard Pen follow.

"I know I disobeyed you, but I was only trying to help," she called out.

"I don't need your help," he rasped, not turning to look at her. "That impetuous hothead might have shot you!"

He urged his horse into a gallop. By the time Pen caught up to him again, they had reached the lane, and he'd once more pressed the lid on his anger.

"But he did not," she said softly, as if to reassure him. "I don't think he is capable of killing a woman."

"He might have pulled the trigger by accident," he said as they trotted across the road and down the drive toward the house. "I'm sending you to the Woodmeres, where you will be safe."

"I won't go," she insisted.

He turned to look at her. "You will," he said coldly. "I won't have your death on my conscience."

He tried to ignore the hurt look in her eyes.

Surprised grooms ran forward to take their horses. Had they heard the pistol shot? He hoped not.

He dismounted quickly, then rushed to help Pen from her horse. He hadn't intended to do it in front of Pascoe, the other grooms and stable boys, but as soon as she was in his arms, he found he could not release her. So he kissed her hotly, giving in to a desperate need to feel her warm body safely in his arms.

When he released her, he could see the others averting their heads and coughing to hide their grins. He looked back at his wife and saw a relieved smile on her lips as well. He shouldn't have kissed her; he'd completely undermined any good his harsh words might have done. His anger boiled up again, but he held it fiercely in check, not wishing anyone to witness their argument.

"Come with me. We are going to talk about this," he said, taking Pen by the arm and pulling her toward the house. Although she broke into a run to keep up, he did not stop until they had reached her bedchamber. Then, helpless dolt that he was, he could not resist taking her into his arms again.

"You are going to the Woodmeres," he said again, kissing her to silence any possible protest.

She returned his kiss, hugging him with a strength he hadn't known she possessed, blunting the edge of his anger. With an oath he released her.

"I am staying with you," she said again.

"You are going, even if I have to bundle you into the carriage myself." He began working on the buttons of her riding habit, a frenzied urgency robbing his fingers of their usual dexterity.

"I'll only come back," she retorted, lifting her chin stubbornly as she removed his riding jacket.

"You are going." He pulled her habit down off her shoulders.

"We are married. I have vows to keep. I am staying." She began to loosen his shirt from his breeches.

"You are going, and we shall not discuss the matter any further," he said, cursing as he fumbled with the laces of her corset. Damn the stupid thing, he was tired of fighting it, could not manage it with the distraction of Pen's hands removing his own garments.

With another oath he pushed Pen toward the bed. Finding Circe curled upon it, he resisted the urge to fling her across the room and instead placed her gently on the floor. Then he turned to his wife and flung *her* onto the bed, corset, stockings, and all.

She called his name, looking up at him in warm invitation, and he groaned. He would not hit her, so all he could do was climb onto the bed with her and release his passion by the only acceptable means. The minx was ready for him, as always, matching him move for move, frenzied breath for frenzied breath, soothing, maddening, healing him, joining him in a peak of frantic ecstasy. He looked down into her beatific face, transformed by rapture, haloed by her fiery hair, and a moment of blinding, agonizing intensity assaulted him.

Good God, he'd fallen in love with her.

And no doubt he was crushing her. He started to withdraw, but she wrapped herself around him, holding him tightly, so he remained where he was, gazing down into her bright eyes, which shone with undimmed affection for his sorry self.

"I'm staying with you, Robert," she said with calm conviction.

He wondered how the frightened creature he'd comforted in Brighton had turned into such a lioness. Her fierce loyalty warmed and humbled him. With gentle words, sweet caresses, and incredible bravery, she'd revived a heart he'd thought died a decade ago. Now he realized with simple clarity that though he'd called it an infatuation, he *had* loved Anne, with the fervency of an eighteen-year-old heart. But it had been nothing like *this*—this feeling he had for Pen was stronger and deeper than anything he could ever have imagined. He did not deserve her, did not know how he would bear her leaving. But it was unthinkable to allow her to continue to risk her life for him.

"Pen. *Darling*," he said hoarsely, shifting and rolling to hold her beside him. "Don't think I am ungrateful for how you shielded me from Edward. It was an extremely brave thing to do, and I thank you for it. But I would never have brought you here if I'd realized this old scandal could put either of us in danger. You know that, don't you?"

"I know. But I'm not sure the danger is as grave as you think. Edward is not a murderer at heart, and Lady Grayshott seems capable of keeping him in check."

There was some sense in what she said, he mused. Mariah had certainly changed from the awkward and mildly annoying girl he remembered from his days of paying court to Anne. Mariah now had all the assurance that came of being the great lady of the district, and she appeared to exercise a powerful control over her impetuous brother. If Verwood was not mistaken, she'd do anything to protect Edward from the consequences of murder. Still, could he take the risk that Mariah might fail?

"I would rather you left," he said. "Perhaps we should both go away."

"I think we should see this through," she replied. "Anne will come soon, or she will write. She *has* to."

He thought about it. It might only be a few weeks before they had some sort of reply from Anne. Perhaps all they needed to do was to take some additional precautions.

"I'll send another letter impressing on her the urgency of the situation," he said. "I think she will not fail us."

"You will let me stay, then?"

He sighed. "I still don't want to take the risk."

She lifted herself on her elbow and looked at him earnestly.

"Robert, listen to what I have to say. We are safe if we stay together. I feel it, *here*," she said, touching her heart. "Besides, I would miss you."

His resolution wavered and crumbled. Not that he set any store by her touchingly naive belief that she could continue to protect him. But perhaps there was no imminent danger, and matters would resolve themselves peacefully with no need for a painful separation.

"Very well, my lady, you have won this argument."

She lowered herself back onto the bed, and he eagerly

gathered her close once more. No, he didn't deserve her, but he could not bear to let her go.

An almost unbearable joy flooded his being, bringing with it excruciating hopes and fears. Against all his expectations, he'd fallen in love. In allowing her to stay, was he allowing passion to cloud his judgment? He held her closer, praying fervently that his love for her would not bring them both into more danger.

Pen hurried into the drawing room later that day, summoned from a discussion with the elderly gardener by the intelligence that Lady Grayshott and Mrs. Finchley, the rector's wife, had come to call upon her.

The other ladies looked up as she entered, and she saw that Lady Grayshott had changed her black riding habit for an equally somber but well-fitted morning dress. Mrs. Finchley, a plump young woman with a friendly face, smiled up at Pen a bit nervously. Despite Robert's notorious reputation, the Verwoods were still the most important landowners in the district, and Mrs. Finchley clearly knew her own husband's living depended on Lord Verwood's goodwill. It was an awkward position, which Pen, as the daughter of a vicar, understood all too well.

As Lady Grayshott made the introductions, Pen smiled reassuringly at Mrs. Finchley. Out of the corner of her eye, she quietly observed her other visitor. Lady Grayshott was clearly accustomed to the role of great lady in the district, and might resent being outranked by Pen, as Robert was a baron and Sir Charles Grayshott had been only a knight. But there was nothing in her expression but polite friendliness.

At that moment Mrs. Symonds appeared, bringing tea and macaroons.

"Lady Verwood," said Mrs. Finchley when the housekeeper had gone, "I trust you understand that it has always been my intent to call upon you on your arrival at Tregaron, not merely because of this morning's—" The poor lady paused, clearly distressed even to speak of the incident.

"What Mrs. Finchley wishes to say, my dear Lady Verwood," continued Lady Grayshott, "is that all of us wish for peace, and to allow bygones to be bygones. We mean to do everything in our power to help you become comfortable in our parish."

"Thank you," she said wholeheartedly, realizing how much these two influential ladies could help turn the tide of resentment against her husband.

"Perhaps I should tell you my father was a vicar back at my old home in Sussex," she added, wishing to make it clear she had no intention of behaving in a proud or condescending manner. "My mother and I were very much involved in various projects for education and assistance to the poor. If there are any such schemes you have in mind, I am certain my husband and I will give you all our support."

Mrs. Finchley looked a little embarrassed. "Since his return to England, Lord Verwood has contributed handsomely to the village school. I believe his tenants have no pressing needs."

Pen nodded, not surprised to learn that despite his reputation, her husband had attended to his duties as a landlord.

"I trust that regular inoculations have been carried out in the parish," she said.

"Yes, of course. Our dear Lady Grayshott has performed most of them herself," said the rector's wife. "She has been more than generous with her time. I daresay there is not a cottage nearby that she has not visited at some time or other to provide sustenance and medicines for the indigent or sickly."

"Oh, you are a gardener?" Pen asked, looking toward the other lady.

"I know a few things about plants," said Lady Grayshott.

"Mariah is being modest, as usual," said Mrs. Finchley. "Even the apothecary defers to her knowledge of herbs and their medicinal properties."

"If you are interested, sometime I shall show you my garden at Norland Manor," said Lady Grayshott.

"Thank you, I should enjoy that," said Pen, shaken by the thought of encountering Edward Norland again. Was it possible to achieve normal relations with their family after such an altercation? But perhaps, as often was the case, the women would prove to be the peacemakers.

"I hope we shall all become great friends," said Lady Grayshott, smiling to reveal perfect small teeth. "You must call me Mariah; your name is Penelope, is it not?"

Pen nodded.

"Yes, and you must call me Amelia," said Mrs. Finchley. "We do not stand upon ceremony here."

"Well, now that that is settled, perhaps, Penelope, you will tell us more about how you and Lord Verwood became acquainted," said Mariah in a conversational manner.

"Quite a love match, is it not?" asked Mrs. Finchley, curiosity written all over her face.

Pen wondered if the servants had already been gossiping about her and Robert. Had someone observed them from the cliffs yesterday? She colored a little, but decided it would be no bad thing if it was seen that they were different from his parents.

"Yes, his lordship and I have become very fond of each other," she temporized. "The marriage was rather sudden. Perhaps I should explain it to you, since you may already have heard some garbled versions of the story."

She proceeded to give them a simplified version of the tale, omitting the details involving the Evertons and the Duke and Duchess of Whitgrave. Mariah listened calmly, almost as if she'd heard parts of the lurid tale already, but the rector's wife looked shocked.

"It must have been dreadful for you," said Mrs. Finchley. "But all's well that ends well, you know. I have heard your husband is very handsome and extremely charming."

"Yes, he is," said Pen, not sure she liked Amelia's tone.

"You must have been the envy of all the ladies in Brighton," continued the rector's wife.

Pen did not know how to even respond to this foolish remark.

"I imagine Lord Verwood has other traits Penelope values more," said Mariah. "I for one am willing to believe that he has reformed his ways, and that in time he will be cleared of any fault regarding past events."

Her words were kind, so Pen did not know why she felt

an inward shiver on hearing them. Did Mariah really believe what she was saying, or did she speak so out of diplomacy? It was difficult to tell. The rector's wife was easier to read. She seemed the sort who enjoyed petty gossip and perhaps hoped Robert would provide food for it.

Though glad of their support, Pen was relieved when the ladies left. She was not convinced that either of them truly believed that Robert was innocent of wrongdoing regarding Anne Norland. Their opinions were probably a fair reflection of the beliefs of everyone in the parish.

She prayed Anne would return, and soon.

Verwood left his steward, with whom he'd spent the past few hours, and found his wife heading out toward the gardens. He knew she'd been speaking with the ladies of the parish, and seeing her tense posture, wondered what they had all been saying. His own shortcomings must have been a favorite subject.

"How are you, my dear?" he asked, searching her face. "You are looking a bit tired. Did the ladies quiz you mercilessly?"

"N-no, well, perhaps a little. They were very kind to me and mean to do all they can to help us become established here. I had not thought to encounter such a welcome."

"You deserve nothing less," he said, thinking he ought to be glad for her sake.

She still looked troubled. What could they have said about him that Pen would have believed? She was not the sort to listen to gossip.

"You know, darling, I am a bit weary from poring over those ledgers all morning. Perhaps we would both find a swim refreshing," he suggested.

She nodded, her face lighting with expectation as he'd hoped it would. But when they descended to the beach a half hour later, they encountered a distressing sight. A gray seal lay dead at the edge of the water, a bit of old fishing net twined around its neck. Beside the corpse flopped a small whitish pup, nudging the body of the larger seal and making sad sounds, something between the bawling of a calf and the barking of a puppy.

"The poor thing," said Pen.

No doubt her sensitive heart was wrung with pity for the little creature. Verwood wasn't completely immune to its appeal, either.

He put his arm around her to comfort her. "I know. It is a sad sight. But seal pups do sometimes lose their mothers. It is just the natural course of things. Let us go now, and try to forget it."

Ominously, she stood her ground.

"Perhaps we can help it," she said.

He sighed. "It might be ill."

"No, look, it appears to be perfectly healthy. I think it is just hungry. We cannot leave it to starve."

Clearly, the suggestion that he put the poor thing out of its misery would find no favor with her. Well, he didn't like the idea himself. He studied the pup, trying to remember what he had learned watching seals as a boy.

"I would guess it is only a week or two old, so it must still have been nursing. I do not know what we could feed it."

"I would imagine seal's milk must be rather rich," said Pen, staring down at the sleek fat body of the mother. "Perhaps some cream, with fish oil added to it?"

"How would you convince the pup to take it?"

She looked thoughtful. "We could try a bottle or a pap boat, like those used to feed infants."

"What if it won't feed?"

"Then it will be no worse off than it is now," she said a bit sharply.

"Very well. I don't know if we can rear it, but we can try."

She hugged him, and he decided it was a worthwhile reward for indulging her whim.

"Where could we put it?" she asked. "Do you think it would need salt water?"

"They bask out of the water for hours sometimes, so I don't think it necessary. Perhaps we can build some sort of enclosure for it near the horse pond."

"That sounds perfect," she said, smiling down at the pup.

"You must remember, though, that it is a wild animal,"

he cautioned her. "We must use leather gloves when handling it, for it will probably bite. And we shall have to release it once it is big enough to fish for itself."

"I understand."

He removed his coat and folded it several times, then used it to catch the pup, protecting his arm from sharp teeth that were all too ready to bite him.

"He or she does seem healthy," he commented, holding the surprisingly heavy, struggling creature tightly in his arms.

Following Pen, he laboriously carried the beast up the path toward the cliffs. On reaching the summit, he stopped to catch his breath and began to chuckle as the pup thrashed about in his arms, yelping.

"What are you laughing about now?" Pen asked.

"You assured me you wished for no exotic animals, but I don't believe even the Duchess of York has a seal pup in her menagerie."

She only laughed.

On their return to Tregaron House, he set a bemused stable boy to the task of building an enclosure around the horse pond that would keep the seal pup in and dogs or other animals out. He set the pup down to flounder about in the grass while Pen ran off to the kitchen to prepare its next meal. He hoped it would survive, for her sake.

A short time later he sat on a crude bench near the pond, trying to hold the pup still while Pen knelt before him and tried to tilt the spout of a pap boat containing cream and ground-up fish organs into its mouth. The creature tossed its head, fussed and spat, spraying them both with the noxious mess.

"Oh dear," said Pen. "Let us try something else."

Undaunted, she set down the small silver dish and from her basket, produced a leather glove with a small hole in the tip of one finger. She filled the glove from the remaining mixture in the bottle, and directed him to hold the seal pup's head still. Kneeling back in front of him, she tried to insert the tip of the glove in the animal's mouth. After several attempts, Pen managed to squirt some food into the creature. The pup sprayed her again, but this time it swallowed some of the mixture.

"Let us try that again," said Pen, working the glove back into the pup's mouth.

This time, the pup took the liquid more willingly.

"Ah, she has realized it is good," he remarked.

Pen smiled, holding the glove steady as the pup began to gulp in earnest. "She?"

"I looked," he said, winking. "What shall we name her?"

She pondered a moment. "I think a Cornish name would be most suitable. Do you know of one?"

"I only know a few words of Cornish, but as a boy I sometimes visited Mrs. Symonds's mother. She used to call Mrs. Symonds 'Tegen.' I think it means 'pretty thing.'"

"Tegen she is," said Pen, smiling down into the creature's lustrous brown eyes.

As he watched his wife ministering to the pup, oblivious to the fact that her dress was spattered with cream and fish parts, he couldn't help thinking what an extraordinary mother she would be. She certainly wouldn't scold her children for running about out-of-doors, playing with animals or dirtying their clothes.

Why the image gave him such a pang he didn't want to think. It was enough to rejoice that they were both still alive, and that he had the amazing good fortune to bask in her warm affection, however little he deserved it.

He was slipping.

Boulders tumbled and plants tore by their roots as he helplessly grasped them, seeking any handhold that might keep him from going over the edge.

There was Pen, the outlines of Corfe Castle behind her. She held out her hand and called to him, her eyes wide with fear. He tried holding on with one hand and reaching the other toward her, but he only slipped farther down.

A heartbeat, and the scene changed around him. The Purbeck hills and the village of Corfe disappeared, and he was on the cliffs near Tregaron. Pen tried to come to him, but he begged her to stay away from the steep precipice.

Waves crashed below him, tumbling about the jagged

rocks that waited to tear his body asunder. Unseen ghostly hands tugged at his ankles, pulling him down to certain death.

He lifted his face, hoping for one more look at Pen, but she was no longer there. Crying out his rage and grief, he gave up the struggle, plummeting to his fate.

Had he screamed aloud? Had anyone heard?

Verwood sat up in bed, shaking. He hadn't had a nightmare in over a year, and never anything so vivid. Could young Norland's attack have affected him so strongly? He'd faced and survived much more determined murderers: Ted Booley and *La Perle* among others. But he had faced them alone. He'd never had to watch a gun trained on someone he loved.

He wondered if Pen had heard him yell. She might be frightened and wish for reassurance, he reasoned, then scoffed at himself. *He* was the one who craved reassurance.

A few minutes later he quietly opened her door. Pen lay peacefully curled up, her ginger kitten beside her. He took a step forward, cursing when the floor creaked beneath him. Pen stirred and he waited, deciding to make certain she was sound asleep again before making another move.

"Is that you, Robert?" she asked drowsily, then lifted her head. "Come here. You'll catch your death of cold standing in the doorway like that."

He let out a sigh at her prosaic words and quickly crossed the floor. He climbed into the bed, on the opposite side from Circe, and arranged himself spoon-fashion around his wife's warm shape. It was wonderful just to feel her against him, to know that she was *his*.

She rolled over, twined her arms around him, and pressed a soft kiss to his cheek. Just feeling her was not enough; he needed more now. He sought her lips, and she blossomed under his kiss. She came awake, her small hands caressing him with newly acquired skill while she returned his kiss with all the innocent ardor of her generous soul. He returned her caresses, stroking and teasing until her desire matched his. Then he entered her, reveling wildly in the almost unbearable rapture of knowing he was still alive, of feeling her warm and alive beneath him. Oh, how he wanted her, wanted to know that they would share countless nights like this together.

Just when he thought he could stand it no longer, the wanting exploded into joy, and he found he was strong enough to bear it.

Chapter Thirteen

Pen sat up in bed, feasting her eyes on her husband's sleeping face. Tenderness overcame her, seeing Robert vulnerable and childlike in his repose and remembering how he had stood almost shyly in the doorway last night. He'd come, not merely wanting her, but needing her as well. It was a marvelous feeling to sleep in such closeness with a lover.

His eyelids fluttered and opened. He gazed at her, his eyes taking a moment to focus.

"Good morning," she whispered, then kissed his nose.

"Good morning," he said, pulling her to lie on top of him.

He had reddened a little under the slight stubble on his cheeks. Pen thought she'd never seen him so beautiful, the sunlight filtering through the curtains and caressing his face.

"Did you sleep well?" she asked, wondering why he looked both embarrassed and deeply moved.

"Quite," he said, his rapt look changing to a grin. "I hope you are not too distressed over my interrupting *your* repose."

"I suppose I could become accustomed," she replied, smiling down at him. "Perhaps it would be easier, husband of mine, if we both started the night in the same bed."

"A delightful idea, wife."

"I should just like to know why you have not slept with me before," she said, laying her head down on his chest and draping an arm around his shoulder.

He tensed beneath her, and she almost regretted her innocent question. So it was not just aristocratic custom that had kept them in separate beds. There was a more serious reason.

"Do you really wish to know?" he asked, sighing.

"Yes."

"It's not a pleasant story."

"Perhaps it will do you good to tell it to me."

He sighed, and she waited patiently for him to begin.

"Over a year ago, I went to a Cyprians' Ball—a party designed to unite gentlemen with mistresses," he explained, then paused. "Are you certain you wish to hear this? It's not a tale that resounds to my credit."

"Go on. I won't despise you for it," she said, inwardly bracing herself for the worst.

"I was in a foul mood at the time, for various reasons. As was my habit, I planned to console myself with all the sensual pleasures attendant on such affairs." He paused again. "There was a woman there who called herself *La Perle*. She had very white skin and black hair, wore a white silk gown with a matching mask and ropes of pearls around her neck and in her hair. Every man there desired her, but she singled me out. I had drunk enough champagne by that point to think her quite desperately attractive. So when she lured me to her lodging, I followed, like a stupid brute, and fell in with her seduction."

She remained quiet, sensing the worst was yet to come.

"I woke to find her holding a gun to my head."

She lay still with shock for a moment, then wrapped her arms around him tightly. "How could any woman who'd been with you do such a thing? How did you survive?"

"I don't know why, but she hesitated and I was able to overpower her and force a confession from her. She'd been sent by a Lord Filey, who had been paying my father to keep secret the fact that he ran a brothel. For some reason Filey suspected I would continue the scheme. As he was beset with gambling debts, he thought it more economical to do away with me."

"What happened then? How did you protect yourself?" she asked, trying to keep the horror from her voice.

"I sent *La Perle* back to him with a warning. For the next few months Filey and I merely avoided one another. Later I heard he shot himself after a streak of particularly bad luck."

"So you are safe from him now," she said, appalled at the extent of the violence stirred up by his father's activities.

"Yes. Since the affair, I was left with a cowardly inability to fall asleep beside any woman, no matter how kind and good-natured. I wanted to try with you, but frankly, my darling, I was afraid even you could not cure me."

She shifted to look down into his face. Seeing his look of self-mockery, she lowered her head to kiss him. His arms tightened around her, and she deepened her kiss. He began to relax, to respond to her caresses. Finally, in her mind, she heard the words *I love you*, as if he'd spoken them aloud.

No, it was wishful thinking. He had not said the words. But he *had* come to care for her, else he would not have been so furious with her for defending him from Edward Norland. And Robert needed her love and understanding. Perhaps it was not the same grand passion she felt for him, but it was far more than she had ever hoped for. It was more than enough.

A blissful interval later, Verwood left his wife's bed-chamber, still wondering if he should have declared his feelings for her. The words had hovered on his lips, then he'd bitten them back. They seemed such a feeble offering. She'd given him everything, risked her life for him, and all he'd done for her were easy, enjoyable things, like giving her pets and pleasuring her with all the skills he'd acquired during a misspent lifetime. She might not believe him if he said the words, and he could not bear to see the trust that shone in her eyes whenever she looked at him fade away.

Pen sat beside Robert in Tregaron's simple stone church, thinking how kind it had been of him to volunteer to ac-company her to services. They both had anticipated the many sullen glances that were directed at him. The service was nearly over; perhaps the fact that no lightning bolt had come down to smite the worshipers would reassure them that Robert had as much of a right to attend as anyone else. But Pen doubted it, and she knew the most difficult part was yet to come.

Together they arose, left the family pew that had been empty for years, and followed the crowd down the aisle. Beside the door, Mr. Finchley, the rector, and his wife waited to exchange greetings with the more important of the churchgoers. As Pen expected, the stout rector greeted Robert politely but nervously while his similarly plump wife eyed him with rampant curiosity.

Mariah, accompanied by a maidservant, also gave them a cordial greeting, for which Pen could only be grateful, knowing their exchange was witnessed by many curious eyes.

Feeling relief that they'd gotten through the trial so easily, she walked through the churchyard on Robert's arm to where their carriage awaited them behind several others.

She sensed a tensing in his arm as they approached an open carriage, in which sat a middle-aged lady and a pretty girl in her teens. A gentleman stood beside the carriage as if he'd just helped the ladies in. As they passed, he turned and Pen saw that he was about her husband's age, a trifle shorter, with brown hair and candid blue eyes in an open, honest-looking face.

"Hello, Nick," said Robert quietly, stopping beside the man.

So this was Mr. Nicholas Dalton, Robert's childhood friend. The one who had not forgiven him for not telling him what had happened to Anne Norland. Robert had said he might be present, along with his mother and sister.

Dalton's face tightened with suspicion as he eyed them. Pen noted a troubled look in his eyes, as if he wanted to believe in Robert but had had his faith shaken by Robert's earlier refusal to confide in him. She pleaded silently that he would at least acknowledge her husband's presence.

Finally, he gave a slight nod toward Robert and a bow in her direction. "Verwood, Lady Verwood. I wish you a good day."

He climbed into the carriage, and as they walked on,

Pen's heart ached for Robert, whose expressionless face masked what she sensed was painful disappointment. While Dalton hadn't cut the acquaintance entirely, he had not introduced his mother or sister or given any sign that he would be willing to resume his friendship with Robert.

"It will get better," she murmured, and was relieved to see him nod in response. As soon as they were out of the village, she would try to kiss away his troubled look.

She prayed Anne would return. *Soon.*

Verwood turned his horse onto the drive approaching Tregaron House, Pen on Melior beside him. They'd been visiting one of his more distant tenants. Undoubtedly she was tired, but her face glowed as it always did on returning home.

Had only a month passed since they had come to Cornwall?

Within that short time, she'd wrought amazing changes in his house as well as his life. She'd cheerfully turned the place upside down, ordering footmen about as they returned ancient pieces of furniture from the attics to their former locations, and gradually brightened the place with splashes of vivid jewel colors. The rooms no longer echoed with the memories of violent arguments between his parents or the months of silence when his father was absent and his mother brooded, occasionally exploding into anger at him over what he now realized were the most venial of offenses.

"Shall we visit Tegen?" Pen asked, reclaiming his attention.

He smiled and nodded, and after they'd left their horses at the stables, they went to the horse pond.

Watching as Pen tossed small fish to the seal pup, he marveled at the creature's growth. Tegen had more than doubled in size, and he privately thought she was ready to return to the sea. But there was no rush, seeing how Pen enjoyed showing the seal pup off to the villagers' children.

Watching her serene expression as she fed the seal, he felt a rush of love for her. He still hadn't dared put it into words; she seemed so perfectly content between her animals and her domestic concerns that he sometimes wondered if she needed him at all. More disturbingly, she had never said the words either, though her every word and gesture and action was loving. Was this how she would have behaved toward any husband, because she took her marital vows seriously and wanted children?

"Silly glutton, there are no more," she said fondly, dropping the empty pail beside Tegen, who yelped and nosed eagerly about searching for still more fish.

Verwood smiled, reminding himself that *he* was the lucky man who awoke with her every morning, not her sanctimonious curate, not those mutton-headed bucks who had pursued her in Brighton. Did it matter that their marriage had not begun as a love match? They were both happy now.

He linked arms with her to return to the house, remembering how he'd consoled her when her courses had come upon her again. He'd felt only relief himself, not because he was unwilling to share her affections with a child, but because their position in the district was still so tenuous.

Over the past month, some of the animosity directed toward him had faded. Most of his tenants were reasonable men who appreciated an honest-dealing landlord. Pen's pleasant ways, as much as the support of Mariah and the rector's wife, were gradually winning her the respect and liking of the villagers. However, he knew Pen felt a bit distressed after every conversation with the ladies, as if their gossip worried her.

As for the gentlemen, Nick maintained his cautious reserve, and Edward Norland glowered at Verwood any time he chanced to catch sight of him. How long could Mariah continue to keep the youth's simmering resentment under control?

He'd written and dispatched another letter to Mrs. Ross, but to his growing unease there was still no sign or word of Anne.

"I wonder who that can be?" Pen exclaimed.

Then he noticed several traveling carriages on the drive directly in front of the house. For an instant, the thought that Anne might have come to Tregaron flashed through his mind. A gentleman descended from the carriage and turned to hand down a tall lady with golden hair peeking from her fashionable bonnet. He'd seen her before, and she was not Anne.

"Juliana!" Pen shrieked and ran across the lawn toward the carriages.

Verwood followed more slowly, taking stock of the man beside his wife's friend. He was tall, brown-haired, handsome, and had a slight limp. Well, well. This could be interesting.

Pen hugged Juliana warmly. She hadn't realized how much she had missed her in the months since her marriage to Marcus Redwyck, the Earl of Amberley.

"How are you, Pen?" asked Juliana, her vivid blue eyes full of affectionate concern.

"Very well, and very happy," Pen replied, making sure she spoke clearly enough that Lord Amberley could hear as well.

She had her own suspicions as to why they'd come and wanted to make sure they did not doubt she was happy in her marriage.

"I don't even need to ask how *you* are doing, Jule," she continued. "You will have to tell me all about Venice."

She turned and saw the men eyeing each other warily. She also caught a hint of amusement on her husband's face.

"Welcome to Tregaron, Amberley," said Robert. "Or should I say . . . Lord Dare?"

So Lord Amberley was the one who had knocked Robert down last spring. Pen instinctively moved between the two men.

"Oh, so it is what Robert and I were thinking," she said before Amberley could reply. "Jule, you and Lord Amberley must have had such an adventure. But I must welcome you both to Tregaron House. I hope you are planning a long stay."

"Thank you, Lady Verwood. We do not wish to be a burden on your hospitality," said Lord Amberley. "The inn in the village appears quite comfortable."

"Nonsense. You will stay here," Pen insisted.

"I am happy to welcome any of my wife's friends to our home," said Robert with the demeanor of a perfect host.

Pen breathed a sigh of relief on seeing both Juliana and her husband relax and accept the invitation.

"Then let us go inside so I can tell Mrs. Symonds to prepare a room," she said. "Dinner will be ready in about an hour."

She led the way into the house, where Mrs. Symonds awaited them, surprised but happy to receive guests. After she'd finished making the arrangements, Robert suggested she and Juliana go for a walk in the gardens.

"I would love to, but . . ." she faltered, looking at the gentlemen worriedly.

"Go on," said Robert. "Amberley and I will have some sherry together and discuss old times. I promise I'll not give him cause to hit me again."

They all laughed, albeit a little nervously.

"Lady Verwood, your husband is safe with me," said Lord Amberley, with a charming smile. "I can see you have become fond of him, so perhaps he is not completely undeserving."

"Go on, you don't need to protect me from Amberley," said Robert. "Our last encounter was clearly a misunderstanding of the most comic order. Why *did* you assume a false name, Amberley?"

Amberley's face reddened slightly. "It began as a foolish lark," he admitted. "If word had gotten out that I had visited the Green Room at the Opera House, I would never have been allowed to pay court to the fastidious and highly respectable Miss Juliana Hutton."

He grinned at Jule, who pretended to frown.

"And if I had not done it," he continued, gazing warmly at his wife, "I would never have lost my heart to the loveliest dancer ever to grace the stage there."

Pen chuckled, remembering how shocked she'd been by Juliana's bold scheme to avoid the marriage. Clearly, it had ended well.

"Now you may go on and have your chat," said Robert, still looking amused. "Amberley and I will promise not to engage in any further fisticuffs."

"You had better not," said Juliana, giving her husband a cautionary look.

"Do you see what I must endure?" said Amberley with a mock sigh as he looked adoringly at his wife.

"I understand completely," said Robert, and grinned sympathetically. "However, you must admit there are rewards for being an obedient husband . . ."

The men smiled wickedly. Pen lifted her chin, linked arms with Juliana, and together they left the Hall.

"Now, you must tell me. What really brings you both here?" Pen asked Jule as soon as they were outside again.

"When we got your letter, we could not resist seeing how you went on."

"I imagine you were ready to drag me off to Redwyck Hall if you thought I was not happy. But I *am*, Jule, happier than I ever have been. I wish you had not curtailed your trip on my account, but now that you are here, I hope you will make it a long visit."

"As to that, I think we may stay only a few days. Grandpapa will be wanting to see us in London, and Marcus is anxious to return to Redwyck Hall for the harvest. But you must tell me everything that has happened. I gather you have been in some danger."

"Perhaps I should tell you the entire story," she said.

As they walked, she recounted the entire tale to Juliana, who looked grave at the end.

"You love Verwood, don't you?"

Pen nodded.

"And now you still fear for his life. I've half a mind to ask Marcus if we can take you with us. I couldn't bear it if anything happened to you."

Pen shook her head. "Robert already tried to make me go to visit Catherine. No, my place is here."

Juliana looked at her for a long moment, then nodded. "I understand. I just can't help but be worried. I wish there was something more we could do."

"I am sure everything will turn out for the best."

Conversation ran easily over dinner, rambling from the Amberleys' travels to politics and news from Catherine and her family. Pen was delighted to see the beginnings of what might be a friendship between the two men.

The next day being Sunday, they all attended services together. Pen was amused to see they had caused something of a stir in the churchyard, an earl and his countess being rarities in the district. Mariah joined them at the door as they all stood chatting with the rector and his wife.

"I hope you will find some time to enjoy some of the sights of this remote corner of England," she said graciously, after Pen had introduced her to the Amberleys.

"I am not sure we will have the time," said Juliana.

"I am not in such a great hurry that we cannot spend a few days here," said Amberley, looking fondly at his wife.

"Perhaps we should make up an expedition to go to Tintagel tomorrow," said Mariah, her eyes darting eagerly around the group. "It is such a romantic spot. A ruined castle atop windy, precipitous cliffs. Legend says it was King Arthur's birthplace. It is only a few hours' drive from here."

"Oh, what a splendid idea!" said Mrs. Finchley, the rector's wife. She was quickly echoed by her husband.

Mr. Dalton, Robert's childhood friend, was just coming out of the church, and somehow Mariah managed to draw him, his mother, and his sister into the discussion. Pen had the opportunity to intercept a brief glance Mr. Dalton threw toward her husband, and a fleeting look in his eyes made her think that perhaps he was beginning to soften toward Robert a little. His sister Cecily gave Pen a shy smile.

Perhaps this was Mariah's way of starting to bring them all together. Pen only wished she knew whether Mariah intended her brother Edward to be one of the party. That would certainly be pushing matters too quickly.

"What do you think, Penelope?" asked Mariah, drawing all eyes toward Pen. "Shall we go to Tintagel?"

Pen hesitated, wishing she could question Mariah but unable to do so politely. Conscious of everyone's attention, she looked toward Mariah and encountered a clear, unspoken message from the lady's steely eyes. Mariah intended the outing to unite them all, and Pen would be in disgrace if she declined it.

Stealing a sidelong glance at Robert, she saw him nod slightly, though he wore what she had come to think of as his "Verwood" expression. Perhaps he felt it unwise to antagonize Mariah, given all that had come between him and her family.

"Yes, I think it a fine idea," she said.

She trusted Mariah would be sensible enough to leave her brother out of the expedition, but the next day, as the carriages gathered at their arranged starting point, she saw that Edward Norland was indeed one of the party.

Worry plagued her throughout the scenic drive, and she was relieved to see the group disperse on arrival at the ruined castle. Mercifully, Edward avoided her and Robert, instead devoting himself to Cecily Dalton. Mr. Dalton stayed with them, protecting his pretty sister's reputation in his mother's absence. Pen and Robert strolled with the Amberleys, while Mariah lagged far behind with the stout rector and his wife. Neither of the Finchleys were vigorous walkers.

Soon Pen relaxed enough to sit down and sketch a view of the castle and coastline. Robert sat beside her, just as he had on their honeymoon, while Juliana and her husband explored the ruins more closely.

About ten minutes later Pen heard a cry and looked up. Mariah had fallen down a steep section of the path. The rector and his wife were nowhere in sight. She and Robert sped to the place where Mariah lay.

"I am afraid I have sprained my ankle," said Mariah, grimacing as she looked up at them.

"Let me see," said Pen. She removed Mariah's half-boot and discovered that her ankle was indeed beginning to swell.

"Yes, it is sprained," she said, looking back at Robert. "She must not put any weight upon it. Perhaps you could help her back to her carriage somehow?"

"Of course," he said. He lifted Mariah up in his arms, and she smiled gratefully and apologetically at Pen.

"No, no, you shall stay here and finish your sketch. I can wait in the carriage until everyone is ready to leave. I would be desolated to know I had ruined the outing for you, too."

Pen returned to her sketchbook, but could not resist another glance at Robert as he carried Mariah's slender form along the path toward the carriages. Something in the way the widow flung her arm around his neck caused a jealous suspicion to dart into Pen's mind.

Fool! Although Pen had heard of ladies feigning injuries to capture a man's attentions, she couldn't imagine one intentionally spraining her ankle to do so. It was quite mortifying. She was jealous and could not bear to see her husband attending in the most innocent way to another female, particularly an ethereal beauty like Mariah.

Pen tried to force her attention back to her drawing, but she could no longer concentrate. She folded up the sketchbook and climbed the slope back up to the carriages. She saw Mariah sitting in the carriage, frowning, no doubt in pain. Robert stood facing the sea, his back to both Mariah and her. He turned around at her approach, and she was disturbed to see a tightness in his expression, a hint of trouble in his eyes. An instant later, his face was impassive and he came toward her and the open carriage where Mariah sat.

"Are you in great pain, Mariah?" she asked. "Is there something we can do to make you more comfortable?"

Mariah smiled with a visible effort and shook her head. "No, no, I would not wish you to trouble yourselves so much over a minor sprain. I can wait until we pass through the village."

"It may be some time before the others return. Perhaps my husband could walk to the village and procure some arnica," she offered. "A cold compress, too, if it could be arranged."

"I would be more than happy to run the errand," said Robert.

Pen caught a hint of anxiety in his voice. Was he worried about Mariah or about what they might discuss in his absence? Yet she sensed he was eager to leave. Why?

"Thank you. You are both being far too kind to me," said Mariah with a strained smile.

Robert set off on foot to the nearby village, while Pen

climbed into the carriage, still disturbed by the undercurrents she sensed around her.

"Thank you so much, Penelope. Your knowledge of medicine is admirable," said Mariah.

"I learned a few things from the apothecary and the midwife in our village, but my knowledge does not compare with yours," she replied, remembering the extensive garden of medicinal plants Mariah had shown her at Norland Manor.

Mariah shifted in her seat and grimaced.

"I am so sorry this happened to you," said Pen sympathetically. "It must hurt terribly."

"You are so kind, but I assure you, the pain is not great," said Mariah, though her voice remained mournful.

"Does something else trouble you then?"

"No, nothing at all. Why should there be?"

"I don't know," said Pen, feeling abashed.

"Well, I am grateful for your concern, dear. And you must know that if anything—or *anyone*—ever causes you pain, I will happily lend you an ear and give you what advice I can."

Pen wondered why she felt oppressed rather than warmed by the offer. Was the other lady implying that *Robert* would cause her grief?

"Thank you, Mariah, but I assure you I am very happy in my marriage," she said firmly.

"Oh, I was not implying otherwise. You must be the happiest of creatures, married to such a charming rogue. I hope you will always be as happy."

"Lord Verwood is a most devoted husband," she said, suppressing a spurt of anger over Mariah's insinuation that Robert might not remain faithful.

"I did not mean to imply otherwise, my dear. It is just that his reputation is so . . . and we still have heard nothing from Anne."

A chill spread through Pen at Mariah's words.

She was relieved to see the Finchleys approaching. The rector and his wife were both puffing and wheezing from the exertion of the climb, and she readily gave up her seat in the carriage to them.

An hour later Pen finally relaxed, back in her own carriage with Robert and the Amberleys. Juliana, hearing her small sigh of relief, asked her frankly if anything was amiss.

"You are not worrying about Lady Grayshott, are you?" asked Jule. "I did not think her injury was serious."

"No, I don't think so," she replied, not wanting to relate the gist of her conversation, particularly with the gentlemen sitting with them.

"You seemed distressed when we rejoined you," Jule insisted. "Did she say something to you?"

Pen stole a glance at Robert, but his expression was closed. He was uncomfortable about something; perhaps it pained him to be the subject of gossip.

"Tell us if something is bothering you, Pen," said Jule. "You know you can trust Marcus to be discreet."

Pen sighed, realizing it was useless to resist Juliana's questioning.

"She reminded me that we have still not heard from her sister," she said at length.

A brief silence ensued. Pen knew everyone present understood the seriousness of the situation. She supposed it was a minor blessing that Edward Norland had not made any aggressive moves toward Robert, but it was frightening to think that Mariah's good intentions toward them might be wavering.

"What else? Is there more?" asked Juliana.

"The rest was just spite, I think," said Pen, not wishing to discuss Mariah's other insinuations.

"I'll tell you what, Pen," said Juliana in a heartening tone. "I think you are right—it was all just spite. It is like what we used to endure at Miss Stratton's School. Do you remember how Lydia Bixley and her set used to try to coerce us all into doing their will?"

Pen nodded, smiling as she remembered how staunchly Juliana and Catherine had defended her against the catty set. "Yes, but in this case I do not think spiders in her bed will serve the purpose."

They all laughed, but Pen sobered quickly, realizing Mariah wielded greater power than the cats at Miss Stratton's school.

"I just don't understand why people must behave that way," she said, sighing.

"Envy," said Juliana after a pause. "Lydia and her set were always envious of the friendship you and Catherine and I shared; I think that is why they delighted in causing trouble for us. I suppose Lady Grayshott envies you your happy marriage, since she is a widow and childless."

Pen thought for a moment, then turned to Robert. He had sat quietly throughout the conversation, only the tension in his body betraying his unease over the matter.

"What sort of man was Sir Charles Grayshott?" she asked him.

"Your typical country squire: an avid huntsman and a hard drinker," replied Robert in a clipped tone. "He was well into his fifties when they married."

"What were her parents thinking to sanction such a match?" Juliana asked, sounding horrified.

"He was the wealthiest man in the district." After a pause Robert added, "He was the man they intended Anne to marry."

Pen clasped her hands tightly in her lap, sensing the pain it caused him to speak of it.

"Perhaps Lady Grayshott was not happy with him," said Juliana pensively. "That would explain a great deal."

"I do feel sorry for her," said Pen. "Children would have been a comfort to her. I wonder why she has not remarried."

"Who can tell?" said Jule. "You may feel sorry for her if you wish, but you should not let her bully you."

Pen forced a smile and changed the subject, but vague fears pressed on her all the way home. She no longer felt at all confident they could rely on Mariah's goodwill. Without it, their position was precarious indeed. Mariah might not wish Edward to cause them trouble, but she had an immense influence over most of the local populace, some of whom still loathed Robert.

Why did Anne not come?

Chapter Fourteen

After bidding farewell to the Amberleys the following morning, Verwood returned to the house, hoping the groom that picked up their mail at the village had already returned. Once more, there was no word from Anne, and no sign that she had communicated with any of her family either. Surely she'd had time to receive his letter and respond to it by now.

Shaking off his disappointment, he decided to seek out his wife. He searched the house and gardens and finally found Pen in the enclosure near the horse pond, wearing sturdy boots and leather gloves, an apron with a knife protruding from its pocket, and holding a bucket of pilchards. Tegen flopped about her feet, yelping greedily.

Then he saw that Pen was standing quite still, with tears running down her cheeks.

"Darling, whatever is the matter?" he asked, hurrying forward. "Do you miss your friend so much already?"

Wordlessly, she reached into the bucket and held up a piece of fish. He came closer and saw a large, nasty-looking fishhook protruding from it.

"I was afraid this fish was too big, and when I cut it, I found . . . this inside. If she had swallowed it . . ."

She caught her breath on a sob. He knew it was no use telling her the hook was there by accident. She knew as well as he did that pilchards were caught in nets and not on fishhooks.

Someone had just tried to kill Tegen.

Anger filled him as he watched the devastated look in Pen's eyes while she looked down at her odd pet. Her hand shook as she carefully picked a small fish out of the bucket and dropped it into Tegen's open mouth, temporarily stilling the pup's yelping.

"Who would do such a thing?" she pleaded.

"I don't know, Pen. Some village louts, perhaps. Boys can be very cruel."

"B-but the children seemed to enjoy watching Tegen," she said, feeding the seal a few more fish. "They liked to throw fish at her and see if she could catch them."

Seeing that Tegen was quiet now, he took the bucket from Pen and set it down. He pulled her into his arms and stroked her back, unable to think of anything more to say. He knew it was not just her fear for the seal that was upsetting her; it was the thought of the malice behind the deed. Most likely it was village children who had carried it out, but they were only acting on hatred they had been taught. Hatred directed against *him*. And Pen was suffering for it.

"Let us go away," he said roughly.

"Go away? Where?" she asked, her voice muffled by his shoulder.

"Anywhere. London, the Continent, back to Sussex, wherever you wish. We could go for a holiday, or if you like, find an entirely new home. Someplace we can start afresh."

For a moment she stared up at him, her reddish-brown eyelashes still damp, then shook her head. "*No*. I won't be driven away from my home. We should see this out."

He held her tighter, amazed at the force in her voice.

"Unless you believe *you* will be attacked again," she faltered, her face twisting with fear.

"I don't think so," he said, hoping to reassure her. "I find this as distressing as you do, but most of the villagers would regard this as a mere prank. Fisherfolk will sometimes kill seals, for they compete for the same fish, you know."

"I know," she said, sounding calmer. She let out a long, shuddering sigh, looking down at Tegen sadly. "I suppose it is time to set her free. I hope she is old enough to fend for herself."

Pen cried again that evening, when they brought Tegen down to the beach and encouraged her to enter the calm waters. At first the seal seemed inclined to return to land, but when they started up the steep path she turned back into the sea and swam off toward a nearby rocky outcropping.

That evening, they sat before the drawing room fire as had become their custom. Pen embroidered a cushion for one of the chairs resurrected from the attic using a pattern of her own devising, a graceful stylized dolphin worked in vibrant shades of blue and green. Meanwhile, he read to her from a novel they had both been enjoying, *Pride and Prejudice*. He would never have guessed that he would come to enjoy such a cozy occupation. Now he treasured every lovely, serene moment he spent with Pen.

However, this particular night he was dismayed to see his wife struggling to set her stitches. When she surreptitiously wiped away a tear, he set the book down and crossed the room to kneel beside her chair. Gently he took the embroidery frame away from her and set it down, then took her hands in his own.

"I'm such a weakling," she said, choking back a tiny sob.

"You are not. I know exactly what this sort of malice can do, darling. It can make you feel that anything you try to do, anything good or useful or beautiful, is in vain."

She nodded, looking down at his hands covering hers, and he knew his words had struck home.

"Pen, there have been people trying to crush the enthusiasm out of me my entire life. They very nearly succeeded. I won't let it happen to you. Embroider your cushions, plant flowers. Decorate the nursery."

"But I am not—" She blushed prettily, looking up from their hands.

"You will be," he said, leaning in closer so he pressed against her knees. "Life is uncertain, but we must plan and strive anyway. Otherwise none of it's worth a damn."

A shaky smile trembled on her lips. "I cannot believe you are saying these things."

"You have taught me well, my wife," he said, grinning. "Let me tell you what I intend to do."

"I am listening." She straightened up, looking more cheerful.

"Within two weeks, the harvest will be over. If Anne does not respond to my letter within that time, I will take you to Scotland with me, and we will bring her back ourselves. Do you like my plan?"

She nodded, an almost painful look of hope in her eyes.

"I trust it will all be over soon, darling, but if it is not, remember we do not have to live here year-round unless we wish. In fact, I am quite resolved that we shall go to London in the new year."

"You are?"

"Of course. How else am I to take my seat in the House of Lords? I expect you to advise me on any and all issues that come up for discussion, of course, and tell me how to vote on every question."

"You may count on me," she said, beaming.

He pulled her down into his lap and kissed her, relieved to see the smile back on her face and determined to ignore the insidious voices that still whispered to him that their happiness was not so easily won.

Later that night, Pen gazed at her sleeping husband. The soft flickering light of the candle beside her bed cast soft shadows over the subtle tracery of dark hair, the shapely lines of his chest, and the handsome contours of his face. Though pleasantly tired, she did not wish to sleep, being possessed by a deep and overwhelming joy.

She reached out a hand and gently stroked Robert's arm, then pressed her hand lightly to her own belly. Somehow she felt certain a new life was growing there.

She returned to contemplate his shuttered eyelids under his dramatically arched brows, the sensual mouth that had kissed her so tenderly a while before, the gentle, rhythmic breathing that proved his trust in her, and she nearly wept with happiness. For the first time since they'd arrived in Cornwall, she knew beyond any doubt that he would not tire of her or leave her alone to raise their children.

She laid her head upon his chest. Drowsily, he put an arm around her and pulled her into him. She pressed closer, tears of joy filling her eyes. As long as they were together, she thought fiercely, they would be happy and safe. *Nothing* else mattered.

Pen surveyed the empty flower bed before her. Which species of tulip would look best here? Some of those red and yellow ones, she decided. The ones that looked as if they'd been carelessly streaked by an artist's brush.

A cool wind enveloped her, reminding her that it was now September. Though less than a week had passed since she thought she had conceived, she had already begun to feel a subtle inner warmth, as if a flame were glowing inside her. Another week, and she would tell Robert her good news.

Lost in happy thoughts, she started when a footman cleared his throat, then announced that Lady Grayshott had come to call upon her and was awaiting her in the drawing room.

"I shall be there directly," she said, stifling her disappointment at being interrupted.

She entered the drawing room as a maid set a tea tray next to the sofa where Mariah awaited her.

"Mariah, what a pleasure to see you," she said, handing Mariah a cup of tea. "I hope this means your ankle is better."

"It is healing quite nicely," said Mariah. "I came as soon as I could, since I heard what nearly happened to your poor darling seal. So dreadful for you!"

"How did you know what happened?" Pen asked, puzzled.

"My dear, have you forgotten that your groom Pascoe's sister is the second housemaid at Norland Manor?" Mariah asked, smiling.

"Of course, I should have remembered," said Pen wryly, remembering how news often traveled in the country.

"I hope you were not too distressed by what happened," said Mariah in a kind tone.

"No actual harm was done. I suppose it was nearly time

to release Tegen back to the sea anyway," Pen replied. For some reason she felt unwilling to reveal her lingering concerns over the vile act to her visitor.

Mariah took a sip of tea, then set her cup down. "Well, I am relieved to hear the incident did not overset you. I must also beg your forgiveness for speaking as I did at Tintagel. My ankle was paining me. I meant well, but I know now I should have kept my concerns to myself."

Pen considered Mariah's words. Pain was no excuse for the insinuations she had made. In fact, she hadn't retracted them; she had merely apologized for voicing them. But it would not be wise to engage Mariah in an argument.

"I am glad you have realized that," she said in a mild tone, hoping Mariah had indeed learned her lesson.

"You are too kind, too forgiving, dear Penelope." Mariah sighed a bit sadly. "I am afraid there is another matter I must bring to your attention."

"What is it?" Pen asked, irritated by the woman's ominous manner.

"There has been some talk in the village regarding what happened at Tintagel," said Mariah, lowering her voice. "I suspect that one of the coachmen who were present when Lord Verwood brought me back to my carriage imagined he saw some sort of impropriety in your husband's solicitous care for me. I tell you this only so that you do not hear it elsewhere."

Pen stared at Mariah for a moment. Why did she tell her such a thing? Did Mariah hope to raise doubts as to what really occurred at Tintagel?

"I hope you denied the rumor," Pen said sternly.

"Of course, but you know how difficult it is to halt the spread of gossip," said Mariah in a plaintive tone.

It occurred to Pen that Mariah might be finding a perverse pleasure in being considered Robert's victim. She certainly enjoyed being the center of everyone's attention. And she held sway not only over her beloved brother Edward, but over so many others in the parish. Much as Pen longed to defend Robert, she could not afford to make an enemy of Mariah.

"Surely you have enough influence over the parish to

convince everyone of the truth," insisted Pen, hoping the compliment would make her statement more palatable.

"Perhaps, Penelope, you do not realize how difficult it is to convince anyone in the parish of your husband's innocence when we still have not seen sign or word from Anne."

The threat in Mariah's voice and the cold light in her eyes caused Pen to wrap her arms around herself. Instinctively, she pressed one hand to her belly, then removed it, hoping Mariah hadn't noticed the gesture.

"I know it is difficult for others to believe it," she said, trying to sound calm. "But I promise you everything will be made clear in time."

"Let us hope so, for all our sakes. In the meantime, I shall continue to do what I can to keep the peace."

"Thank you," said Pen, relieved to see the angry light fade from Mariah's eyes.

After Mariah departed, Pen returned to the gardens, needing a happy occupation to dispel her lingering anger and unease over Mariah's whisperings. Why did the woman have to indulge in such petty, spiteful behavior?

Pen thought over what Juliana had said on the way back from Tintagel, and her anger faded to annoyance. She had a devoted husband and a child growing inside her. She was so blessed in comparison with Mariah, who cared for no one but Edward, whom she spoiled shockingly, keeping him at home at an age when many young men of good family were sent to Oxford or Cambridge. Still, her devotion to Edward would keep him out of trouble, and Pen could not help but be glad of that.

As she returned to the flower bed she had been designing, Pen cheered herself with the thought that Robert would take her to Scotland in another week or so. Much as she had become attached to Tregaron House itself, it was high time they lifted the cloud of suspicion that hung over them all.

Three days after Mariah's visit, a premonition of trouble assailed Pen as she left the cottage of one of her husband's pensioners. She headed quickly toward the village green, where she was to rejoin Robert, who was meeting with Mr. Nicholas Dalton at the Red Anchor to discuss some boundary issue.

From a distance she saw young Cecily Dalton begin to make her way across the main road, bearing a small parcel, perhaps some trifle purchased at the village shop. The girl stumbled on the stony road, fell and dropped her package. At the same time Robert emerged from the door of the inn. He quickly bent to help Cecily, handing her up with a polite smile.

An instant later Edward Norland burst out of the adjacent blacksmith's yard and set upon Robert from behind, landing a swinging blow to the back of Robert's head that knocked him onto his face in the stony road.

"Blackguard! Don't you dare touch Miss Dalton again!" shouted Edward, falling upon Robert and viciously pummeling him wile Cecily stood by screaming.

"Stop!" shouted Pen, running toward them and feeling each blow as if it had been directed at her.

Robert turned over and began to wrestle with Norland, and a crowd quickly gathered to watch the fight. Pen saw Dalton come out of the Red Anchor and run toward the fighting men, clearly intending to break them apart.

His efforts were not needed, however. By the time Pen had reached the group in front of the inn, Robert had pinned his opponent to the ground. There were bruises on his face, and his coat was torn, but thank goodness, he did not look to be seriously hurt.

"Damn you, Verwood! You'll not play off your tricks on Cecily, do you hear me?" Edward continued to rave, lifting his head. "I demand satisfaction!"

"As a justice of the peace, Norland, I must remind you that dueling has been outlawed," said Dalton in an authoritative tone.

"Damn you, too! He must be brought to justice. He's seduced both my sisters, or tried to. Are you going to sit idly by while he tries out his tricks on *your* sister?"

Pen flinched at his ugly words and his patent belief in all the lies and rumors surrounding her husband. She looked around, terrified the crowd might turn against Robert. She prayed that Dalton would be able to prevent a riot.

"I have seduced neither of your sisters," said Robert. "I don't wish to hurt you, but I will if you force me. If you could only be patient, I will do my best to explain everything."

His quickened breath betrayed the effort it cost him to remain calm and hold down the angry young man.

"Let's not bandy words in the street, Norland," said Dalton. "If you promise not to fight, we can go into the Red Anchor and discuss the matter privately."

"I refuse to talk to this scoundrel! I want justice!" shouted Edward, renewing his struggles to free himself.

"What is going on? Edward?" a feminine voice called out, loud and frightened.

Pen turned her head and saw that a post chaise had arrived at the inn while everyone's attention had been focused on the fight. A couple came forward, apparently just having alighted from the chaise. Edward stopped thrashing about. For a moment he and everyone else just stared at the newcomers. Then Robert broke the silence, addressing the lady.

"Anne," he said in a steady voice, but his eyes glowed with excitement. "It appears you have arrived just in time."

Chapter Fifteen

"Anne, it is you, isn't it?" Edward breathed, staring up at the lady.

"My little Edward. You are so *tall*," she said, voice breaking.

Now Pen had the leisure to see how much the lady resembled both Edward and Mariah. She had the same pale hair and blue-gray eyes, but she was a little taller than her sister, her features a little stronger. She had the look of one who had suffered and was wiser for it.

Robert released Edward, who ran to his sister's open arms. At the same time, Pen went to her husband.

"Are you badly hurt?" she asked, putting her arms around him and studying his bruised face. He shook his head, passively accepting her embrace, his gaze fixed on Edward and his sister.

A moment later Anne turned from her brother and looked at Pen. "Lady Verwood, I am so happy to meet you. Lord Verwood mentioned you in his letter."

"I am glad you have come home, Miss Norland," she replied, trying to hide her unease over the way Robert stared at Anne, as if watching a ghost.

"I am Mrs. Ross now," said Anne, smiling. "Dr. Ross and I have been married for about a month."

The gentleman beside her bowed and introduced himself as Dr. James Ross. "We were on our honeymoon in the Highlands, which is why it took your letter a while to reach us," he said. "We came as quickly as we could, and not a

moment too soon, it seems. Well, it's a long tale, but Anne
is ready to tell it to you all."

A few minutes later they were all gathered in one of the
Red Anchor's private parlors. Anne sat in the center of the
sofa, her husband holding her hand protectively on one side
and Edward sitting on the other, looking stunned.

Pen, Robert, and the Daltons sat across from them. She
wished she could touch Robert, to sense what he was feeling. It struck her forcibly that fond as he had become of
her, he might still be in love with Anne. She folded her
hands in her lap, trying to remain calm. At last his reputation would be cleared, and he would be safe from further
threats. That was all that mattered.

Anne paled a little before beginning, but her husband
gave her hand a squeeze, and she cleared her throat.

"Some of you may already know that my father wished
me to marry Sir Charles Grayshott. I did not wish to marry
him, but my father was quite . . . adamantly in favor of the
match, since Sir Charles had promised to pay handsomely
for my hand. So I asked Robert—Lord Verwood, now—to
help me run away."

Anne paused. Pen watched Edward's gaze move from his
sister's face to Robert's.

"Lord Verwood asked me to go to Gretna Green with
him, so we could be married," Anne continued.

"Why didn't you marry him, then?" asked Edward, looking at Robert suspiciously.

"He tried to persuade me, but I refused his offer."

Anne paused again, her breath tumultuous, her face pale.
The rest of her words came out in a torrent. "I could not
bear the thought of being his wife, for I thought myself ruined already. Sir Charles Grayshott had . . . defiled me.
With my father's sanction. They thought it would serve to
bend me to their will."

A stunned silence fell upon the room. Pen reeled with
horror. For a moment she stared at Anne, whose husband
had put a protective, comforting arm around her. Then she
looked at Edward, whose face showed shock and disbelief.

"It can't be. Papa would never have done such a thing!"
he blurted out after a moment.

"He did, Edward. You were the son, his favorite. You do not know," Anne replied flatly. "When I rebelled against his plans, he beat me and then left me alone with Sir Charles."

Pen looked toward Robert. His face had contorted in a bitter expression of self-blame.

"Why did you not tell me, Anne?" he implored. "I saw those bruises, but I never imagined anything quite like . . . I would have tried anything in my power to help you. I would have—"

"There was nothing you could have done. Not then," Anne said softly, recovering some of her color. "At the time I was too ashamed, too wounded to even talk about it. I felt I had become as loathsome as Sir Charles and unworthy of the love you offered me. You did all you could by leaving me with James's aunt. If you had not done so I should not have met him, and we would not now be married."

Anne looked up into her husband's kind, rugged face, her eyes alight with love and gratitude. Pen was relieved to see a little of the anguish fade from Robert's expression.

"I am happy for you, then," he said, his voice strained.

"Thank you for keeping my secret all these years," Anne replied. "With the Rosses I was safe, and had the opportunity to recover my spirits. But it was not fair to you. When I asked you to promise not to tell what had become of me, I had not realized what this would do to your reputation and your prospects. I am so sorry."

Edward turned to Robert, hanging his head.

"I am sorry to have misjudged you, Verwood. It was just that I missed Anne so much, and no one would tell me anything."

"Your actions were understandable, Norland," said Robert. "I'm willing to let bygones be bygones."

"Damn good of you, after the fool I've made of myself," Edward said dejectedly. Then he paled.

"What is it?" asked Anne.

"You have not heard," Edward replied. "Mariah married Sir Charles a little over a year after you ran away."

"Good God, she would have been just sixteen! I had not thought . . ." Anne put her face in her hands for a moment, then lifted it. "How is she? Do you know if he has mistreated her?"

"Sir Charles died a few years after they married," explained Dalton, "and Lady Grayshott returned to Norland Manor."

"She said she was happy to marry him," said Edward in a troubled voice. "She said she liked being the richest lady in the district and the opportunities it gave her to do good."

"I find it hard to believe," said Anne. "Mariah and I always did have differing views and preferences, but still . . ."

"Mariah is very strong," offered Edward.

"I shall have to talk to her," said Anne, looking troubled.

"There's one thing that confuses me," said Cecily Dalton, turning all heads her way. Pen had nearly forgotten she was there. "Surely, Edward—I mean Mr. Norland," she corrected herself hurriedly, with an apologetic glance at her brother, "you did not mean it when you said Lord Verwood had tried to seduce *both* your sisters."

"Mariah seemed rather blue-deviled after our visit to Tintagel, but she refused to tell me why," said Edward. "Later I heard that Verwood had tried to impose on her, and I believed the rumor. You must accept my apologies, Verwood."

"Accepted," Robert said quietly.

There was a brief silence. Pen looked around, realizing that now everyone present believed in her husband's innocence. It should have been a great relief, but Robert's frozen demeanor troubled her.

"Well, I hope you will both stay at Norland Manor as long as you wish," said Edward, looking at Anne and her husband. "If Mariah needs to unburden herself, I'm sure you will know what to say to her, Anne."

Anne nodded and embraced him again, her expression sweet and grave.

"With Mrs. Ross's permission," said Mr. Dalton, "I think some version of this story should be made public."

"Yes, I agree," said Anne, looking at her brother and her husband.

Dalton paused a moment before continuing. "We could say simply that Lord Verwood helped you to escape an unwanted marriage with Sir Charles, but that once you reached Scotland you decided to marry Dr. Ross instead. We need not dwell too much on the timing of all these events."

"I'll support the story, if you think it will serve," said Dr. Ross.

"I hope it will," said Dalton, his gaze passing from Robert back to the group on the sofa. "If we are all seen to be on cordial terms with Lord and Lady Verwood, it would help to ease the tensions in this parish."

The Rosses and Edward nodded their agreement, and Mr. Dalton turned to look at Robert. He was doing all he could to help them, and now Pen could see he longed for a reconciliation with his onetime friend. She prayed Robert would be open to it; he needed trusty friends like Nicholas Dalton.

"Thank you, Nick," he said with a half smile, and Pen sighed with relief.

"Then we are in agreement," said Dalton. "I think it is time we all returned home."

Their horses were brought around from the stables a few minutes later, and Robert helped Pen onto Melior rather mechanically. He remained silent as they turned toward Tregaron House, and she could not decide whether he needed some time to absorb all that had happened or whether it would be a healing thing for him to talk about it. As they left the outskirts of the village, she blurted out the question topmost in her mind.

"Are you still in love with her?" she asked, and immediately reproached herself for being so tactless.

"What? With Anne?" he asked, as if his thoughts had been far away, then shook his head. "No, not now."

His words should have been reassuring. Why did he look so withdrawn?

"It was generous of you to keep her secret for so long," she ventured.

"I am no martyr," he said harshly. "My father paid George Norland to pretend Anne had run away and died, and you already know what I did with my life after that."

He looked ahead, and Pen watched his profile for a moment. He must have been such a passionate young man.

How must he have felt when Anne rejected his love and all his attempts to comfort her? It was not surprising that he had plunged into excess afterward, seeking consolation in the arms of more willing women.

Pen was still trying to think of the proper words to console him when he spoke again.

"I keep wondering if there was something I should have done differently."

"Stop tormenting yourself," she pleaded. "You were only eighteen; how could you have guessed what those horrible men had done to Anne? If you think you must read minds and always know exactly what to do for everyone you care for, you are setting yourself an impossible task. It is enough that you tried."

"Perhaps you are right," he said in a subdued tone.

"I am always right," she said with a smile, hoping to lighten his mood.

"I shall endeavor to remember that in the future, my wife," he said, sighing. "Only tell me if I have succeeded in pleasing *you*."

She shook her head and gave him a saucy smile.

"If I told you how you please me, you would become far too full of your own perfections."

Thank Heaven, his roguish smile reappeared. It would take time for him to recover from the revelations of the day, but he'd made a start.

Seeing the gates of Tregaron House, she spurred Melior into a gallop and flew down the drive. Robert soon caught up and passed her, reaching the stable yard just in time to help her dismount and snatch a kiss in the process.

He was slipping. Again.

This time the wind was stronger, whipping around him. Sea spray pelted him, softening the earth under his fingers, loosening his grip. Below him the waves pounded ever higher, and sharp rocks awaited him. As before, ghostly hands tugged at his ankles.

Pen was there again, her face full of loving concern. This time she held an infant in one arm and held the other out to help him. This time he didn't dare reach out to her. If he took her hand, he would only pull her and the babe over the edge with him.

She came closer and knelt down near him, putting her hand around his. He felt the ground give under him. With all his might he pushed her away, before plunging off the cliff. He cried out her name one last time before the darkness claimed him.

From across the bed, Pen reached out a hand and gently touched her husband's shoulder.

"Robert, Robert," she whispered. "Wake up. You are dreaming."

In the light of the fire, she watched him raise himself up on one elbow.

"Lord, did I hurt you?" he asked gruffly.

So he was conscious of having thrust her away from him. "Not at all," she replied, relieved when he opened his arms and gathered her close again. "What did you dream?"

She wasn't surprised when he did not reply. He probably wished to protect her from even the thought of anything horrible enough to make him cry out as he had.

"Was someone trying to kill you again?"

"Something like that."

She had hoped for more, but straightforward questioning did not always succeed with her husband. She laid her head onto his chest, put an arm over him, and lay still, treasuring the sound of his heart thumping away steadily beneath her ear, the feel of his chest rising and falling under her arm.

"Dreams are not omens, you know," she said after a minute. "They are just fears coming to plague us at night. It may take time for them to fade away, but you are safe now."

She hugged him closer, but could not suppress a shiver as she remembered the violent way Edward had rained blows on Robert and the ugly look of the crowd that had surrounded them. Nameless fears still weighed on her, too, but she would not give them form by voicing them. In time, they would pass.

"Yes. *We* are safe now," he echoed, as if willing himself to believe it. Then he began to stroke her back softly.

She was drifting off to sleep when he spoke again.

"Pen, do you truly think we go to Heaven when we die?"

She almost gasped, the question was so unexpected. But it was only natural he should begin to think about his own mortality, after so many attacks on his life.

"Yes, I do," she said firmly.

"I'm an irreligious scoundrel, you know. I've never really thought about it before, but I always had the conviction that when we die, we are gone. Now I should like to think there is more to the whole business."

"I don't really know what Heaven is, of course, whether it is some beautiful place in the sky or some different state of being. What I do know is that you and I are more than just these mortal bodies," she said, giving him a squeeze. "Our spirits live on. There are times that I feel the presence of my parents and know they still love me and are watching over me."

He was silent for a moment. She wondered if he thought her foolish and sentimental.

"No one watches or waits for me, Pen."

Said in a flat, matter-of-fact tone, the words brought tears to her eyes. She turned her head a little, hoping he would not feel the one sliding down her cheek land on his chest.

"In fact it is quite likely my mother pushed my father off that cliff," he said, his voice still impassive. She sensed the effort it cost him to make the revelation.

"Why do you think that?"

"She said she blamed herself for his death. When I returned to England she was like a lost person, wandering about at all hours, in any weather. She suffered an inflammation of the lungs that proved fatal, despite careful nursing. She had lost her will to live."

"Despite everything you did to try to help."

"Yes."

The weary hopelessness in his voice struck her to the core.

"My dear, I think your mother must always have had a tendency to melancholy. She loved your father, else she would not have been so bitter over his infidelities. Perhaps she said she wished him dead, which is why she became so distraught with grief and guilt when her wish came true. Whatever the truth, you are not to blame. Not for her sins, not for his, and certainly not for their unhappy marriage."

"Perhaps you are right."

"I know I am. I also know we can choose to create our own happiness."

Again, there was a pause. Did he think she belittled his suffering with her cheerful predictions?

"I count on you to help me do so."

He let out a deep, shuddering sigh Pen felt in her innermost heart. What pain he must have suffered over what he believed to be his failures with his mother and Anne. Was it any wonder he craved the company of a loving and loyal wife?

It was time she lightened his mood. Time to resume the natural, happy life they had already begun to forge between them.

"You may rely on me." With her fingertip she began to trace a little circle on his chest, in a way she knew teased and aroused him. As she did so, she smiled a secret smile. Was it time to tell him her news? No, not yet. Better to save it for a happier moment, unalloyed with grief and unspoken fears. Now it was time to forget those fears in simple, loving play.

Her husband let out another deep sigh, this time of pleasure. When he began to tease and caress her in turn, Pen smiled again, knowing the healing had begun.

In the soft morning light, Verwood watched Penelope's face as she slept curled up beside him. His heart swelled at the pure, innocent beauty of her. At the same time his conscience pricked him, just a little. She was usually an early riser, but no doubt she was still tired from consoling him over his nightmare. Well, he would make sure nothing interrupted her sleep now.

He looked about, marveling again at the lovely haven she'd made of what had been a drab, forbidding room. Blue-and-white pottery graced the elaborately plastered mantelpiece, and hangings in the same pure, honest colors made a brilliant contrast to the dark wood of the four-poster.

Clouds must be rolling in, he thought, for the room suddenly dimmed. A few moments later rain began to patter against the windows, and he was almost sorry to see his wife stir and wake at the sound. He opened his arms, and she settled into them, laying her head on his chest and smiling drowsily up at him.

"I don't know what it is about rainy mornings," she murmured. "I feel as if I could stay in bed all day."

"Then stay," he said. "You have earned a day of sloth, I think." He chuckled at her shocked expression, then held her tightly for a few minutes before releasing her and getting out of bed.

"Do not bestir yourself," he said, going to the door. "I shall see about the fire and breakfast. There's no need to leave this room until you wish."

A short while later, he'd rebuilt the fire and brought in a breakfast tray they both shared. They spent the rest of the morning alternating between leisurely love play and peaceful slumber, cocooned in warmth and safety while the wind and rain pelted harmlessly at the windows.

Hours later, the sun came out, and like children, they allowed it to lure them outdoors. Donning their oldest clothing and sturdy boots, they went for a long ramble through the damp meadows and cliff tops. They enjoyed the fresh breeze, with a snap of autumnal cold to it, and noted small signs of the changing season in each hedge and grove.

They returned to Tregaron House, comfortably tired, and both retreated to their rooms to bathe and dress for dinner. Seeing he was ready before her, he went down to his desk in the library to see if any mail had arrived that needed his attention. He sat down to his desk, and there on the corner lay a twist of paper with his name written upon it in an unknown hand.

With a sense of foreboding, he opened it and read the brief message written inside.

Come alone to the fogou *at sunset. Do not fail.*

He stared at it for a few moments, his mind stupidly repeating the words, unwilling to accept their import.

Come alone to the fogou *at sunset. Do not fail.*

He crushed it in his hand, in a futile gesture of denial, then opened it back up, forcing himself to look upon the words and accept the bitter truth: that while he and Pen had frolicked like children, a malignant force had been rising against them once more, ready to burst the lovely, fragile bubble in which they had enveloped themselves.

Damned fool that he was! To allow wishful thinking to cloud his judgment, to blind him to the signs that were there all along. Now his mind raced, putting together clues that resolved themselves into an ugly threat that menaced not only his and Pen's innocent hopes and plans for the future, but possibly their lives as well.

He cast his head down upon his arms, trying to keep from roaring with the anger and despair that flooded his soul. For a few moments he lay still, allowing the blackness to take him, then lifted his head again.

He might have allowed his imagination to run riot. But even if there was danger involved, they had come too far for him to give up. If there was the slightest chance that he could protect the life they were forging together, he had to try. At least he would do everything in his power to keep Pen safe, and make sure no one else came to harm over his affairs.

He stared absently down at the paper in his hands, forcing down his rage and despair, calling upon the cool composure he had learned through years of threats against his life. He might need all of it tonight.

He got up and stared out of the window, repressing panic at the position of the sun. He crossed the room to the hearth and threw in the note, watching just long enough to be certain it was consumed by the flames. So little time left, and he must use it wisely.

Half an hour later, he'd done all he could to prepare, and it was time to rejoin Pen for dinner. It was all he could do to smile and embrace her as usual when she came down to the dining room, looking more ripe and enticing than ever in a dark green gown with long sleeves, cut low across her lovely bosom.

He feasted his eyes on the sight of her, and took pleasure in the sweet sound of her voice as she chatted over the meal. Foreknowledge of the evil to come somehow intensified all his senses. He'd never tasted such succulent duck, such rich Burgundy, and the blackberry tart they had for dessert fairly burst with sour-sweet flavor. And throughout, he was painfully conscious of his wife's loving gaze upon him, so that it was all he could do to keep from going around the table and kissing her like a madman.

As usual, they went to the drawing room after dinner, but when he sat down and reached for the latest volume they'd been reading, Pen came to kneel beside him and stayed his hand.

"There is something I wish to tell you," she said, holding his hand in both her small ones and looking a bit shy.

Good God. The meaning of her look struck him like a blow. *Not this. Not now.*

He struggled to keep his expression blank, hoping she would think him surprised, and not feeling as if a knife had just been thrust into his heart.

"I think I can guess what it is," he said, forcing warmth into his voice, hoping she would be deceived.

"Sometime in May, or perhaps early June, we will have a child," she said, a smile hovering about her mouth as she looked up at him expectantly.

"How—how are you feeling?" Perhaps he could hide his fears in concern for her health.

"Very well," she said, happiness and reassurance glowing in her eyes. "Just a bit sleepy at times."

He turned his hand, grasped hers, and bent forward to kiss it. "I cannot tell you how happy you have made me, Pen," he said, praying she would mistake the raging emotion in his voice for joy. "You know you will have to teach me to be a good father."

She nodded, tears coming to her eyes, and the knife in his heart twisted. Would she have the opportunity to teach him, or he to learn from her? God help him, he had to keep her safe. If he himself did not survive the night, at least the babe would be a comfort to her.

He rose from the chair, helped her up, and gathered her close for the kiss he'd been wanting the past hour. It was sweet, achingly sweet, and already she was making little sounds of desire and pressing herself against him in entreaty. Dear God, how he wanted her. Was there time, or did he risk ruining everything for what might be his last chance to make love to her?

He broke the kiss and looked down at her. Out of the corner of his eyes he noted the light still entering the room through the bay window. An hour, perhaps, before he must leave.

"Are you—certain this will not hurt you, or the babe?" he asked, looking down at her.

She shook her head, her eyes alight with laughing affection. He looked down at the soft Oriental carpet before the hearth and decided against it. If they went to her bedchamber, she might fall asleep and he would not have to lie to her about his reason for leaving.

So he lifted her up and carried her, softly protesting, to her room. As the light failed, he caressed her in all the ways she liked best, savoring the scent of lavender on her soft skin, the love shining from her aquamarine eyes, and every twist, expression, and coo that proved how he pleased her. He held back his own release until the last possible moment, praying that whatever ugliness came afterward, she would remember him with love.

He held her curled in his arms a few minutes, and as he'd hoped, she fell asleep, exhausted by her exertions and her pregnancy. He got out of bed and dressed quickly, watching the day go down in flames through the window.

He was late, and their enemy would not appreciate that.

Yet he could not help one glance back at Pen's sleeping form. Even in repose her face held a loving expression. What an idiot he'd been to think she cared for him only as a father to her children. She'd come to love him for himself, and he hadn't even recognized the miracle until it was too late. Beef-witted brute! He hadn't even told her he loved her in return.

He could not risk waking her.

"I love you," he whispered, praying she would hear the words somehow, then turned and left the room.

Chapter Sixteen

I love you. Had she heard the words, Pen wondered, dreamily rolling over in the softness of her bed. She reached out for Robert, but could not find him. She opened her eyes. He was not there. Her heart turned over in a sudden panic, then she decided she was being foolish. There was probably a perfectly mundane reason for him to have left. He would be back in minutes.

She lay thinking about how lovingly he had reacted to her news, but a sense of impending trouble intruded on her serenity. Something had been pressing upon him; she was sure of it now. Perhaps it was just misgivings about fatherhood, but she would not feel easy until she saw him again.

A few minutes later, Robert still had not returned. Overcome with dread, she rose from the bed and hurried to dress herself in the garments that she'd worn earlier.

She opened the door, only to encounter Will Symonds.

"Where is his lordship?" she asked without preamble.

"He wished me to tell you he had gone out to see about Zethar. He thinks the colt may have strained a hock today out at pasture."

"He didn't mention it," said Pen, frowning. "I think I shall go out and see if there is any way I can help."

"There's no need for that, my lady. I am certain his lordship means to return quickly," Symonds assured her as she turned to go back into her room.

She passed through it to her dressing room and found her

cloak. Putting it on, she returned to the doorway to find Symonds still there, his brow furrowed.

"There is no need for you to go out, my lady. 'Tis a windy night, and I'm sure the master will be back soon."

"I'll go out to him," she insisted, her anxiety mounting at the valet's evident desire to keep her indoors.

"His lordship particularly stated he did not wish you to go out. Likely there's another storm brewing," he said, sounding agitated as he followed her down the staircase.

She entered the Hall, and a gust of wind blew in as the massive wooden door opened. The head groom, Pascoe, entered, bearing something in his hand.

"Have you seen his lordship, Pascoe?" she asked.

"He went for a walk," he said, as if it were a normal occurrence at such an hour. "I found this in the stable yard and thought he might be glad if it was returned to the house."

She took the paper from him and opened it.

Come alone to the fogou at sunset. Do not fail.

Her heart clenched with fear as she read the words. Good God, someone threatened Robert again. Hard on the heels of her terror came the conviction that he would not be safe until she was with him again.

"I must go to him," she cried.

"You're not to go out," said Symonds, who sidled around her to block her way.

"I must. You can go with me, if you wish."

She tried to go around him, and with a desperate look Symonds grasped her and pulled her into an impersonal but relentless hold.

"I must go to him," she begged.

"Here, you can't treat her ladyship like that," Pascoe cried out indignantly and tried to pull Symonds away from her.

"You're not to go out, my lady. His lordship's orders," said Symonds, turning toward Pascoe. Pen broke free from his hold, then cried out as Pascoe flung the smaller man across the room. Symonds landed hard on the stone floor and remained there, motionless.

Pen stared at him for an instant, terrified that he might be badly injured.

"I didn't mean to hurt him, m'lady," said Pascoe, looking down at Symonds, his expression a strange mix of guilt and defiance.

She ran to Symonds and knelt down beside him. She felt his breathing and his pulse and was relieved to find both steady. Then she glanced up at Pascoe, wondering why he'd gone so far as to hit Symonds. There was a strange glint in his eyes. Something inside her screamed a warning. Was he in league with whoever had summoned Robert to the *fogou*? Had he delivered the note so she would go there as well?

She lowered her gaze, hoping he hadn't seen her fear. She felt Symonds's head and found a lump on the back of it. What should she do? If she stayed to assist Symonds, who knew what might happen to Robert? Pascoe might take her away forcibly, if he had orders to make sure she arrived at the *fogou*. Or would he kill Symonds if left behind with him?

"I think he is not seriously harmed," she said, forcing the words through dry lips. "But he is not likely to awake before morning."

She prayed it would be enough for Pascoe to leave Symonds alone for the evening and that Symonds would awake in time to fetch help.

"Shall I lay him down somewhere?" asked Pascoe.

She hated the thought of moving the injured man, but nodded. "Perhaps you can carry him to the drawing room sofa."

She followed Pascoe as he fulfilled her order, then a thought occurred to her.

"I must check his breathing again," she said. Shielding Symonds's body with her own, she slipped the note in between his shirt and his waistcoat. If he didn't know Robert's destination, it might prove useful.

She stood up and thanked Pascoe for his assistance. Trembling, she went back into the Hall and toward the door, Pascoe following her.

"Shall I escort you, my lady?" he asked, holding the door for her.

"No, thank you," she said.

She ran down the steps and then the drive, holding her cloak around her, a cold wind whipping her cheeks. When she reached the road, she risked a glance behind to see if Pascoe was following her. She saw nothing, but it was possible he was hidden among the elms that lined the drive.

There was nothing to do but continue. Only a slight remnant of light remained in the west. Robert might already be with their enemy. Her fingers shook as she opened the gate to the fields, nearly crippled by dread of the malignant threat they faced. She was a simple vicar's daughter; nothing in her life had prepared her for walking into what was very likely a trap. She hadn't even been able to bring a gun, not that she would have known what to do with one if she had. She touched her belly. Was she wrong to disregard Robert's attempts to protect her and their child?

She stared up at the stars beginning to appear through the shifting clouds. The conviction that she and Robert would be safe if they were together sent her dashing onward, while sending prayers to God to keep him alive until she reached him.

"You are late."

Mariah's cold accusation was backed up by the pistol she pointed at Verwood.

Verwood held his own gun aimed at her, maintaining the stalemate they had established a moment ago when he'd entered the central chamber of the *fogou*. A diplomatic answer would serve him best, but diplomacy was a tricky business when dealing with a jealous woman wielding a gun.

"My apologies, Lady Grayshott. It was quite a tedious task disengaging myself from my wife this evening," he said casually, stifling the memory of Pen sleeping in her bedchamber. He needed a cool head.

"It is most rude to point a pistol at a lady," she chided him, her smile revealing pearly teeth that matched her pale skin, ghostly against the somber black of her hooded cloak. "If you lower yours, I shall lower mine."

She let out a laugh, a sound completely devoid of joy, and lowered her gun to her side. He followed suit.

"Why so cold?" she asked in an injured tone. "Have you nothing to say? No words of gratitude to me for setting the stage for our romantic tryst?"

She waved behind her, where blankets and cushions covered the dirt floor and several branches of candles cast a fitful light through the stony chamber. There was even a tray bearing a decanter of wine and a pair of glasses. He'd had a suspicion that something of the sort awaited him, considering the way Mariah had pressed herself against him at Tintagel and complained suggestively of her loneliness. When he'd read the note and first suspected that she was the author, he'd still cherished a faint hope that she was not so far gone in her obsession as to use weapons.

"I am . . . quite overcome with all the pains you have taken."

"Then show your appreciation by dropping your gun."

"Only if you drop yours," he said with a coaxing smile.

Her gray-blue eyes flickered with a cold light. "I think not. I offered you everything at Tintagel. I even sprained my own ankle to be with you, and you snubbed me most cruelly. I must make quite certain that you will be kinder now."

"I never meant to be unkind. Forgive me, I was merely concerned for your reputation, particularly since my own is so badly tarnished. I did not dare to jeopardize your high position in the parish, though of course there were times I have wished things were different . . ."

He hoped he'd put enough silky seduction into his voice to fool her. If she accepted his excuse for not responding to her advances, he might be able to wrest the gun from her.

"You have given me no reason to think you find me attractive," she said, pouting. "I have decided to go into half-mourning. Do you think it pretty?"

She unfastened her cloak and let it fall, revealing a pale gray silk gown with a tiny bodice, matching gloves on her arms and pearls at her ears and throat. She had unfastened her hair and allowed it to fall in an alabaster stream down her shoulders, but what might have been a sight to gladden a man's heart was marred by the glitter of madness in her eyes. Madness brought on by years of marriage to a monster, built to a peak by jealousy of her sister's present happiness, and his own. Why had he not seen it before today?

Anger, horror, and pity roiled within him as he looked at her. He would as soon embrace a corpse. And Mariah was much more dangerous.

"I find you beautiful, as always," he replied carefully.

"Prove it to me, then," she said with a brittle, challenging smile. "Kiss me."

He ran through his limited choices. Reject her, and risk being shot outright. There was the pistol in his hand, but he hoped not to have to resort to it. He didn't wish to shoot her, and would anyone—even Pen—believe he had pulled the trigger to defend himself from a madwoman? Given the way Mariah was revered in the district, he might not survive to stand trial. That is, if she did not manage to shoot him in return, which would be easy enough at such close range.

No, for now the wisest course would be to play her game.

He came forward to the center of the chamber, where the ceiling was highest. Suddenly, Mariah lifted her gun and pressed it directly against his chest. She snaked her other hand inside his coat and pulled him closer to her, her fingers cold against his back.

Quickly, he lifted his gun and pressed it to her side, reestablishing the balance of fear. Oddly, she only laughed.

"Is that any way to treat a lover?" she asked, flinging her head back and eyeing him with the bold look of a courtesan.

He broke out in a cold sweat. She must have gone further into insanity than he would have guessed, to smile so casually with a pistol pressed to her side.

"You have not shown you trusted me, *ma belle*," he said, putting all the charm he could muster into the endearment, conscious that at any moment she could pull her trigger.

"I do not trust you. Kiss me," she repeated, the pitch of her voice rising slightly.

He lowered his head, closed his eyes, and brushed her

lips with his. Her mouth opened greedily, sucking as if to draw the very life from his body, making a bizarre mockery of what should be a loving act or at least a pleasurable one.

"Your heart is not in this, I see," she said, chiding him softly. "Perhaps you will be more enthusiastic when Penelope joins us."

A new horror seized him, but he did not trust himself to say anything. Any sign of his love for Pen would endanger her more. He hoped Symonds would be able to keep her safe.

"Yes, I have arranged for your wife to join our game. She should be here soon," she said in a satisfied tone.

He kept his face still, struggling to think. He didn't want to shoot this vile, pathetic creature. But the alternative was unbearable. Death or exile would be better than leaving Pen prey to Mariah's insane malice. Revulsion, pity, grief, and above all, a desperate longing for Pen ripped through him. He sent a quick prayer heavenward for her safety and pulled the trigger.

Nothing happened.

Damned fool! He should have realized Mariah had an accomplice at Tregaron House. He should have checked the pistol again, instead of rushing out of the house dazed by lovemaking. Now Pen might be at the mercy of Mariah's henchman. Or would Symonds be able to keep her from this hellish trap?

"Pascoe did his job well, I see," said Mariah, with a laugh that echoed strangely through the *fogou.*

Once again, Verwood forced his mind to work. Perhaps Mariah would be content to destroy their happiness by allowing Pen to witness what might look like adultery. If so, he would go along and hope that Pen would flee the scene. In any case, he had to comply with Mariah's wishes, else she might kill him. Then only the devil knew what she might do to Pen. Kill her, too, or make a misery of her life. The twisted creature probably knew exactly which herbs would cause a miscarriage.

Somehow he had to stay alive, at least long enough to know Pen was safe.

He dropped the gun, gave Mariah a comic, rueful look, and joined in her laughter.

"I see you have the advantage of me, Mariah," he said admiringly.

"Of course. Kiss me again, and do it properly this time. *Now*," she commanded, pressing the pistol painfully into his chest.

There was an undercurrent of frenzy in her voice. Perhaps he could distract her enough to get the gun away from her. It was his only remaining chance to protect himself, and more importantly, Pen and their unborn child. So he lowered his head again. He forced his lips and tongue to return the assault of her rapacious mouth and his hands to rove over her cold, perverted body, all the while praying she would succumb to desire and relax her hold on the gun.

Pen took a last look up at the sky, praying for strength, then plunged into the black opening of the *fogou*. It was dark, and the passage was so narrow she had to proceed slowly. About ten feet farther, the passage curved and there was a faint glow, but still, ominously, no sounds.

A few steps more and she stopped short, transfixed by the sight of a woman whose long white hair streamed down her back and glowed in the light of several candelabras. Mariah. Holding her in a lascivious embrace, his arms working over her perfectly formed body with expert skill, was Robert.

He's seduced both my sisters.

Meet me alone at the fogou *at sunset.*

His lordship particularly stated you were not to go out.

The words spun through her head, and she sagged against the stone wall, battling nausea as her world shattered.

Unable to draw her eyes away, she caught Robert's gaze as he opened his eyes briefly, his head at an angle to Mariah's. His eyes blazed, but not with guilt. With horror.

Her world reformed itself as the look of horror changed to one of frantic warning, a silent plea for her to leave for

her own protection. He was still the same man who had
made love to her so tenderly just an hour before.

But now they were both menaced by a jealous madwoman.

When Mariah twisted and opened her eyes, Pen saw her
suspicion confirmed in the strange smile that played about the
woman's lips. The woman *had* gone mad. The signs had all
been there, and Pen had foolishly ignored them, as had everyone else who knew the ordeal it must have been for a young
girl to be forced into marriage with Sir Charles Grayshott.

"Ah, I see your little pet has arrived, Robert," Mariah
purred, her triumphant smile widening.

Pen could not tell for certain, but it seemed Mariah held
a hand tightly against Robert's chest. She swallowed, wondering if there was a gun pressed against him. What did
Mariah want? Merely to see her humiliated? Would that be
enough?

"Robert, what does this mean?" she pleaded, allowing
some of her fear and outrage to show, hoping Mariah would
take them as signs of defeat.

"My dear, you were not supposed to come out. It is quite
your own fault if what you see distresses you," he chided
her in a callous drawl that was horribly convincing.

Mariah laughed. "Did you think he would not tire of
you? Perhaps you should go back to your embroidery, and
your pets, child."

Pen still could not see what the woman was doing with
her left hand. Out of the corner of her eyes, she saw covert
warnings flash from Robert's eyes. Should she go? Perhaps
Mariah would be content thinking she had succeeded in de-
stroying their love. Perhaps Robert would free himself, or
she could bring back someone who could help. Nicholas
Dalton, perhaps?

She let out a sob and covered her face.

"Yes, I am leaving now. I will go to Catherine tomorrow,
Robert," she said in a low voice.

She didn't dare look to see whether he understood what
she was doing. She turned to leave, but Mariah's voice rang
out sharply.

"I have changed my mind," she said, then her voice softened. "I should like to discover whether Verwood is truly as indifferent to you as he claims."

Pen stopped, not wanting to imagine what Mariah intended.

"If you take another step, my dear Penelope, I'll send a bullet right through his heart."

Pen turned. Mariah leaned back slightly, providing a clear view of the gun she held against Robert's chest. Somehow, he maintained a cynical, unconcerned smile.

"What say you, my darling? Will you show me how you desire me, with that freckled thing you call a wife watching us? Remember, I have two bullets ready."

His forehead shone with sweat, but he bent obediently, and Pen watched, agonized, as his mouth and hands worked over Mariah once more. She prayed he would be able to distract the woman and seize the gun.

Instead, Mariah withdrew from the kiss and gave them both a coldly delighted smile.

"That was quite charming, my darling. What shall we do next?" she asked. "Surely you know many more ways to pleasure a woman than mere kissing."

A spark of pure rage showed in Robert's eyes, and his very stance betrayed that he was close to the breaking point. Pen had to do something to distract Mariah.

"Why are you doing this, Mariah?" she asked gently. "I know life must have been horrible for you, married to Sir Charles, but—"

"What can you know?" Mariah spat, fury darting from her eyes. "What can any of you know? Not even Anne can imagine what it was like to lie night after night with that drunken brute."

"No, we cannot imagine what you suffered," Pen said in a low voice, shaken by pity and horror, but disappointed to see that Mariah continued to hold her gun steadily against Robert's heart.

"I had my revenge, though," continued Mariah. "Perhaps you are aware that there are herbs that can help to bring on one's womanly courses. I made sure to use them, denying Sir Charles the heir he wanted. But even after a year it was not enough to keep the brute out of my bed, so I was obliged to prepare a special mixture for *him*. Ingredients to make him more tractable, to cause him to weaken and vomit and lose flesh. So obliging of dear Sir Charles to drink so heavily. No one suspected it was not a liver complaint that finally struck him down."

"Very clever of you," Pen replied, struggling to keep her voice from shaking. She silently blessed Mrs. Symonds and Cook for their vigilance in the kitchen.

"Yes, I thought I was quite clever," said Mariah. "Afterward it was far too easy to dispose of my father. A little preparation of foxglove can stimulate the heart, and just a bit more can bring on . . . palpitations. A common ailment in a man of his age, and no one wondered at that, either."

"So you have revenged yourself on all of them. They deserved to die," Pen said in a soothing voice. "Now there is no one left who wishes you harm, and you have a brother and sister who love you. Perhaps it is time you sought their comfort."

"I don't need your pity! I don't want anyone's pity!" Venom suffused Mariah's voice, and she began to shake. "Anne ran away, leaving me to Father's tender mercies, and your precious Robert helped her to do it. Now she has returned, flaunting her husband and soliciting everyone's pity over her ordeal. Ordeal! She knows nothing of it, and neither do either of you!"

Her voice and her entire frame shook with jealous fury. Pen shuddered, but in a sudden, lithe movement, Robert twisted and flung Mariah against the wall. Pen blinked and saw the woman's gloved arm pinned against the stone, her pistol pointed at the roof of the chamber.

Within another heartbeat, strong arms seized Pen from behind, and something hard and cold pressed against her temple.

Chapter Seventeen

"*U*nhand me, or your wife dies," Mariah commanded, with a victorious glance in Pen's direction.

Pen's heart thudded as Pascoe continued to press his pistol against her head, holding her securely with his other arm. Robert's face twisted in defeat and he released Mariah. Immediately, she pointed her pistol back at his chest.

"Well done, Pascoe," said Mariah, sidling over to Pen and her captor. "Now, give me your gun and tie her up."

Pascoe lowered his hand, pointing his pistol at Pen's chest until Mariah came forward and took it from him. Then while Mariah gloated over her and Robert, a gun in each hand, Pascoe seized Pen's arms, bound them behind her back and pushed her roughly down against the wall. In her terror, she barely felt the pain of the impact against the cold stone. Then Pascoe bound her ankles together. Despair washed over her. She was helpless, and she might have made matters worse for Robert.

"Shall we shoot 'em now?" asked Pascoe.

"Is there a reason we must rush this?" Mariah asked. "You are quite certain you were not observed leaving Tregaron House, are you not?"

"No one saw us leave," he said, his face shadowy in the uncertain candlelight. "No one knows we are here."

"Very good," said Mariah, and Pen let out the breath she'd been holding. There was at least a small chance that Symonds would revive in time to send help.

"Why waste any more time playing games with *him*?"

asked Pascoe, looking impatiently toward Robert. "When do I get my reward? I spied for you in Brighton, I went to Norland Manor and fetched you, I delivered all those messages for you, just as you bade me. Now I want what's coming to me. If we kill 'em both now, there'll be plenty of time for a bit o' real fun before we leave this place."

The lustful way he looked at Mariah made it clear how she had bent him to her purposes.

"We will kill them when and if I say so," said Mariah reprovingly, a hint of steel in her voice.

Pen's heart chilled at Mariah's words.

"You promised we would run away together. I say kill 'em now," Pascoe snarled, going toward Mariah as if to take one of the guns back.

Pen recoiled as a shot reverberated around the chamber. Pascoe fell backward, blood spurting from a hole in the center of his forehead. She shuddered helplessly at the sight, horrified by Mariah's ruthless act.

"A stupid brute," said Mariah, lowering the gun she'd taken from Pascoe. "But he did keep me well informed of all that occurred in Brighton, and executed certain tasks for me here."

"Tegen." Pen wished she hadn't said it aloud.

"Yes, that smelly creature you cared for so slavishly. You should be grateful to me and Pascoe for trying to rid you of it and spare you from being ridiculed as a mad eccentric. Ah, one meets with so little gratitude in the world."

Pen could not stop shaking now, as the seeming pettiness of the attack on Tegen resolved itself into part of a more sinister pattern. She looked up at Robert, who stood completely still, his face impassive except for the tormented look in his eyes.

Mariah glanced down at the corpse again, then raised her eyes to Robert. "What a fool Pascoe was; he actually believed I was going to kill you and run away with him."

Pen struggled to calm her mind. There had to be something she could do, or she and Robert would meet the same fate as Pascoe.

"He was a clumsy lover, too," continued Mariah. "There was only one man who ever did bring me pleasure."

Pen's stomach churned as Mariah stared over toward Robert like a carrion bird.

"It was your father, of course," Mariah said with a wintry smile.

Verwood stiffened with shock at the bizarre revelation. But he sensed that Mariah was speaking the truth.

"We were accustomed to meeting in this very spot, the autumn before he died," said Mariah pensively. "He loved me so. He would have missed me dreadfully had he returned to London as he planned. What a shame he fell off that cliff."

By the time she made this new revelation, Verwood was not surprised. So his mother had *not* killed his father. Small comfort when a murderess had him and Pen in her clutches.

"How lucky of him to have been spared the pain of separation," he replied, struggling to sound unaffected.

"I always thought so. But like Pascoe, he had his uses. After I killed Sir Charles, I knew it was my responsibility to avenge Anne. Your dear father gave me such useful information with which to do it. He told me all about poor Lord Filey's woes, for instance."

"*You* warned Filey I would continue my father's arrangement with him?" he asked, stunned out of his false composure.

"Of course," she said, smiling. "I wish I could have been there to see you awaken to see *La Perle*'s gun at your head! I was so disappointed to learn you had overcome her, for it took me some time to come up with a new scheme."

"Everton. And Whitgrave," he breathed, his mind reeling at the malignancy of the woman.

"Of course. Pascoe was good enough to inform me they were both in Brighton, and I had learned enough about them to realize just how delightfully they might play off one another. It was rather amusing to try to guess which would be your downfall: Everton's jealousy or Whitgrave's fear of being made a laughingstock. When your father gave me that necklace, he could never have imagined I would put it to such clever use. The only thing I don't understand is how you survived. Perhaps you will enlighten me," she mused, her gun never wavering.

What a keen intelligence it had taken to set off all these attacks! And now it was directed at both of them. Verwood struggled to keep all expression from his face as he looked down at his wife lying bound against the wall beside him, endangered by her very love for him.

She'd tried so bravely to soothe Mariah. Had she thought she might succeed, or had she been stalling for time in hope of a rescue? Did she have reason to think help would arrive?

"I was able to return the letters in question to His Grace," he replied after pausing as long as he dared. "Still, it was an extremely clever plan. You have an amazing mind, Mariah."

"Ah, I had thought those letters were lost," she said, looking pleased with his compliment. "Well, all's well that ends well. This is much more amusing than my earlier schemes. Shall we resume where we left off, my dear Verwood? Your kisses are so intoxicating."

He had guessed that was why she had left him unbound. Mariah knew keeping Pen at gunpoint was enough to keep him tractable.

He stepped cautiously forward, fighting down his loathing. Once again, he put his arms around her again, noting how she pressed one pistol against his chest while pointing the other at Pen. One wrong move, and Pen would die.

So he forced himself to kiss Mariah again. Her body was as cold as the air in the dank chamber and her mauve lips not much warmer. He stifled the nausea that burned inside him and concentrated on finding the touches and caresses that would satisfy her, drawing on years of experience in trying to please women. Finally, she began to warm and melt in his arms. A little moan escaped her, then she jerked away from him, her pistol up again.

"Faugh! This is too easy; it affords me no entertainment," she said, but a quaver in her voice betrayed her. Then she straightened and commanded him back against the wall.

He obeyed, tasting the bitterness of failure.

"Three bullets," said Mariah with a brief look down at

the two pistols. "All that remains now is for me to decide which of you to shoot first."

"But how will you explain what you've done?" Pen asked quickly.

Verwood couldn't help but look down at her. She trembled slightly, but her face was grave and composed. She must have some reason to keep Mariah talking. His heart swelled at her bravery. He prayed it would be rewarded.

"Oh, the last bullet is for me."

His heart plummeted. If Mariah was desperate enough for suicide, she would not balk at murder.

"Oh, *my* wound shall not be a fatal one, just enough to convince everyone of the truth of my story."

"Your story?" asked Pen, as if making conversation.

"I pride myself on my inventiveness," Mariah replied. "I shot Pascoe as he helped your husband to abduct me. You, my little Penelope, are so on fire with jealousy—knowing your husband had already imposed on me at Tintagel—that upon discovering us together you will shoot us both. Then, overcome with remorse, you will shoot yourself."

While Mariah was watching Pen, Verwood stole another glance at his wife. She remained serenely calm, except for a minute trembling. From the fervent look in her eyes he could see she was praying, but whether for a rescue or for a quick deliverance, he could not tell.

"Shall I shoot you first, Verwood?" asked Mariah, looking back at him. "Then I may deal with your wife at my leisure. No, perhaps it would be more amusing to watch your face as I kill her. Shall I shoot her in the heart? Or perhaps kill the babe first?"

Pen let out a gasp as Mariah lowered her aim. He barely contained his own cry of rage. Dear God, was there anything he could do? Should he just rush upon Mariah? But even if she emptied all three bullets into him, Pen was still bound and at her mercy.

Mariah laughed as she looked down at Pen. "Did you think I didn't know? When you touched your belly in that tedious gesture women adopt when they are in the family way?"

"You are acute, as always, Mariah," he said, hoping for some way to reach her.

"Your plan is most ingenious," he continued. "But I think I have a better one. Let us leave this godforsaken place and flee to the Continent. Think what a life we could lead there, with my money, and both our brains and good looks."

Mariah stared, an arrested expression on her face, then shook her head. "Ever since you returned to Tregaron, you've behaved like a veritable moonling over this wife of yours. If you had taken up my offer at Tintagel things would have been different. Why should I believe you now?"

"Oh, there was a certain piquancy to seducing an innocent, Mariah. But it palls on one eventually. I am ready for a change. When the choice is between death at gunpoint and life with a beautiful woman, I'm no fool."

"How can you say that? How could you even think of leaving me?" Pen cried out.

Brave girl, he thought. She had caught on to his plan. Would it work?

"Then we shall go," said Mariah after a pause. "After I kill her." She pointed the gun in her left hand at Pen.

"Would it not be more amusing to leave her to suffer?" he asked quickly. "With everyone knowing I left her for you?"

Mariah cocked her head, as if considering the plan, then shook it. "A valiant effort, but not quite convincing, my dear Verwood."

"Mariah," he said forcefully, to make sure she kept her gaze directed at him. "There is no more need for revenge. You are so beautiful, so brilliant. The perfect woman I'd never thought to meet. I was a fool not to realize it when I first met you, but I was so infatuated with Anne, and you were so young. At the age of eighteen, I had not the wit to predict that an awkward fourteen-year-old girl would grow into such a Beauty. And I had not yet learned to appreciate intelligence in a woman. I didn't know you'd be wed to Sir Charles so soon. I wish I could have saved you."

He had her complete attention now; the pistol pointed at his wife had started to droop toward the floor.

"Don't you see, Mariah? We were fated to be together, but your father's plans for Anne interfered. Now is our chance to enjoy what destiny intended for us."

He took a step forward. She did not shoot, but merely stared at him, a wild, impassioned look in her eyes. Revulsion, pity, and guilt churned inside him as he remembered the troublesome young girl who had interrupted all his calls on Anne. The one whose youthful infatuation with him had twisted over the years into a fearful, maddening obsession.

There was nothing he could do but continue the lie he'd started, if he wished to save his wife and their unborn child.

"Come with me. It is all you ever wanted, isn't it, for me to pleasure you and care for you as you deserve? Let me care for you, Mariah."

He took another step forward, pleading with his eyes, loathing himself for what he had to do. Mariah's entire body began to shake, and her face crumpled with grief and longing. Finally, he had his moment. He sprang toward her and knocked the pistol from her left hand.

"Liar!" she shrieked, suddenly backing from him and lifting the other pistol.

He sprang to one side as a shot rang through the cavern.

"Liar! Bastard!" shouted Mariah.

He dove to the ground desperately as she fired another shot. Searing heat burned his arm. A welcome sensation, for it proved that her last bullet had only grazed him. He looked up to see Mariah's furious expression change to pure dismay.

"Edward!" she cried out.

He looked behind him. Edward Norland lay at the entrance to the chamber, Dr. Ross and Anne behind him, their faces pale with shock.

"Edward, my baby, what have I done?" said Mariah, stumbling over Verwood to cast herself on her brother.

"Let me examine him, Mariah," ordered Dr. Ross. He lifted her off of Edward and pushed her toward Anne's waiting arms.

"I have killed him. Damn you, Verwood! It is all your fault!" she sobbed.

Anne struggled to hold her back from him. Quickly, Verwood snatched up the pistol that was still lying on the ground and placed it in his pocket. Seeing Mariah subside, hysterically sobbing, into Anne's arms, he went to Pen.

"You are bleeding," she said, her eyes huge in her pale face.

"It is just a graze," he said, glancing at the trickle of blood on his arm, and knelt down to untie her.

"Pen . . . my dear one . . ." he said, voice breaking. "I'd have done anything to spare you this."

He gathered her into his arms, and she began to weep the tears she must have been holding back throughout the entire hellish ordeal. She must hate him for having drawn her into such ugliness, for all the loathsome things he'd said and done. But no, she only hugged him back fiercely, then withdrew a little, looking up at him with undimmed love.

"I know," she said, her voice shaking. "Let me tend to your arm."

She struggled to get up, cramped from having been bound, and he helped her. When they started toward the others, Mariah cried out once more.

"He's dead! You're not to touch him, you murderers!" she shrieked to Dr. Ross. "Let me go!"

She twisted, broke free of her sister's hold and turned to face them all. Verwood put an arm around Pen, secure in the knowledge that he had all the guns.

"Damn you, Anne!" shouted Mariah. "You have ruined everything. I wish you had never come back! You and that wretched Scotsman of yours, with your pity and your sneering offers to *comfort* me! I would have shown you *comfort*, once I'd disposed of these two! And now Edward is dying! Damn you! Damn you!"

"Compose yourself, Mariah," Anne said in a trembling voice that she tried to make soothing. "You are distraught. James is doing all he can to save Edward."

"It is all your fault! If you had only married Sir Charles as you were supposed to, none of this would have happened! Verwood was meant for me, do you hear? But you stole him from me, you took him away and then you cast him aside. I would have loved him more than anyone has ever loved. And Edward would not be bleeding to death now! Damn you all!"

She glared at Pen and Verwood, screamed again, and dashed toward the seaside entrance to the chamber.

"Robert, stop her!" Anne begged. "Please. She is just a poor mad creature; let us help her if we can."

He stared at her for a heartbeat, then nodded.

"Be careful!" he heard Pen shout behind him as he ducked to leave the chamber.

He tried to hurry down the passage, hampered by having to bend to fit under the low ceiling. When he emerged from the *fogou*, Mariah was far ahead of him, heading toward the cliffs, as he'd expected.

"Mariah! Stop! Let us help you," he shouted.

"Damn you!" she screamed, turning briefly toward him. Then she ran on, her pale gown floating eerily behind her. She staggered at the edge, then disappeared over it.

He was too late to stop her. Poor Mariah; perhaps this was the most merciful end for her.

He stood for a moment, staring out over the water. Could it really all be over?

He walked slowly to the precipice and looked down. There was nothing to be seen but small white curls of waves around the rocks. A sudden sense of dread gripped him, and he turned quickly to leave.

Too late, he realized, as slender, relentless hands gripped his ankles and pulled him over the edge.

Chapter Eighteen

*V*erwood clawed desperately at the cliff as he fell, tearing small plants out by their roots, banging and scraping his face along the rock wall. Seconds later, he found a handhold on the narrow ledge Mariah must have used to waylay him. He came to a stop, holding onto the stone with all his strength while she dangled below him, maintaining a death-grip on his ankles.

"For pity's sake, Mariah, stay still!" he shouted above the sound of the waves. "Someone will come to help us."

"I don't want anyone's help!" she shrieked. She started to thrash about, kicking off the cliff to make them swing. Verwood's muscles protested; the graze on his arm burned. Twice he almost lost his grip.

"Robert! Hold tight! Help is coming!" Pen cried out above them.

He could just make out her head peering out over the edge. She disappeared, and he heard her calling for a rope.

Mariah kicked out and swung them violently again. "You were right, my darling Verwood," she shouted. "We *are* destined for each other."

He managed to hold tight, but the next swing would surely send them to a rocky death below. Perhaps Mariah was right, and fate did mean for him to perish with her off these cliffs. Perhaps he'd never been meant to experience the joys and concerns of the lovely, ordinary life he and Pen had just begun. At least he'd managed to save her and the child. Pen was brave; she would mourn him, but she would live on.

He looked up and saw her face above him.

"Hold tight! Please," she pleaded. "I love you! Hold on!"

The passionate entreaty in her voice sent renewed strength coursing through his body. He had a firm grip on the solid stony outcropping. All he had to do was maintain his hold, and a future with Pen awaited him.

"Come join me in Hell!" screamed Mariah with another kick.

They swung out at a giddy angle, but he kept hold of the sturdy rock. Mariah's body slammed back against the cliff. She lost her grip on his ankle and screamed. An instant later, her scream cut off, and all he heard was the sound of waves.

He let out a shuddering breath, then looked up again. Now two heads were silhouetted along the edge.

"Steady, Rob," Nick shouted. "I'm sending a rope down."

Verwood found a foothold on the cliff and managed to hoist himself up onto the narrow ledge and grasp the end of the rope Nick had lowered to him. The cliff face above him offered few footholds, but he worked his way back up, using the rope. Finally, Nick and his wife both reached out to haul him over the edge.

He collapsed on the damp grass, struggling to regain his breath, but feeling safe for the first time in ages. Pen fell to her knees beside him and pulled his head and shoulders into her lap. She leaned down to cover him with tears and kisses that miraculously began to wipe away the pain and horror of all that had happened. He basked in her loving care for a few moments, then sat up and hugged her convulsively.

"I love you," he said, his voice shaking. Then he kissed her forehead, her cheeks, and her plump, sweet lips, thanking his Maker that he was alive to say the words.

His wife kissed him, then drew back. The moon shone through a break in the clouds, allowing him to see the wise, mischievous smile on her tear-streaked face.

"I thought you'd never get up the courage to tell me," she said in a low, husky voice.

"I was a fool," he said, and pulled her close to savor her

sweet, warm mouth under his, her vital womanly form in his arms.

"You must let me see to your arm," she insisted, drawing back after another long, healing kiss.

"To hell with my arm," he muttered, kissing her again.

Then he felt her small fists gently pummeling his chest, and opened his eyes.

"Why did you come here by yourself?" she demanded. "You should have told me; we could have thought of a way to face this together."

"I didn't want you to be harmed."

"You didn't think losing you would hurt me? Did you want our child to grow up not knowing his father?" she retorted. "Now, the least you can do is let me care for your wound."

"Pen, you saved my life. I would have fallen off that cliff if you hadn't been there urging me to hold on," he said, pulling her tightly against his chest. "Don't worry about this stupid scratch."

"I'm your wife! Let me take care of you," she scolded him softly.

She withdrew from his arms and somehow pulled him to his feet. Putting an arm around her, he started to walk with her back toward the *fogou*. Halfway back, Nick joined them.

"You look awful, Rob," he said, the moonlight showing his lopsided smile. "But I'm glad to see you still in the land of the living."

"Thanks for pulling me up off the cliff," he replied.

"You should thank your wife. And your man Symonds for alerting us all to what was going forward."

"Is Symonds all right, then?" asked Pen. "Pascoe dealt him a dreadful blow to the head."

Nick nodded. "He'll do."

"How did he guess where to go?"

"Your wife left a message in Symonds's waistcoat. My compliments on your presence of mind, Lady Verwood. You are a brave woman."

"She is indeed." Robert pulled her closer against his side, deeply thankful for all she'd done.

"How is Edward?" asked Pen.

"Dr. Ross has stopped the bleeding. Now he must extract the bullet, which he says is close to a lung," Nick replied.

"Perhaps I can assist him," said Pen. "I hope Edward survives; it would be terrible for Anne to lose him, too."

They went down into the *fogou* once more, where clean water, cloth for bandages and other items requested by the doctor had just been brought from the house. Verwood allowed Pen to tend to his arm, then she conferred with the doctor about Edward.

While Dr. Ross and Pen labored in the fogou, Verwood and Nick comforted Anne and attended to various other necessary matters, such as sending a boat to retrieve Mariah's body and deciding how much of the tale to make public.

Dawn was breaking by the time Pen finally emerged from the *fogou* to announce that Edward was out of danger. There was blood on her dress, dark rings etched under her eyes, and her fiery hair hung tangled down her back. In the soft morning light, she was the loveliest sight Verwood had ever beheld.

He opened his arms. She staggered into them, looking so exhausted he could not help worrying.

"Are you all right, darling?" he asked, holding her close.

She nodded, feeling reassuringly warm and solid in his embrace.

"It's hard to believe it's all over," she murmured against his chest.

"It is all over now," he said. "We are safe."

"Yes, we are safe. I feel it in my heart."

She looked up at him, tired but happy, and he knew he'd been blessed beyond anything he had ever imagined. Yes, they were safe. They'd enjoy the harvest celebrations, sit reading together by the fire on cold winter evenings, make passionate love to each other in the nights that followed. In the spring, they'd watch flowers she'd planted emerge. All the while their child would grow in her belly, to bring them new worries and new joys next summer.

She yawned. He realized that for the present, all he wished was to curl up with his wife in the peaceful haven of her bedchamber, to sleep with her tucked inside his embrace.

"Let's go home," he said, smiling down at her.

She returned his smile, her eyes glowing.

"Yes. Let us go *home*."

Epilogue

*T*he cries of seabirds mingled with the delighted shrieks of the little Woodmeres. Strolling arm in arm with Juliana and Catherine, Pen watched the children frolic in the shallows farther down the beach. Mr. Woodmere waded among them, keeping a watchful eye on his young sisters and brothers, carrying his own little daughter on his shoulders and maintaining a lively discussion with Lord Amberley and Robert, both of whom stood just out of range of the children's splashes.

During the past session of Parliament, the two had joined with Lord Everton and become a force to be reckoned with. No doubt they were busily encouraging Philip Woodmere to run for office in order to gain an ally in the Commons. Lord Amberley waved his hands vigorously as he made his points. The only thing that prevented Robert from doing the same was two-month-old Christopher, squirming in his father's arms.

"Do they ever tire?" asked Juliana, staring at the children.

Catherine's dark curls bobbed as she shook her head. "Only once they have gone to bed," she replied, a smile in her deep blue eyes. "Then a full regimental band could not rouse them. They'll sleep soundly this evening."

"I am so glad you were all able to come for the christening," said Pen contentedly. "Somehow it makes my happiness complete to have you all here."

"You look a bit tired, Pen," said Cat. "Did Christopher keep you up all night?"

"Part of it," she admitted, blushing a little. "Yes, I'm tired, but it's a happy sort of tired."

"Who would have pictured Verwood as a father?" Jule mused, looking toward the gentleman. "He seems quite a devoted one."

Pen nodded, holding back the happy tears that flowed so easily since Christopher's birth. "He is determined not to fail his son as his own parents failed *him*."

"Well, I have no doubt Marcus will prove an excellent father. I suppose if you both advise me I shall manage somehow, too," said Juliana, her expression a droll mixture of happiness and nervous anticipation.

Pen smiled, seeing Juliana's glowing complexion and how she swayed slightly with the welcome burden of her pregnancy.

"You should have seen Jule when my Elinor was born!" said Catherine, laughing. "I never saw anyone so frightened of an infant. You managed perfectly well, though, and it is different when it is your own. You will see."

"You must all promise to come to Redwyck Hall for Christmas," said Juliana.

"And everyone must come to the Lakes next summer," said Catherine.

"A seal! A seal!"

They turned to see the children shouting, jumping up and down and pointing excitedly toward a rocky outcropping near the entrance to the cove, where a seal had just climbed out of the water to bask on one of the rocks.

"Is it the one you told us about?" asked Juliana. "Tegen?"

"It is hard to tell. She behaves like a wild creature, just as she should. I like to think it *is* Tegen."

They watched the sleek animal for a few moments, then continued making their plans as they took another turn along the quieter end of the beach. Pen delighted in the sunshine, the feel of sand between her toes, and the company of her friends. As they approached the gentlemen and children again, Robert came toward them. Pen noticed that Christopher was fiercely sucking on his fingers.

"This little glutton wants his mother," said Robert, smiling apologetically. "I'd hoped to keep him occupied a bit longer, but our son has other ideas."

He handed her the child. Christopher smiled up at her for a moment, then began to nuzzle her. Catherine and Juliana rejoined the others, and Robert went with Pen toward the shade of a small boulder, where a blanket had been spread. She sat down, leaning against the stone, while Robert placed cushions around her, then tilted the brim of her bonnet up to give her a quick kiss. She adjusted her dress and shawl to bring her son to her breast, and a rush of pure joy spread through her as Christopher began to suckle and Robert lounged on the blanket beside her.

"What impeccable timing," he said with a wry grin.

Pen turned her head and saw the servants coming down the path bearing hampers of food for the picnic.

"Little scoundrel, must you always interfere with your mother's meals?" he said, chiding his son lovingly before looking back at her. "I'll fetch you something, darling."

Her happiness deepened as she watched him get up and head down the beach toward the spot where the servants were spreading more blankets and unpacking the hampers. Robert had certainly embraced fatherhood in a way she would never have predicted a year ago. A year ago, she had yet to learn what forces had conspired to dim his spirit. She understood them now.

Fears still troubled him at times, she knew. Fear of failure, of pain and loss. But he'd learned to face life with the same courage he'd shown in facing death. Now the passion he had formerly reserved for lovemaking showed in all he did: his estate management, the way he discharged his Parliamentary duties, his tenderness toward his son and heir.

A few minutes later, he returned bearing a plate loaded with sandwiches and fruit and a tall goblet of lemonade. In a maneuver they'd perfected over the past few months, he held the goblet to her lips and she drank thirstily from it, her own hands occupied in keeping her wriggling son in place. Bit by bit, Robert fed her a sandwich, and when she'd finished it, popped a ripe, juicy strawberry into her mouth. She lifted Christopher and coaxed him to bring up a bubble before putting him to her other breast. She leaned back against the boulder with a sigh of contentment, and Robert fed her another strawberry.

"We are beasts, little one, to tire your poor mother with our insatiable demands," Robert said, watching her with a look of tender concern.

"Perhaps you should recall that what we did last night was my idea," she said, smiling as she remembered how gently he had made love to her, their first time since Christopher's birth.

His roguish smile appeared, then deepened. The tender, vulnerable joy in his eyes brought ready tears into her own. She knew he was basking in a moment of joy so real and powerful as to be almost painful in its intensity. Through much suffering, he'd learned what she had always known: that such moments were to be seized and treasured, that they provided consolation for past sorrows and hope for the future.

Pen looked down at Christopher, who dozed contentedly at her breast, then back up at Robert. He leaned over to give her a warm, deep kiss, and she, too, lost herself in the sunlit moment.